She DIED

FAMOUS

KYLE RUTKIN

Published by Greater Path LLC

Cover design by Anamaria Stefan

ISBN: 978-0-9836833-2-2 (Hardback)

ISBN: 978-0-9836833-3-9 (Paperback)

ISBN: 978-0-9836833-4-6 (E-book)

To my wife, Mo.

"The public perception is that I'm young, naive, and thoughtless, and these performances are part of some rebellious chapter in my life. But I don't give a shit about public opinion. There's always a bigger purpose. Always."

—KELLY TROZZO, *THEINSIDEJUICE.COM* INTERVIEW, 2019

On July 15, superstar Kelly Trozzo and her manager, Barry Monroe, were found dead at Trozzo's Hollywood mansion. In the days that followed, the LAPD turned its attention to best-selling author Kaleb Reed as the primary suspect in the murders. What follows is an account of the events leading up to and following that infamous night.

I am a "person of interest"—the first stop on the road to "prime suspect," if not already the latter. I'm a little tipsy right now. Maybe I shouldn't be writing. Or, I'm sorry, blogging. I can hear the bloodsuckers outside my apartment. Paparazzi. Gossip vacuums, waiting like hungry zombies. They make me restless. Angry.

It's 2:34 a.m. Another sleepless night spent in the company of online trolls. Blame. Death threats. Disgust. I don't know why I keep reading. Maybe I relish my new title. The most despised man in America, certainly on Twitter. In this bizarre world of celebrity fixation, I can feel the enthrallment and intrigue beneath your disgust.

You want more of me.

Soon enough, I will be charged with murder. It feels good to say it. Get that off my chest. I'm irrational, violent, obsessive, and destructive. I'm a monster. #Monster. Better? At least that one is true. I've done bad things, yes. Evil things, one could say. I'm responsible for the death of your leader. Your beloved princess. You need justice. Don't we all?

If you're scanning for a quick confession, you've come to

the wrong place. I wish it were that simple. You see, I've always been more of a "gray area" kind of guy. I like to understand the history of things. The motivations. The stuff that can't be answered by a simple yes or no. I have a flair for the dramatic. I am a writer by profession. I tell stories. And this story…it deserves more. More than two hundred and eighty characters.

I digress.

I have just returned from a three-day detainment at the Los Angeles Police Department. It was a lively interrogation with Detective Donaldson, scrutinizing my relationship with Kelly. Recalling my account of that infamous night. I certainly have motive. Jealous lover. Besotted fame junkie. A history of irrational violence . . . I could go on. But in the end, no charges were filed. With a case this big, there can be no doubt. No errors in procedure. There are still things the detective and his friends must uncover.

Including a murder weapon.

As a result, I walked out of the police station as a free man, wearing a borrowed hoodie and oversized jeans. The bloody clothes I came in with are now property of the state. I was greeted on the front steps by a swarm of fans, reporters, and TV cameras. Their stares and anger were like a vice tightening around my neck. There is remorse. There is always remorse.

I don't deserve it, but I ask that you hold off judgment. At least for now. There are things I must tell you. Truths I must reveal.

Stay tuned for the next act. I promise I won't disappoint.

CNN

MURDER OF A HOLLYWOOD PRINCESS: THE FINAL DAYS OF KELLY TROZZO

TOMORROW AT 8/7 CENTRAL

She was one of the biggest child stars the world has ever seen. As the quirky, fun-loving Zoe Claireborn on the sitcom *Zoe Loves*, Kelly Trozzo fostered an unstoppable brand that captured the hearts of tweens and teenagers alike. From multiplatinum albums to box office smash hits, best-selling books, and sold-out arena tours, everything Kelly touched turned to gold, including her award-winning performance in the animated feature Castle Heart, a role that earned her the title of "America's Princess" and secured her place among Hollywood's elite.

And then it all came crashing down.

Where did it all go wrong for Kelly Trozzo? With tales of sex and drugs and scandalous headlines circulating this past year, how did America's Princess end up dead outside her Hollywood mansion? Tonight, we talk to Jez Bransen, an inside source close to Trozzo, who believes negative influences brought her to this fate. We discuss Trozzo's successful comeback, and all her hopes for the future. We analyze the last days leading up to her murder, and the controversy that surrounded her.

Will there be justice for Kelly Trozzo? Tune in tonight at 8/7 Central.

HUFFINGTON POST

PAY ME, ALICE HITS #1 ON NEW YORK
TIMES BESTSELLER LIST
JULY 20, 2019

Amid rumors and allegations of author Kaleb Reed's involvement in the deaths of Kelly Trozzo and her manager, Barry Monroe, the author's book sales have soared in the last two days. Reed's novel, *Pay Me, Alice*, will land at the top spot of this week's *New York Times* Best Sellers list.

Although the book debuted in 2017, it first hit the list in July 2018 after Trozzo endorsed it, stating, "This is not only a once-in-a-generation masterpiece, it's one of those rare books that transformed my life. It will make you believe in love." While the book peaked at number five in the year following the endorsement, Trozzo's death—as well as Reed's role as a suspect in the case, and reports of a copy of the novel being found at the crime scene—has propelled *Pay Me, Alice* to the number-one spot.

Rumors that Kaleb Reed was more than an innocent bystander in the July 15 murders have been swirling since that night. Reed, who has a history of drug abuse and violence, has been connected to several incidents involving Kelly this past year, including an attack on a fan after a concert, as well as a reporter during a red-carpet event. Moreover, sources say that Reed assaulted Barry Monroe backstage at Trozzo's last concert in Los Angeles, though no charges were filed. Numerous sources also say the author's behavior and relationship with Kelly was erratic and obsessive.

The eerie final scene of *Pay Me, Alice* has set the stage for speculations about the author, as well as questions about Trozzo's fascination with the controversial novel.

As the mystery continues to grow, so does the author's fame. Only time will tell how much of the novel is fiction and how much is actually true.

HUFFINGTON POST

KELLY'S SECRET "TELL ALL" INTERVIEW
JULY 20, 2019

Celebrity gossip site TheInsideJuice.com has confirmed rumors of a shocking unpublished tell-all interview with fallen superstar Kelly Trozzo. Inside sources at the site revealed that last week, its team was secretly invited to Trozzo's Hollywood mansion to conduct the first sit-down interview with the pop star since her comeback.

The website finally responded to the rumors with a series of tweets:

@theinsidejuice: Our team had the privilege of speaking with @KellyTrozzo three days before her tragic death. Kelly divulged extremely personal details about her life, including specifics about her relationship with @KalebReedAuthor, and her sensational return to showbiz.

@theinsidejuice: The interview will answer many of the public's questions, as well as provide insight into Kelly's volatile mental state prior to her murder. Her words will leave you in disbelief. @KTroops.

@theinsidejuice: The full interview will be released on our website on Wednesday, July 24.

Kelly's fans are abuzz about the mysterious interview. What spurred Kelly to arrange this secret meeting only three days before her murder? Did she know that her life was in danger? Did she provide information that could identify her killer?

TheInsideJuice.com declined to comment further for this story.

In all the hoopla, I forgot to introduce myself. My name is Kaleb Reed. Bestselling author. Convicted felon. Addict. Public enemy #1. In a past life, I've carried other titles. The son of a governor. A big brother. Struggling writer. I'm 6'1", with broad shoulders and a cleft chin. My green eyes are from my mother. My rage, demons, and build are from my father. I have the Serenity Prayer tattooed on my right forearm. I've loved two women in my life.

One of them is still alive.

At times, I have been sober. I have been strong. Most importantly, I have been faithful to the people I love. To my role as a protector.

I'm not blogging from my home, in case you were wondering. I'm typing this from a highway rest stop, a hundred miles east. It's nice to be away. The small-town server refilled my coffee and dropped off my check with a smile. She has no idea who I am, or that my face is plastered on every television in America.

I won't be a free man much longer.

Detective Donaldson won't rest until I'm back in handcuffs.

Even now, I imagine he's fantasizing about his big speech on the podium. He'll stand there with a self-righteous grin, addressing the public in his best suit. *We got him, folks. We got him.* I enjoy that his bushy white caterpillar eyebrows have become pseudo-celebrities, even translated to GIF form on BuzzFeed's "The 22 Eyebrows of Detective Donaldson."

So, there you have it, America. The next time you'll see me? I'm not quite sure. Perhaps I'll go out in a blaze of glory. Frankly, I don't feel like surrendering. Not yet. I have places to be, drugs to take, work to do. I'm heading deeper into the abyss. A place that's very near and dear to my heart.

I need solitude to finish Kelly's masterpiece.

A while back, I started an interesting project. Some of it involved writing. Some of it, not so much. It's rather complicated. Let's call it *He's Coming for Me: The Final Act of Kelly Trozzo.* Not a bad title. I'm sure my publisher would have agreed. Not so long ago, they would have paid a large sum of money for this book. Now they wouldn't touch me with a ten-foot pole.

They leave me no choice.

Against my lawyer's wishes, I'd like to share my story on my least favorite platform. The fucking Internet. You deserve to know what happened to your leader. The truth. Not the version you want. Not the warm and fuzzy plot where light overcomes darkness and heroes prevail.

This is Hollywood. Your princess is cunning. Prince Charming is evil. Dragons, demons, and darkness are hidden in us all. There are no bluebirds, no fairy godmothers. No shortage of monsters. We must save ourselves. Yes, I will tell you what I did to her. What we all did to her. And maybe, what she did to me.

What she did to us…

THE DEATH OF A HOLLYWOOD HITMAKER
JULY 20, 2019

In the wake of the media frenzy surrounding Kelly Trozzo's death, there is another victim that has been an afterthought in the press, Kelly's legendary manager, Barry Monroe, a man whose hulking stature and signature yellow framed sunglasses were a symbol of the Hollywood machine.

While the official cause of death has not been announced, inside sources claim that the mogul was shot down in the foyer of Trozzo's mansion. Police pronounced both Monroe and Trozzo dead upon arrival.

And while the country mourns for the fallen popstar, there is little fanfare for Monroe, who many consider the mastermind behind scores of child stars and boy bands in the past decade. This might have something to do with the scandal that surrounded him—at the time of his death, Barry Monroe had fifteen pending lawsuits, with the majority of plaintiffs being under the age of thirty. Allegations of his wrongdoings range from extortion, embezzlement, fraud, even assault, with detailed reports of the mogul using physical force to coerce young artists and their guardians into signing unlawful contracts.

On a *Dateline* episode last year, five former child stars spoke out about their time under Monroe's tutelage, claiming that they lived in a constant state of fear of their former manager. All five said they were subjected to physical and verbal abuse, stating that Barry had fits of rage where he threatened to destroy their careers if they didn't adhere to his rules, which included mandatory attendance at wild Hollywood parties with prostitutes and drugs.

In spite of the controversy, Barry Monroe's legacy as a skilled manager and producer cannot be questioned. As the CEO and founder of Monroe INT, he created a thriving media conglomerate with an astonishing track record for finding, developing, and launching new talent.

One of those stars included Kelly Trozzo, whom Monroe first discovered in an audition room a decade ago. Since that day, Trozzo had been fiercely loyal to her formidable manager, even speaking out publicly in support of him when allegations first rose to the surface.

For insiders, the star's allegiance didn't come as a surprise. In the same *Dateline* expose, singer Nate Conley of the former teen hitmakers, Blue Rockers, claimed that Trozzo was "in on the scheme" and was "just as manipulative and controlling as Monroe himself." Conley went as far as to say that Kelly was a "wolf in sheep's clothing" who convinced him to sign the contract that would ultimately leave him penniless.

With so many enemies, and accusations of fraud and conspiracy, is it possible that Barry and Kelly's death came at the hand of a jilted client or business associate? As wild fan theories circulate on the web, there should be no shortage of new suspects with the strongest motive of them all—revenge.

FOR IMMEDIATE RELEASE
PAY ME, ALICE: A NOVEL
AUGUST 2017

To AJ Daniels, Alice Summers has always been the perfect girl. The only girl. He gets a summer internship to be closer to her. He accepts a job at the law firm where she works so they become cubicle-mates, and then he buys a three-bedroom home with their future in mind.

The only problem? Alice's tough and tattooed husband doesn't agree with AJ's sentiments, nor does he treat his wife nearly as well as her would-be suitor thinks she deserves. First, there are bruises. Then cuts. Then broken bones. And then, one day, Alice disappears. Shortly after, AJ follows suit.

In a twisted tale of obsession and love, AJ decides to embrace the darker side of romance, the side requiring true sacrifice and suffering. In the end, the question isn't whether or not he can find Alice and save her from her terrible marriage, but whether or not he can save both of them from their own destructive impulses. How far would you go for the woman you love?

Pay Me, Alice will be released on September 15, 2017.

KELLY'S ENTOURAGE SPOTTED AT POLICE STATION!

JULY 20, 2019

Will Kelly's inner circle be sporting orange jumpsuits soon? Check out these candid photos of Kelly's closest friends strolling into the Los Angeles police station for questioning!

First on the scene, **Lizzy Anne Michaels**—Kelly's self-proclaimed best friend, who all-too-quickly stole the leading role on Kelly's show after her mental breakdown last year. That doesn't seem very bestie-like, does it? From this picture, Lizzy looks like she hasn't slept in weeks. Guilty conscience, anyone?

Next to arrive, **Jez Branson**—Kelly's fanatical assistant who has been posting pictures with the pop star on Instagram incessantly, including three #throwbackthursday photos from her wild make-out session with Kelly at the VMAs. Obsessed much? Jilted lover *does* seem like a good motive.

Lead detective on the case Charles Donaldson refused to comment on the matter. Business as usual. We'll have to wait and see which of these girls leaves the station in handcuffs!

I check into a motel this morning, pay cash. You should see this lobby. Flies buzz around spoiled fruit. There are holes in the windows. The front desk attendant doesn't look up from his cartoons. Not even for the Most Wanted Man in America. Tsk. Tsk.

Soon enough, he'll realize his mistake.

I unlock the door of room 232 and take in a deep breath of the stale, musty air. A real piece of shit. Exactly what I remember. What I deserve. Stained carpets and walls, a threadbare comforter, a dogeared Bible in the nightstand drawer. I'm glad it will end here. Far away from the glitz and glamour. Far away from the scene of the crime. Out here, the rage dissipates. The guilt and grief settle. The truth will rise to the surface.

I take a shower, unpack a few things—three grams of coke, a bottle of pills, three bottles of vodka, a bag of assorted drugs. A few other goodies. I have five photographs.

One silver sparrow necklace.

A copy of my book.

I run my shaky hands over the sleek matte cover, tracing

17

my fingers along the embossed letters to the very bottom, where the words "a novel" almost disappear into the background. It's all here, detective. Everything you need to know.

Keep reading.

I believe in you.

I pour myself a drink. A coffee mug full of vodka steadies the hands. I flip through the crème pages until I get to the final scene. It's been almost three years since I wrote this, deep in the Oregon wilderness. The scene depicts my best self. A man with a real purpose, strength. A man who overcame his past. Kelly saw something in these pages that others couldn't. A fallen hero. A knight seeking redemption.

I pour another drink.

I failed her.

I failed them all.

My father was right about me.

My demons are relentless.

I thought I could outrun them.

I thought I could protect her.

Alas, my story will end in this motel room. This is where I'll make my final stand.

I open the curtain. A warm breeze rolls in through the cracked window, bringing me back to better times. I open my computer on the wobbly desk. Rituals are in order. I scatter four of the photographs across the desktop. I tuck one between the pages of the Bible. Each one represents a piece of this tragedy. I lay the silver sparrow necklace to the left of the computer. My novel to the right. I crack my knuckles, then hover my hands over the keys.

A disclaimer before we begin. Much of what you read will be shocking, disturbing. Exaggerated. Dare I say, unbelievable. Fear not. It's all part of the grand illusion. And if I've learned anything from my time in Hollywood, it's this: Illusion is everything.

And I learned from the best.
To our atonement, America.
Welcome to my confession.

ACT I

My confession begins less than twenty-four hours after Kelly's death. I was detained and taken to the Los Angeles Police Department in handcuffs.

I was poked and prodded. Photographs were taken. Swabs were taken. I was confined to a cold room with a metal table and a mirrored glass window for Detective Donaldson's viewing pleasure. By dawn, the world would know. The great circus would begin. But if I confessed…much less stress on the department. They wouldn't need much. I was sleep-deprived and dazed. My hands were trembling.

Hours went by before Detective Donaldson entered the interrogation room. He was just what I expected: middle aged and overweight, with a receding hairline and thick, animated eyebrows. He slammed my file down in front of me. Cliché. Just like his cheap button-down and baggy blue slacks. Just like his overwhelming aftershave and self-assured smile.

"So, how do you want to do this?" he asked, leaning back in his chair.

I didn't respond.

"It's not going to take long to put the pieces together."

I didn't respond.

"We looked you up," he said, opening my file. "A year ago, you were a nobody." He flipped through the pages. "You have a few priors, don't you? Possession. Assault. Jeez. These pictures of your last victim…disturbing."

I didn't respond.

He pulled out a pack of cigarettes, unfazed. "You don't mind if I smoke, do you? It's been one of those nights." He lit the cigarette, took a drag, exhaled.

"Well, I'm just going ask the question on everyone's minds… How on earth did some degenerate like you end up with Kelly Trozzo?" His caterpillar eyebrows arched in amusement.

I didn't respond.

"Hey, I'm not going to knock you. She was a hot little thing, wasn't she?" He chuckled. "I see you Hollywood creeps all the time. Anything for a little notoriety…a few extra followers on your fucking profiles, right? Guess they won't forget you now."

I didn't respond.

"Not much of a talker. We don't have to start with the juicy stuff yet. Just relax. Want some coffee?"

I nodded.

"Good. Good." He beckoned to the window.

A small Styrofoam cup was brought in.

"Let's just talk. Why don't you tell me how you guys met? How you weaseled your way into Kelly's life?"

Weaseled my way into her life. I laughed. That first one slipped out. The second one was intentional. I met our detective's gaze, smirking.

"Oh, that's funny to you, is it?" He smashed his cigarette onto the table. "You twisted fuck."

For the first time that night, my mind was lucid. I was poised, strong. I didn't back down. His intimidating eyebrows couldn't fool me. It was all an act. Overworked and underpaid, this case was going to ruin him. He had no idea what I had in store for him. This was going to be fun.

"You have it all wrong." I took a slow sip of the lukewarm coffee. "I didn't weasel my way into anything, detective." I smiled.

"She found *me*."

Ten months prior to the night in question. I was huddled in a rundown gymnasium, amongst folding chairs, stale coffee, and recovering addicts. The air reeked of moldy tennis shoes and puberty. There were eight of us at the meeting, each one dark and tan from the Orange County sun. Some over a decade sober. Some trying to make it through day one. And me...

"I'm eighty-seven days sober," I said, glancing over to my sponsor, Nathan. He had a newspaper under his nose, a greasy ballcap pulled low over his stringy gray hair. He rarely paid attention, though none of us objected. I continued. "Still, I can't seem to get my latest relapse out of my head. It lingers like static in the background. Reminding me who I am. What I'm capable of."

Thank you for sharing.

The meeting ended and I went to refill my coffee. My phone buzzed in my pocket. It had been that way all night. New email alerts. Notifications from apps I never used. I glanced down at my splintered display screen.

A familiar grunt snorted behind me. "Eighty-seven days. Impressive."

Nathan's calloused fingers reached for a stir stick. He was in his usual attire, a flannel shirt with a pair of worn-down Dickies. He was an alpha male through and through, no time for bullshit. Nathan was an incredible writer, a stern man. He had taken a while to warm up to me, if ever. He was my sponsor, though he wouldn't describe our relationship that formally. Still, he helped me in my darkest hour.

I didn't respond. Secretly, I hoped he would be pleased with my progress. Even if he didn't approve of my methods. The results spoke for themselves.

My phone buzzed.

Ding.

Ding.

"How's the new book coming along?" He stirred his coffee.

"A new one?" I laughed, unable to meet his gaze. "I couldn't sell the first one."

Nathan drained the last of the coffee. Threw the stick in the trash. "You never fucking learn."

Ding.

Ding.

Shit.

I looked down at my phone. A text message from my agent, who I hadn't spoken to in months. *What the hell is going on?*

When I looked up, the doors of the gymnasium door shut. Nathan was gone.

I lived on the rundown side of Santa Ana, amongst abandoned storefronts and a steady stream of police sirens. Fifteen minutes from the happiest place on earth. The only light in my barren studio apartment was the glow of the laptop screen. I was staring at my inbox, two hundred new emails and counting. Not the typical fanfare for a no-name author. But there they were. Shiny new messages, pouring in like water bursting through a submarine hatch. Messages from fans who bought my book. Messages from my forsaken website, a few reporters. Mostly Twitter notifications. I opened up my profile. My last login was over three months ago.

I clicked till I found the source.

A tweet from a user of significance.

@KellyTrozzo.

The post was an image of her lying on a bed, holding my novel. The book jacket concealed her face. The tweet read: *Pay Me, Alice is a masterpiece. Suspense. Love. Real sacrifice. All KTroops must read and follow the author.* She tagged my username. Added hashtags.

I knew who she was. Not to be smug, but Kelly Trozzo wasn't exactly my cup of tea. I didn't understand her world, her fans. And truthfully, I wasn't optimistic that an online plug with hashtags could help me sell books. The youth of America likes GIFs, texts, grams, and snaps. Not four-hundred-page novels. Only Oprah can sell those.

I stared at the picture, then her profile, verified with a blue seal. *Fearless Leader of the KTroops* in her bio. In her profile picture, she was staring off to the side, a seductive grin, with long blonde hair engulfing half the circular frame. A face that once saturated toy stores—dolls, backpacks, you name it. But things had changed. No more tiaras, bubble gum, and sundresses. The new Kelly Trozzo had tattoos and tabloid covers. She was pretty; a cute freckly nose, sharp blue eyes. Cryptic blue eyes. Eighty-nine million followers. A fruitful transformation.

I clicked a link I was tagged in. Kelly's thirty-five-second book review had garnered 217,000 views. It was strange seeing her grown up, but not nearly as strange as seeing her holding my book. The little girl America fell in love with was gone. She was sexy, provocative—undeniably adult. There was something about her. Her mannerisms, her gestures. She was trained to lure you in. Trained to make you watch. Trained to make you feel.

She told her fans that she *loved* this book, *Pay Me, Alice.* It made her cry, laugh, and then text her ex-boyfriend. In that order. She laughed after she said "ex-boyfriend," rolling her eyes and falling back onto the bed. She was lying on her sheets in the video, wearing booty shorts and a white tank top. She twirled a silver necklace as she stared into the camera. She told her fans that it was a modern-day fairy tale. A manifesto for her KTroops. She told them to buy my book. Link below.

I closed the video. Whatever that was, it would blow over. It always did. That shit wasn't real. None of it was. A flash in the pan. The tweets would be swept away with the digital tide. My novel would stay hidden. My career would stay buried.

My secrets were safe.

Speaking of secrets...My cursor hovered over a special folder on my desktop filled with photos of *my* ex, my good life. She was real—Sara. I clicked on the most recent pictures, taken earlier that night. From my preferred viewpoint, less than a block away from her suburban house, my former residence. She wore a black tank top, dirty blonde hair tied back in a messy bun as she washed the dishes. Her faded tattoo on her left forearm, a black sparrow.

I clicked the next photo. She was gazing out the kitchen window, biting her lip. Her light brown eyes ensnared in fantasies. I liked to imagine where she went. Back to our favorite diner in that sleepy old town. The place we fell in love. Before the secrets. Before my sins. Before I ever published my novel.

Perhaps I was seeing things the night I destroyed our life together. When I let my rage consume me. I had my reasons. A shadow from my past had paid me a visit, warning me of his return. I saw the outline of his dark boater hat from the bedroom. Then I did something bad. Sara had every right to kick me out.

Checking on her every night was all I had left. Protecting her gave me a purpose. A reason to stay sober. Eighty-seven days and counting. Old habits die hard.

More notifications from my laptop interrupted my thoughts. I toggled back to Kelly Trozzo's profile.

@KellyTrozzo
This is just the beginning. @KalebReedAuthor #KTbookclub
3.4K Comments 16K Retweets 80K Likes

A new photo appeared on her feed. Kelly with her blonde hair swept to the side, holding a finger to her lips. As if she was hiding from someone in the room. She was still gripping her silver necklace. I wasn't the only one with secrets. I scrolled, stared, clicked. The glow of my laptop screen shone for hours.

Please state your name for the record.

My name is Lizzy Anne Michaels and I was Kelly Trozzo's best friend and co-star on her show *Zoe Loves*. We met in 2015 when I was cast for a small part, a two-episode stint as an up-and-coming country singer. I was a nobody back then. Just a glorified extra. But she was the biggest star on the network. Every child actor wanted to be Kelly Trozzo. Especially me. She was my idol. My character was there to help Zoe write a ballad, maybe one or two scenes, four speaking lines total. If Kelly hadn't begged the directors to make the song a duet, I don't think—I mean, I know for a fact, I wouldn't be where I am. I owe everything to Kelly, everything.

Please state your name for the record.

Jez Danielle Branson. Formally, I was Kelly's assistant. But seriously…it was *so* much more than that. My friendship with Kelly was a total fairy tale. I was such a die-hard fan. I had every poster on my wall. Every album, everything. So you can imagine my excitement when fate handed me an invitation to an exclusive party at her mansion! Oh, my gosh. The universe was aligning for us, just like Kelly always said. As soon as I got there, I made sure to mix her favorite drink, exactly how she described in her *Rolling Stone* interview, October issue, page 57. See? I remember everything.

Lizzy: The other cast members didn't know her like I did.

Maybe they were jealous of her success. Kelly and I had an undeniable chemistry. Neither of us had parents, so we had that in common. But there were other things. We just clicked. She liked being a big sister to me. She always wanted to teach me things. She always wanted to be there for me, look out for me—but if I'm being truthful, it was usually the other way around. I was the one looking out for her. I was the one keeping her safe. But in the end, I let her down...Can you give me a minute?

Jez: Did you see her performance at the VMAs? Oh my gosh. Like I said, I wasn't *just* her assistant. I love that picture of Kelly and me kissing on stage. It was *such* a beautiful moment. I have it framed and everything. We were inseparable this past year.

Lizzy: I want to tell you everything I know about the man who killed her. I will not say his name because he is a monster. I warned her. I really did. Every time he acted out, I told her... What if one day it goes too far? What if you can't undo this? You owe him nothing. He had a darkness inside him, detective. He was pure evil. I want him to pay for what he did.

Jez: I am here on behalf of Kelly herself. Before this is over, they will all atone for what they did to her. The KTroops shall have their victory.

THEINSIDEJUICE.COM
An Interview with Kelly Trozzo

A candid conversation with pop's newest bad girl about her meltdown, her transformation, and the comeback that changed everything

Child star gone rogue or misunderstood icon?

Two years ago, Kelly Trozzo's career was on the brink of extinction. After wrapping her eighth season of the hit show *Zoe Loves*, the star was abruptly fired. While producers claimed they wanted to take the show in a new direction, a string of leaked photos of an inebriated Kelly told a different story. Rumors began to swirl of a drug-addled Trozzo struggling to make it through her lines on set; a pill-popping diva who spent hours in her trailer crying. Tabloids celebrated. Her fans mourned. Then, Kelly Trozzo disappeared.

For eight months, she was absent from the public eye—no interviews, no public appearances, not a single post on social media. Most assumed she had become another Hollywood casualty. Wrecked hotel rooms. Failed stints in rehab. Mediocre comebacks. Eventually, an E! Hollywood True Story to top it off. We had seen it all before.

Or had we?

Last August, Kelly emerged onto the VMA stage like a phoenix rising from the ashes. Dressed in a leather bikini and performing a sultry new single advocating bathroom sex, Kelly detonated a media firestorm that broke the Internet. The gamble paid off. With intrigue and shock value in her corner, Kelly has done anything but fade into the Hollywood sunset.

Her comeback album *He's Coming for Me* became the most

streamed album in the world. Her Reborn Tour is sold out in every city, every country. Even more impressive, she mobilized the largest online following of any pop star elite, with some of the most ruthless and loyal fans the world has ever seen. To them, Kelly Trozzo is much more than a singer. She is the leader of a mythical battle against bullies and oppressors. Those who have enlisted in this fandom call themselves the "KTtroops."

Despite her reemergence into the spotlight, Kelly has maintained a safe distance from the media. In fact, short of a fluff piece on *Good Morning America* and one late-night chat with Jimmy Kimmel, Kelly has declined any interviews to discuss her hiatus and electrifying comeback.

Until now.

INSIDEJUICE: Let's just get into it, shall we? Why did you ask for this interview? Why now?

TROZZO: It felt like the right time to shed light on my actions this past year.

INSIDEJUICE: From an outside perspective, it seems like you've been very intentional about this transformation. What does this comeback mean to you?

TROZZO: For the majority of my career, I've had two alter egos, both weaker, punier, more pathetic versions of myself. I have been Zoe Claireborn, a careless, quirky, ever-trusting girl who squealed over nail polish and cried over boys. I have also been Princess Jade—the naive little bitch who worshiped fairy tales. But now, those alter egos have been destroyed. And in their ashes, I have been reborn. The real Kelly Trozzo.

Only those in the literary community truly understood how unexpected my sudden rise to stardom really was. Authors don't become overnight sensations, or casually land on the *New York Times* Best Sellers list. We are supposed to fight, claw, write until we outlast the amateurs, master the craft. Cast aside our demons. Confront our darkest fears. Triumph over the compulsion to self-destruct and evade the blank page. The first one doesn't sell, fine. Write the next one.

I was handed a shortcut.

As my publisher can attest, *Pay Me, Alice* was an utter disappointment. Forty-four measly reviews on Amazon, split evenly between one star and five stars. One-star reviews said the same thing: *Pay Me, Alice* was too long and whiny, disheartening, and tragic. One reader claimed she wanted to cut herself after she read it. My publisher wasn't exactly eager for a sequel. I wasn't eager to write it.

My agent forwarded me a clip of Kelly mentioning the book on *Good Morning America*. She was sitting with George Stephanopoulos, bullshitting back and forth. He asked her what she had been up to. Reading a lot. Anything good? She mentioned her new book club. She raved about my novel. Next subject. I had my doubts. It was her mannerisms. The conservative black-and-white blouse with tight leather pants, a far cry from the half-naked pictures that flooded the Internet. It was her hair, combed neatly to one side, her makeup soft, not overdone. There was something about her I didn't trust.

Either way, my book soared up the charts. Reviews sprang from Kelly's infinite well of cohorts. New editions appeared with refreshed jacket art and fluffed-up endorsements. Only one mattered: "A masterpiece." —*Kelly Trozzo.*

Her fans asked questions. They tweeted, emailed, demanding insights. Commented. Posted. *What happened to Alice? What happened to AJ?* They searched every crack and crevice of the Internet. There was nowhere to hide. Critics were dumbfounded. *It reads more like a stalker handbook than a literary novel.* To them, the *New York Times* Best Sellers list was sacred, impervious to pop stars tweeting out Amazon links.

I agreed.

Despite the literary world's rejection, people were reading my words. That scared the shit out of me. There was something unnerving about it. Something I couldn't shake. There was something rewarding about not selling books. Staying in the shadows. No critics, no limelight, no offers to speak at graduations. No one was calling for interviews. My past would stay buried.

My first public appearance after Kelly's endorsement was at the Grove in Los Angeles. I was standing next to a giant cardboard cutout of my book cover, my hands gripping the podium. Nerves rattled in my gut like an overworked dryer. The crowd was a mix of young girls and older moms, a few guys scattered throughout. Girls with Kelly Trozzo-branded crop tops smiled in the front row. I opened my book, cleared my throat. Scanned the crowd for a familiar face. Sara wasn't there.

I closed my eyes and pictured her in the fifth row, smiling brightly. *Much better.* She came to my first book signing. Only ten people showed, but she was the only one that mattered. She was proud of me that day. I was sober. I had written a book. She had never seen that side of me. She had this gorgeous smile. I wish you could have seen it. Her presence always calmed me. Everything was going to be okay. Even when it wasn't. I had a good life, once.

"Did you miss me?"

The memory of Sara vanished.

My eyes bolted open. It was *his* voice. The packed bookstore crowd moved in and out of focus. Ice in my veins. Knees buckled. My hand slipped off the podium. The girls in the front row stared at me with horror. *Where did that voice come from?* My eyes shifted back and forth, scanning the seats. He would be in his usual attire, dark trench coat, and a low-brimmed hat that covered his dark and menacing eyes. He would be doing his crossword puzzle. *Where are you? Show yourself.*

"Sir, are you okay?" A bookstore employee was holding my arm, steadying me. "Would you like a glass of water?"

A few people coughed to fill the silence. I took a sip of water, gazed back at the crowd. It was nothing. Just my imagination. This was exhaustion, stress. Of course it was. It made sense. I wasn't sleeping. I locked eyes with a pretty redhead in the back. She had a playful smile, a copy of my book clutched to her chest. I cleared my throat, opening to the marked page.

"I chose this scene because it reveals AJ's transformation to his role as protector . . ."

"The storm came quicker than expected. The bartender warned him as much. A lone leaf scatters onto the shoulder of Alice's coat. AJ grabs the leaf, and she leans into his hand. He moves closer, placing his cheek gently on the side of her cold, bruised face. As if his own warmth could heal the tissue aching from her husband's fist. She turns away, ashamed. AJ's willpower is weakening. There are a million things he wants to say. A

million memories he wants to bring up. The late nights at the law firm. The weekend they got stranded in Maysville. The night he found her in that diner. Anything to make this moment last longer. One last smile, that's all he wanted.

No. No. No. He can't. He must be resolute. One day, she will know. One day, she will understand. It wasn't just words. He would do anything for her. Anything.

'Take care, Alice.'

He puts one foot in front of the other. No matter how badly he wants to turn back. He had trained for this. He pulls up the collar of his coat. He is a new man. A determined man. He walks away with things unsaid. From a girl that stole ten years of his life without truly conceding her heart. Every dream, every waking thought, she governed it all. But it's okay now. He would gladly do it again. Repeat every mistake. She was worth every moment. He doesn't look back. He doesn't turn. This was never that type of story. His eyes become as cold as the winter air. He's made up his mind. A surge of determination and strength courses through him. He checks the pocket of his coat. The gun is still there."

Applause.

The attractive redhead raised her hand. "Hi, my name is Jez, and I just wanted you to know how much my friend and I enjoyed your book," she said, blushing.

"Thank you," I responded.

"And we actually had a question about Alice's husband."

My throat clenched.

"Why did you choose to make him a tattoo artist?" she asked.

I shifted in the silence. That was an unexpected question. Frankly, I didn't want to answer. Why should I? They are my characters. My words. My secrets. The pain, the suffering, the love. Straight from my basement. All mine. Wrapped with some half-assed over-photoshopped cover that I didn't approve. Blanketed with some disclaimer that it was a work of fiction.

That's what I wanted. Layers and walls. No connection to its source. I hated feeling vulnerable.

The truth wasn't that simple. My characters are products of my past.

The crowd needed something, anything. I grinned. "Actually, there's not much to it. The hours of a tattoo artist made it a convenient occupation for the plotline. Anyone else have a question?"

Hands raised. I was just about to call on a girl in the front row when the redhead interjected. "How about Alice? She was based on a real person, right?"

Hands lowered.

I turned back to the incessant girl. There was something peculiar about her interest. I didn't like it. These were hardball questions. I would never give her the truth. She was undeserving. None of them could understand. I gripped my book tightly, gazing back to the crowd.

"Alice is a symbol. The definition of something elusive and intangible in human form. She is the perfect person, mate, friend, or possession. Alice isn't real. It's the fantasy we seek but never find."

The redhead and I stared at each other as if she was still waiting for my confession.

"I'm sorry to disappoint you. But this story is a work of fiction."

Lizzy: Fiction? Please. That book was filled with that man's skeletons.

Jez: You won't find one KTroop that didn't love that novel!

Lizzy: It was an obsession for Kelly. *You don't understand, Lizzy. You just need to read it. This tragic but endearing conclusion.* That's how she put it. I finally bought the book—just to shut her up. I read the ending, and it was some grade-A psycho killer shit. Just like the author. Did you read it? Honestly, it wasn't my thing. A little too dramatic for my taste. But Kelly ate that kind of stuff up. Why else would you love a four-hundred-page book about some guy's creepy obsession with a married woman?

Jez: The book signing? Oh goodness. Drunk, stoned. Whatever. He still looked hot. Kelly asked me to attend. She always relied on me to do the important stuff. My job was to invite him to lunch. Oh, and to ask him a few questions if I had the chance. Trust me, I didn't let her down. She loved that book. She used to read it to me at bedtime. It was so adorable. Then one day she leaped up from her bed and said, "Let's do something different. Let's start a book club."

Lizzy: How did she come across the book? You know, she never told me. That's one thing I never asked.

Jez: Maybe she picked it up at the airport. No, that's not right. That's when I first noticed her reading it. She was so cute when she was reading. I loved watching her little brow furrow when she was concentrating. We were on a flight to Miami. That's right. I remember seeing the skull on the cover. I thought it was so cool. Kelly wanted a tattoo of it. She was totally obsessed. Read the entire flight. Wouldn't even drink the free champagne. Then straight to the hotel room to finish. At breakfast, she had this really passionate look in her eyes, even though she must've gotten like two hours of sleep. She told me that this book was going to change my life.

Lizzy: Her motive? Easy. She wanted to help him. Kelly believed that every artist had a duty to share their talents, even authors who wrote stalker novels. The guy had like four hundred Twitter followers before Kelly. He was a nobody. His book was a total flop before she got her hands on it. That's why she gave it her stamp of approval. But he didn't deserve the attention. And he definitely wasn't ready for it.

Jez: She was right. That book changed my life. It changed all our lives. Look where we are, detective. And there's so much more to uncover.

The Real Kelly Trozzo
TheInsideJuice.com Interview 2019

INSIDEJUICE: Since your comeback, your entire image has changed. The clothes, the hair, the tattoos. Yet, you've worn the same silver sparrow necklace since you were a child. Where did you get it?

TROZZO: I got this necklace from my manager, Barry. I remember the day he put it around my neck. "The sparrow has many meanings," he said. "A sparrow is vigilant in its goals. It's a symbol of protection and love. It's also a symbol of resurrection and life."

INSIDEJUICE: So why is it so important to you?

TROZZO: Barry is more than my manager. He is my mentor. He empowered me to aspire to greatness. He taught me how to be resolute in my agenda, to not concern myself with the small-minded and weak-willed. To me, this sparrow represents the power to safeguard my bigger purpose. Zoe wrapped that precious sparrow around her fingers before each show. The same necklace Princess Jade wore when she was in the recording studio. The same one I wore when I was sick and depressed, alone in my bathtub. It was around my neck when my true self emerged from the ashes of my weaker existence. Now it's a symbol of my inner strength. It was, and always will be, my favorite piece of jewelry.

My motel balcony is a thing of beauty. Rusty patio furniture. An ashtray filled with cigarette butts. The smell of bacon and greasy burgers wafts over from the diner next door. Trucks skid out of the gravel parking lot below, a constant stream of dust swirling in their departure. But most importantly, the balcony is the perfect vantage point to watch the sunset over this sleepy old town. It makes me sentimental. The fantasies I used to have in this very spot. Those were special times. Looking out across the horizon, imagining the perfect life. Growing old.

My fantasies are much different now. Nothing about the future. Only the finale. I know what happens if I stay in this forsaken motel. I can picture the sirens blaring from the parking lot below.

Like father, like son. Once upon a time, the news vans came for him. My brother and I opened the curtain to find the local reporters camped out on our front lawn. His affair had been leaked after domestic abuse had been reported. The great governor was resigning. My family lined up in the foyer, backs straight, chins up. My father came downstairs with a crisp white dress shirt, suit jacket, slicked brown hair. I always stared at his fists. I knew what they did. He gave my mother a cold kiss. Patted my brother on the top of his head. He didn't look at me. Then he walked out to the flashing cameras. Nothing would be the same after that.

It's my turn now.

My reckoning will be so much grander. Helicopters. Breaking news. Thousands of bloodsuckers standing in the parking lot outside, broadcasting live. The locals will come out to see the chaos. They will talk about it for years. Long after I rot in prison.

Don't worry.

We're not there yet.

There's still much work to be done.

I turn on the television, prop my head against the headboard. Crack open a new bottle of vodka. The first gulp makes me shiver. My apartment is in the news again. The yellow caution tape draped across my banister. I take another swig. Snort another line. I change the channel: *The Murder of a Hollywood Princess* flashes across the screen. I love the special effects, the ticking hourglass. The host theatrically strolls through downtown Los Angeles with her inside source.

"Jez Bransen was not only a close friend of Kelly Trozzo's, but her personal assistant and backup dancer. She appeared in several live shows, including Kelly's provocative performance at the VMAs last year. Tonight, we talk with Jez about the night of the murder."

If I close my eyes, I can still see Jez's face in the bookstore. I see her in line at the signing, handing me my invitation. I can picture her in that low-cut shirt, opening the door to Kelly's mansion. Welcoming me into their world.

No. Not yet. The fantasies must wait. I must keep my eyes open. Just a little longer.

The camera pans to the restaurant. Jez and the host are sitting across from each other at a patio table. The table linens are crisp and white, expensive silverware, porcelain bread plates. A rusted metal cage that encloses the patio blocks the sun. Green ivy runs through the gaps.

I met Kelly at that restaurant. The camera zooms in on Jez's young, freckly face as she dabs at her eyes with a tissue. The picture of innocence. If they only knew. I want to hear her speak. I can't. The drugs are taking over. The fog rolls in. I close my eyes. I can feel them numbing my body. The dreams and the fantasies will resume shortly. The voices begin to slow down. I look at the screen. It's the pivotal moment.

"Do you think Kaleb Reed murdered Kelly?"

I turn the television off. Another swig. Another line. I won't see the light of day. Not for a long time. I want to see her. I want to escape. I want to go back. I want to see the sun splash across her face.

Kelly was bright and alive in person. Pictures don't do her justice. It was her eyes that caught me, crystal blue, too big for her face, but in the right way. Long blonde hair swept over to one side, tiny ears, smooth neck.

That day at the restaurant, she was wearing a white V-neck shirt with faded jeans. The silver sparrow necklace dangled from her neck. Long pink acrylic nails and bright gold jewelry on her fingers. Black tattoos scattered around her arms.

Kelly took a sip of a cocktail and set the glass down on the white tablecloth. Sunshine gleamed through the open roof, illuminating her smile. The aroma of overpriced salads and perfume wafted over the patio.

She burst out laughing, shaking her head. "Sorry. I'm nervous. I'm a fan. I just…I loved your book."

I took a sip of coffee and nodded appreciatively. "Thank you."

"I can't put my finger on it, but there was something, it was just so personal, so moving. It was just…just so real."

"Thanks. I'm a fan of yours, too," I lied.

"But I do have one question…about your book, that is," she said.

"Something your assistant didn't ask?"

Smiling, she continued. "I believe I understand the literal meaning of the title, that Alice owed you forty-five dollars for a delinquent video bill, as well as a couple thousand for lunch dates—"

"You mean the main character, not me?" I interrupted.

"Sorry." She combed loose strands of hair behind her ears. "Alice owed *AJ* forty-five dollars. But on a more symbolic level, AJ thought Alice owed him for four years of not reciprocating the love you…I'm sorry…*he* gave her."

I nodded hesitantly.

"And here's my *only* problem with your main character," she said, tapping her nails on the table. "I found him kind of pitiful."

Shadows rolled across the metal cage.

"Hear me out," she went on. "Alice made her position perfectly clear. And yet, AJ grew increasingly obsessed and attached to her and, in my opinion, he was extremely selfish by projecting his fixation onto her. He demands that she expend the same amount of energy on this delusional love story that he created. And because he does it in such a passive-aggressive way, it makes me dislike him."

"Is there a question?" I asked.

She took a tiny sip from her glass. "Well, isn't everything that transpired his own fault? Furthermore, did Alice even love him or did she just pity him?"

My hands clenched beneath the table.

Entitled motherfucking pop star.

"Well, I guess I would have to disagree with you, respectfully, because they are my fucking characters and you don't know shit," I snapped. "And, to address your question, neither of them are—" I stopped midsentence. People at the tables around us were snapping pictures, pointing. There was a ringing in my ear, a constricting in my chest.

"Innocent," I mumbled, then cleared my throat, shifting my gaze back and forth. They were all staring, whispering, laughing. What did they want? I reached for a sip of water. The glass trembled in my hands.

"Are you okay?" Kelly asked.

"I'm fine," I choked out. "You see, AJ thought he could exploit love to eradicate his. . ."

Demons.

I heard his voice again, hissing in my ear. Slithering into my veins. He was here. I could feel his shadow lingering in the background. A wave of hollowness settled deep inside my gut. I scanned the tables. *Where are you?* The feeling was too familiar. That dread. That fear. Pulsing to the surface, throbbing. He was in the restaurant, somewhere. He had to be.

People were still snapping photos of Kelly.

My eyes moved wildly across the bar. A man in a dark jacket materialized, his back facing me. *Could it be him?* The man turned. He was laughing with the guy next to him, a long-neck bottle in his hand. My body and mind calmed. It was just my imagination. Yes. Everything was going to be fine.

Kelly grabbed my hand. "Kaleb, what were you saying?"

"Huh?"

"You were talking about Alice and AJ? That neither of them is innocent."

"Yes." I regained my poise. "I was saying that AJ's love for Alice is flawed, and in some regards, not genuine, because it is entirely self-serving. So, obviously, I agree with your dull epiphany, but how can you say Alice is innocent?"

She shrugged, grasping her silver sparrow necklace.

I continued, "Do you think that blanketing your actions with 'I didn't ask you to fall in love' gives you immunity to act recklessly with someone else's emotions? That it gives you the right to let someone grow increasingly closer to you when you know there is no fairy-tale ending?"

"Fairy-tale ending." She grinned.

"Yes. True love," I was heating up, regaining conviction, "does not exploit another's vulnerability and limitations. To me, Alice and AJ share accountability. It's not Alice's job to coddle him, but she should have been willing to risk their relationship and not enable a guy whose obsession transcended rationality. So, forgive me for being rude, but your assessment is wrong. They are both at fault. And furthermore, how could you possibly interpret Alice's love for him as pity? Did you even read the whole book? It was love. In the end, she loved him."

A triumphant smile swept across Kelly's face.

And that's when I knew.

"You're fucking with me?"

"A little bit," she admitted.

I took a sip of water, a deep breath.

"I just wanted to know that the main character *was* you," she said. Her voice was warm and soft, calm, gentle. "You don't have a good poker face, do you?" Kelly crossed her legs. She glanced back for the waiter, then reached under the table and grabbed my knee. "Sorry I got you all riled up."

"I have a question for you," I said.

She traced her fingers on her glass.

"I think your endorsement was deliberate. You want me indebted to you. You're going to ask me for something."

She nodded. "Yes."

I snickered. "I appreciate everything you've done for me. Your fans are truly something else. But memoirs aren't my thing. Especially if it's one of those self-help ones with a bullshit title like—" I swept my arms dramatically across the air, "*Redemption.*"

Her eyes narrowed. "Kaleb, have you seen some of my recent projects? A self-help book wouldn't quite . . ." She paused to find the right words. "Fit my brand." She paused again. "Can I be blunt with you?"

"Don't stop now."

"If you don't write something for me, your next book, if there even is a next book, is going to be a shitty 'poor me' love story for a dwindling fanbase that I created. They won't give two shits about anything you have to say. I didn't endorse you to help you sell books. I want to push you. I want you to evolve as a person and as an artist. You're limiting yourself, Kaleb. You're talented, but you can do better. We can help each other."

I straightened up in my seat.

"Your book was good, Kaleb. I meant that. It was beautiful. But no one would have discovered you if it wasn't for me. Which means you're hiding."

I scoffed.

"You can't bullshit me," she said. "You wrote that book for yourself. You never wanted the world to read it. You hate that book clubs are discussing it." She smiled as she put a crisp hundred-dollar bill in the black bill folder.

"Come to my house tomorrow night," she said. "I'm having a few people over. I'll tell you about it then." She got up and slid her nails along my shoulder.

I snapped out of my daze. "Can I ask you another question?"

She was standing beside me.

"How did you get ahold of my book?"

She looked off into the distance, and then met my gaze.

"You wouldn't believe me if I told you."

I stared at her ass as she walked away. My jeans tightened around the crotch.

Lizzy: Kelly had a history of shitty guys. I imagine it was an unhealthy attachment to abuse, or not having a real father figure in her life. You didn't have to be a therapist to figure that out. Being treated like shit was enjoyable for her, plain and simple. And guess who was there for all the breakups, the crazy ex-boyfriends, the stalkers...me. I was the one who had to clean up the mess. And just so we're clear, when I say crazy, I mean clinically insane. That was Kelly's type. Like it was some prerequisite. It didn't matter if they were singers, actors, photographers, authors, whatever. They were all nuts, plain and simple. But the author...he was a whole different breed of crazy.

Jez: Oh my gosh. She was so nervous before that lunch date. As if Kaleb wouldn't like her. Please. It was so cute. She even came up with a list of thoughtful questions about the book to impress him. I helped pick out her outfit, a black maxi dress with her favorite gold earrings. She looked so hot. I'll say this. Kelly knew how to get a guy's attention.

Lizzy: Strangely, I think she worshipped him. The way she talked about those damn characters. He was guarded at first, according to Kelly. Then he opened up after the second beer. He admitted that Alice was real. Surprise, surprise.

Jez: Drinking? Not sure. When was Kaleb not drunk or stoned?

Lizzy: I hoped that confession would have scared her. But no, how could AJ and Alice's tragic love story be disturbing? *It's a* *modern fairy tale, Lizzy*. Honestly, it makes me sad. Because no matter how awful things got, Kelly still believed in happily ever after. She had this unshakeable belief that she would ride off into the sunset with Prince Charming. She always found the best in people—even if they were ex-felons with a history of drug abuse. You know how hard it is to watch your best friend put her faith into a man like that?

Jez: Kelly came home from lunch in such a good mood, skipping around the house. We were going to throw a huge party to launch the new book club! A *Pay Me, Alice*-themed party with Kaleb as our guest of honor. We even got a cake with the cover of his book on it!

Lizzy: Yes. I went to her little party. Once I saw the cake, I left.

The Real Kelly Trozzo
TheInsideJuice.com Interview 2019

INSIDEJUICE: Is this the first time you've spoken out about your suicide attempt?

TROZZO: In the press…yes. But I've been very open about it in my music.

INSIDEJUICE: Any song in particular?

TROZZO: My new single, "He's Coming for Me." The song is about our inner monster. It's about the darkness we've all buried. Sometimes, you think that you're safe. You think that you've shoved him in the basement and padlocked the door… or locked him in a tower. But eventually, he'll break down that door. He'll come for you. And when he does, you better be ready. Because there will be no mercy.

My dreams are becoming more and more vivid. Perhaps it's the drugs. Perhaps it's the things I've done. The things I've seen. Everything feels so real, so severe. There is no filter.

In last night's visions, I found myself in the backseat of a police car. The lights of downtown Los Angeles whizzed by. Neon signs. Vagrants pushing shopping carts. Girls in short dresses smoking cigarettes standing next to guys in ripped jeans yelling, stumbling.

I felt the vinyl seats. The dried blood caked on my hands. The police were talking over the squeak of the windshield wipers. They knew who the victim was. *This is going to be a fucking frenzy.* Static from the police scanner. "Craziest shit I've ever seen. Found her naked. Thrown across the driveway. Slashed up with a knife. This guy is one twisted fuck."

I slammed my head against the steel cage that separated us. I was desperate, frantic. I needed to go back. I needed to see her. The officer in the passenger seat turned around. Kelly's beautiful face came into focus. Blood dripped down her forehead, running into her eyes. "I'm dead, Kaleb."

I jolt awake. I'm in the cheap motel room.

Rays of sun drip through the blinds.

I decide to get out for some fresh air. I take precautions. Hat. Sunglasses. I even bleached my hair blonde. Getting outside is worth the risk. I need it. Food and water before my next binge, for starters. At the store, a mother of two is reading a magazine with my face plastered on the cover, along with Kelly's. She looks up from her magazine, then quickly turns her gaze. Pulls her kids closer. I can tell she doesn't recognize me. How could she? Besides the hat and glasses, I don't look like the author in the photo. That was a better time. Since then, I've lost a few pounds. The stress, the drugs. It's not my best look.

Kelly's face was glowing in the photo. Your sweet, innocent princess. I can't recall the exact headline—*Kaleb Reed's Wicked Sex Games?* Sounds about right. You guys love that shit. I can relate. Gossip is no different than my favorite drugs. It feeds your hunger. Offers a little rush, a twinge of excitement.

The next chapter of our fairy tale begins in the hills of Los Angeles, far from the smog and congestion of the city. The fortress that Kelly called home, perched on the Mt. Olympus of Hollywood. I was sitting in my car, staring at the turrets of a castle built on television royalties. Engine still running. The threshold between worlds. Dragons, demons, and monsters lay on the path ahead. I wasn't equipped for the fight. I needed meetings. I needed my sponsor, Nathan. I needed to start writing again. Work the steps. Stay in the light. Go back and check on Sara.

I put the car in drive.

I was prepared to leave.

Then I saw him.

His dark trench coat and low-brimmed hat. He was in the crowd of partygoers, ascending the steps, entering the castle. Fear crept down my spine, prickled beneath my skin. It wasn't my imagination. Not this time. Not just stress, nor lack of sleep. It was him. He had some nerve showing his face. I turned the engine off. I opened the car door. I had to find out why he came back.

I stepped across the line.

Clouds of smoke swirled through the air.

Lights flashed and spun.

Tattooed skateboarders flew across the marble floors. The child stars had grown up. They wore brightly colored clothes and sunglasses, scruffy facial hair, oversized beanies. Heavy mist rolled through the castle. I moved past cocaine piled upon a glass coffee table. Past prescription bottles filled with my favorite white pills. My body shuddered, perked up. A familiar chuckle echoed through the room.

Welcome back, Kaleb.

I would recognize that voice anywhere. His breath. Oh, that evil, cold, menacing breath. Crawling down my neck. Where was he? I spun around and around, frantically scanning the room. I spotted his black boater hat amongst the crowd. He was weaving in and out, smiling. Bob. That motherfucker. He wasn't real. But he was real. He was the manifestation of every pain and fear inside me. He tipped his dark hat. *You missed this, didn't you?* He knew. Oh, he knew everything.

Yes, I missed this shit. Of course I did. It was my life, once. I missed how it stifled the darkness. I missed the thrill. The shakiness. The chaos. Excitement. Vigor. Yes. Give it back to me. All of it. Kids were laughing and rubbing their coke-numbed noses, placing pills on each other's tongues. I missed the anticipation.

Bob disappeared into the crowd.

The music shook every wall. Strobe lights, black lights. Beats pulsed and echoed. A dark voice boomed through the speakers.

"CHAIN ME TO THE ROCK, BABY."

THROW AWAY THE KEY.
THE MONSTER'S ON THE LOOSE.
AND HE'S COMING FOR ME."

Young girls danced in glowing bathing suits. They gyrated in slow motion, drifting in and out of the fog. Lollipops attached to their mouths. Their hips turned and twisted like they were luring me in. Faces fixed in ecstasy. Their tongues slid across their lips. All extras in my beautiful fantasy.

The chorus repeated.

"HE'S COMING FOR ME.
HE'S COMING FOR ME."

A kid bumped into me in the flashing lights. He scowled, then blew smoke in my face. I spun around. Lively faces. Blurred faces. Neon faces.

The kids laughed.

They toasted.

They screamed.

"HE'S COMING FOR ME."

I should have tried harder to resist. I should have turned down Kelly's invitation.

"HE'S COMING FOR ME."

I should have signed her book and moved on. I could have driven back to Sara's house. I could have stayed sober. I could have fought back.

I shoved my way through kids jumping, dancing, screaming.

"THE MONSTER'S ON THE LOOSE…"

They chanted.

"AND HE'S COMING FOR ME."

I saw Kelly.

She was lying on an inflatable raft in the pool, wearing a white bikini and holding a red cup in her hand. This was what I came for. I wanted her. Oh, I wanted her badly. The way her wet hair was swept wildly to the side. The brightness in her eyes. The way the world revolved around her. Most of all, I missed the excitement. That craving. It made me feel alive.

Three girls squealed with laughter and dove naked into the pool. Jez walked up to me, dripping wet. She pointed to a towel hanging up beside me. Her breasts were completely exposed. They were incredibly large and perfect. Of course they were. This was a trap, a test. I *was* the main character from your favorite book, Kelly. I was AJ. And you were right. He was selfish. And weak. He was always chasing. It's so laughable, how predictable I am.

Kelly climbed out of the pool.

Her tiny bathing suit dripped onto the cement, her bottoms scrunched, flaunting her ass—small, not overly toned, more natural. She walked over and threw her arms around Jez.

"Kelly, I didn't realize this would be a party," I said, beckoning to the door.

She looked at me suspiciously.

"Maybe we can just get coffee, or—"

"Kaleb," she said firmly. "Relax. We can go somewhere quiet."

She pulled back her wet hair. She had little makeup on. Her face perfect like a doll—soft, diminutive features. Her body was small and petite. She was stunning. She was twenty-one. Not too young. What am I saying? She *was* too young. What did it matter? This was my fantasy. She created this all for me.

She grabbed a red cup from a friend, her eyes never leaving mine.

"Follow me."

I shadowed her through the smoke and chaos. I felt the envious stares of everyone at the party. I was chosen by their leader. I knew Bob was watching me from afar. I would deal with him later. My eyes were glued to Kelly's backside as we climbed the stairs. It bounced up and down with each step, and my mind wandered.

We were in her bedroom.

In her tower.

"Will you excuse me for a moment, Kaleb?"

She disappeared.

I paced the room, taking in my surroundings. Marble sculptures. Medieval oil paintings. Elegant furniture. All props. Everything was shiny and new. Nothing from her childhood, no photos of friends or family. I sat on the bed, hands drenched in sweat.

Music pounded through the walls. *"HE'S COMING FOR ME."*

Kelly came back into the room wearing navy pajama bottoms and a white tank top, no socks, her hair up in a messy bun. A description from my novel. Chapter ten. They were stuck overnight before a client meeting. A storm kept them in a hotel. Alice came out of the shower, drying her hair. AJ had never loved her more. Pajama bottoms. White tank top. No makeup. He liked her hair up in a messy bun. Something about the state of sleep readiness.

But this was a new story.

New characters.

New villains.

New plot twists.

A new lead.

I wanted Kelly to undress. I wanted to be inside her. My heartbeat thumped in rhythm to the pulsing music. Drumming against my ribcage. It was calling to her. It bothered me that she commanded so much power.

"Tell me about the project."

She examined me from the mirror where she was fixing her hair. "You're so tense."

58

"I'm sober," I said. "And I have somewhere I need to be."

She laughed, looking at me intently. "Do you want me?" she asked.

"HE'S COMING FOR ME."

"Yes," I admitted. "But you already know that. And I'm not big on these games."

Suddenly, she was on the bed next to me. Her tiny waist peeked through her white top. It was perfect and flat, soft and tight.

"Games?"

"We live different lives."

"How so?"

"I don't have teenagers snorting and screaming all over my house."

She snickered.

"And don't forget the part where you take me up to your room and ask me if I want you," I added. "You think this is normal?"

She walked over to a small bar area built into an alcove in the tower room.

"How do you normally conduct business?" she teased.

"Not like this."

She pulled out a bottle of vodka.

"How about this?"

"HE'S COMING FOR ME."

I stared at the bottle. What about all your hard work? What about Sara?

Are you kidding? Sara doesn't want you anymore. You think showing up at her house is going to keep you sober? That's not a damn purpose. That's desperation. She doesn't want you. This is where you belong.

What about the people you love? Your brother?

Please. He's dead. It was your fault. Just ask your father.

What about your sponsor? What about Nathan?

I don't see him. He can't help you now.

What if I give in? Will you leave Sara alone?

I will. Bob entered the room.

I took a swig and passed the bottle back to Kelly. The warmth from the alcohol slowed my heart rate, calmed my breathing. It wasn't my favorite, but I missed it. The voices dulled. She took a swig. Fell back onto the bed. We made small talk between swigs. She kept pushing loose strands of blonde hair behind her ear. Another description from my book.

She asked me if I still partied. I used to. I told her about my past. The arrests. Rock bottom. Leaving my family. I told her that cocaine and pills were my favorite. She asked if Alice was still in my life, and I shook my head. I felt vulnerable. Not starstruck, but intimidated. It was hard to tell. I wanted to please her. I wish she had been immature and selfish, pertinacious, and snobby. I wish she had asked me to write some shitty, juvenile screenplay. Then I could say no because it was an absurd idea and I wouldn't compromise. That wasn't Kelly.

She touched my arm, running her nails down to my hands. Our fingers interlaced. She stared up at me with doe-like eyes. Her nails moved back up my arms. Chills trailed. She got up from the bed and walked over to the dresser. Her pajamas dropped, revealing a pink thong and a perfect ass. My heart raced past the numbing alcohol.

"HE'S COMING FOR ME."

The elastic bands of her thong were high on her hips; my eyes stuck on her soft cheeks. Why was I really here? I was so far out of place, and seven swigs deep in vodka. She hoisted herself onto her dresser and opened her legs as I walked toward her. She reached for me. The height of the furniture was perfect. Our bodies aligned with ease. She had either done her homework or done this before. I assumed the latter.

I put my index finger on top of her pink cotton panties. Slid my fingers under and touched the soft skin beneath, moving up and down, my breath hovering on her neck. She moaned. I pulled her panties to the side. Smooth skin. Wet lips. No hair.

"HE'S COMING FOR ME."

I pulsed and surged onward. I stripped her thong down, staring at her hairless crotch. *What about Sara? What about Nathan?* They pulled me out of this mess, once. They wouldn't be there again.

Fuck them.

They left you.

I placed my hands on Kelly's knees. I half expected her to shove me off, but she didn't. The innocence was gone. Her gaze was direct, provocative, leading. She knew what she wanted. I let her reach for my waist. Our lips touched. We kissed. My thumbs slid down her delicate jaw. I wanted every part of her. She tugged at my belt and pants until my erection was out in the open. I took my shirt off. Hers followed.

Her hips moved closer to the tip of my cock resting against her vagina. I buried my forehead in the crook of her neck, feeling the warmth of her body. She was already so wet. I shouldn't be doing this. *Keep going.* I knew this ending. *You have no idea.* She took one more slide forward. My penis slipped inside of her.

The warmth devoured me. Completely. No more resistance. Down the rabbit hole. Into the fantasy. I begged for more. I pushed. Again and again, I pushed as deep as I could. Jaw locked. Teeth grinding. Thrusting madly. Into the darkness. My hands lowered to her ass, pulling, squeezing, pushing until I couldn't possibly go any farther. Until I took in every part of that warmth.

She moaned with every thrust. My hands went back to her neck. I tried to pull her head into my chest, but she pushed away. She wanted my gaze. Her wide blue eyes consumed me, scared me. I averted mine...too much. She grabbed my neck tightly, challenged me to stare back. She was in control. She bit her lip, looked down. Then back up to my eyes.

She was posing. Her hips gyrated perfectly with my thrusts, and I reached down and grabbed her ass. She moved in closer. I pushed deeper and deeper. I kissed her again. I couldn't resist.

My penis thickened as I got ready to come. I didn't want to go so fast, but I couldn't stop. I tried to pull out, but she dug her nails into my back and didn't let me move. I didn't fight it, pumping one last thrust into her small frame and letting it go. My heartbeat slowed. My body relaxed. Still inside of her. She rubbed her nails through my hair and then put my head on her shoulder.

Bob chuckled from across the room as he got up to leave. He smiled, tipped his hat, and slid the crossword under his arm. *Welcome back.*

Lizzy: I never trusted his eyes. They were just...filled with darkness. Like his soul was at a crossroads. I saw him that night at the book party, before I left. Did he tell you that? I don't think he recognized me. He was pale, grossly sweaty. He was okay-looking when he wasn't strung out, not my type, definitely not good enough for Kelly. I warned her not to be alone with him. I should have known better...you couldn't tell Kelly what to do.

Jez: That was such an amazing night! I knew they were going to hook up. How could they not? Kaleb was hot. We spent two days shopping for outfits. A whole day just on bathing suits. I thought she was going to go for something slutty, like a scrunched bottom or a skimpy thong. Kelly's ass was seriously the best. But instead, she chose a conservative two-piece and a few Alice-inspired outfits for later. She looked so gorgeous dressed up as Alice. Look at me, I'm crying just thinking about it.

Lizzy: I don't want you to get the wrong impression of Kelly…it's not like she was a slut. Contrary to the gossip, she didn't have a ton of one-night stands. All that stuff onstage is a complete act. Kelly had a heart of gold. But dressing up as Alice from his book? That was a horrible decision. No matter how tough that girl was, she could be naive. It was just another acting role for Kelly. A night of dress-up and hanging out with the guy she likes. How could she know what he was capable of?

Jez: Oh please. It was a *Pay Me, Alice*-themed party, for heaven's sake! Of course she was going to dress up like Alice! I knew Lizzy wouldn't approve. It was awkward when she came. Kelly tried to be nice to her, but Lizzy had a giant stick up her butt. She was jealous. Just so you know, she and Kelly were not that close this past year. I'm not going to gossip, Kelly wouldn't want that. So that's all I'll say.

Lizzy: She said he was pretty pushy. Forceful? I wouldn't say that. Not sure she would have admitted that. But when I pressed for more details, she gave a long pause. She said she liked it. And that *didn't* shock me. Typical of someone who craves abuse. I asked her what her next move was, and she said that Kaleb wanted to write her story…

Jez: Not a story, detective. Stories come and go. But legends… those last forever.

THE REAL KELLY TROZZO
TheInsideJuice.com Interview 2019

INSIDEJUICE: Let's switch gears for a minute. I look around at the statues in the driveway, the paintings on the wall. You're obsessed with Greek mythology. Why?

TROZZO: It started when I was a child. I would beg my mother to read me the tale of Andromeda, even though I'd heard it a million times. I liked how she told it, how the universe could sometimes seem unfair and cold, but everything happens in accordance to this higher plan, something bigger than us.

The story is very similar to the plot of my movie, but I'll recap. Andromeda is the gorgeous daughter of cruel Cepheus, king of Aethiopia, and Queen Cassiopeia. When the queen opens her fat mouth and brags that their daughter is prettier than the nymph daughters of the sea, the great Poseidon sends a sea monster to destroy the city. In response, King Cepheus goes to the Oracle of Apollo, and decides to appease Poseidon by sacrificing his only daughter.

So, there's Andromeda, chained to a rock, betrayed by her father and mother, at the mercy of this human-eating monster. What on earth will she do? Then the dashing Perseus comes strolling in from his escapades with Medusa, and lo and behold, he sees Andromeda chained to the rock. Our hero can't have that. With a swift swing of his sword, Perseus kills the monster, frees Andromeda, and then—because what else happens after you save a damsel in distress?—he marries her.

My mother used to say that some terrible things are supposed to happen in our lives. It is the universe's way of correcting itself, and that everything will unfold the way it needs to. It just makes sense to me. Only when we are chained can we discover our true strength, our destiny in this world.

It was 4:00 a.m., and I was still at Kelly's house, polishing off the bottle of vodka. Our bodies propped against the head-board. The party was over, and the house was still. The window was open. A gentle breeze rolled over the bed. My book was sitting on her nightstand. I liked that. I took a swig, my eyelids closing. I was tired and numb, but alert enough when she spoke.

"I told you I wanted you to write something." She curled her silver sparrow necklace around her fingers, her naked body twisted toward me. "I loved that your book was the love story of someone you would never end up with."

It jolted me awake.

"The hopelessness of it all. You loved her more than she loved you," Kelly said, gazing into the darkness. "It was so real. You knew everything about that girl. I knew her better than the narrator."

She grabbed the bottle from me with a mischievous grin. "I want our book to be a love story, not a memoir. I want you to fall in love with me, Kaleb. I want you to know everything. The

67

good, the bad, the secrets that I've hidden from the world. And in the end, I'm going to break your fucking heart."

And then she kissed me softly on the lips.

Lizzy: She called me in the morning on her way to the airport. She was weary, but also strangely enthralled. A recovering druggie with a rap sheet? I mean, c'mon, how could she resist? And not just any rap sheet. When I read about what he did to that poor tattoo artist in Massachusetts…It was beyond gruesome. He beat that guy to a bloody pulp. Did you see that man's face? Google it. Who wouldn't be scared? There was something horrible inside him.

Jez: As usual, I found her deep in meditation the next morning. I was freaking out. Tell me what happened? Did you guys hook up? Spill it! That's when she opened her eyes and grabbed my hand. It was so intense. I was thinking, oh my gosh, something bad happened. She can't even get the words out. Then a huge smile broke out on her face. She screamed, "He wants to write our book!" Oh my gosh. I've never seen her so excited! Her favorite author was promising to capture her in a way that no one else could!

Lizzy: Kelly believed in all that universe crap. She was always looking for signs of a bigger purpose. The author knew that. I wasn't a fan of his book, but the guy was a good storyteller. You should have heard some of the garbage he fed her. Stars aligning, sharing missions, all sorts of New Age mumbo jumbo. Absolute bullshit if you ask me.

Jez: Kelly was adamant that the universe had grand plans for her and Kaleb. She found his book for a reason. Just like I served that drink to her for a reason. She believed we were all meant for something bigger. But she also taught me something else—it only takes one bad seed to poison the entire apple.

The Real Kelly Trozzo
TheInsideJuice.com Interview 2019

INSIDEJUICE: What is your relationship with your mother?

TROZZO: I don't have one.

INSIDEJUICE: Why is that?

TROZZO: My mother was a sick woman. I'm not sure what it was, bipolar disorder, schizophrenia. All I remember is the hysterics. When I was a kid, she would have these episodes, and her face would be as red as a cherry tomato. I would ask if she was okay, but she couldn't answer me because she was another person—even her eyes looked different, just dark and scary. She'd lock herself in her room for a week straight, and I would hear picture frames and other stuff crash against the wall. I had no idea what was going on. But there was something wrong with her. The drugs helped ease her suffering.

INSIDEJUICE: What kind of effect did that have on you?

TROZZO: Believe it or not, I owe my success to my mother. Most nights, after she got high, she would stroke my hair and stare at me in the mirror. She would tell me that I was a beacon of light, a burning star that would never die out. My mother took me to my first audition. She found this red velvet dress at a Salvation Army, holes in the skirt, and she twirled it around like it was designed by Coco Chanel herself. I held her hand as we walked into the casting room to find twenty blonde dolls dressed to perfection, next to their chic parents. And there I was, in some dirty hand-me-down, next to my strung-out mom.

In a moment of weakness, I told her that I wanted to leave, and I'll never forget what she did. She squeezed my hand with real strength. Suddenly, her eyes became clear and lucid. Then she said the words that came to define me: *You're going to be better than me, darling. You're going to shine brighter than all of them. Because you have something they don't—pure light. Now step forward, my beautiful daughter, my beautiful star.*

Then they called my name to audition, and she pushed me forward. Permitting me to shine.

I opened my eyes, the sun blanketing my face. I was naked. Kelly was gone. The sheets were too crisp, the comforter too large and expensive. Her bed felt good. I hadn't slept on good, clean sheets in a long time. A copy of *Pay Me, Alice* was on the nightstand. I grabbed the book, browsed the pages for any clue to its origin—an advanced copy stamp, a name, anything. There were no notes. No dog-eared pages. No signs of wear. The pages were crisp, the matte black cover unscathed. Placed for decoration. Just like everything else.

Kelly's house was always still and silent in the light of day. The sins of the night washed clean. I walked out to the staircase overlooking the foyer, expecting to find passed-out teenagers lying on the marble, amid whippets and empty Solo cups. Instead it was spotless. The cleanliness was almost eerie. My bare feet slipped across the polished tiles.

There was something familiar about Kelly's house. It reminded me of my childhood home. That same sorrow. Coldness. A shiny political family with a hollow center. My father's scandal punctured the surface. My brother's death imploded us. My mom locked herself in her room. My dad abandoned

72

her. She was safer that way. He couldn't hurt her anymore. I haven't been back in over a decade. I never forgave my dad for being a coward. For his rage. For leaving. But in all fairness, that was what I did, too.

What I've always done.

I'm just like him.

I found Kelly in her study. Books were stacked along the walls alongside medieval suits of armor and oil paintings of Greek Gods. My eyes fell upon the largest one, stretching across the entire wall. A monster rose out of the sea, its fangs primed to devour a pale woman chained to a rock. Andromeda. A strapping Greek hero was on the horizon. Perseus. He was riding on a Pegasus, his sword held triumphantly in the air. The scene was painted in a classical style, but bright colors were smeared wildly around the canvas, with the words: *Love, pain, sacrifice, grace, mercy.*

"Kaleb."

Kelly was sitting on the floor surrounded by fan mail and letters. She had her headphones on, sporadically scribbling in a notepad as she swayed to the beat.

"Good morning," she said over the music in her ears. "You sleep well?"

"What's all this?" I asked, looking at the scribbled-upon pages.

"My routine."

"Routine?"

She was fully dressed in a long, black cotton skirt and a white tube top, no makeup. Her hair was wet, tied into a bun. She took off her headphones and looked up at me.

"You don't have a creative routine?"

"Not really," I said.

"One book at the age of thirty-three. Why am I not surprised?" She pointed over to the desk. "There's your offer."

I grabbed the thick stack of papers. An official book

contract. Fully thought out and detailed. A minimum of twelve months. Page one: "Rules and Regulations." I flipped through, skimming over the details. I couldn't make our relationship public…I couldn't do this…I couldn't do that…Page after page of clauses. My eyes went to the bolded dollar amount. She would give me a $200,000 advance to complete a manuscript within a year of the date of signature. Six months of research, six months of writing.

There was nothing about falling in love. A last-minute verbal addition, no doubt.

It was a lot of money. More than I'd ever had to my own name. The fine print said she would pay for plane tickets, hotels, trips, and miscellaneous expenses. The money was for my total commitment. Both of us had final approval over the finished manuscript. Publication required two signatures. She had the right to stop this project at any time. One of the guest bedrooms would be available for me during the project.

She wanted me to live there, at her mansion.

A spot for a signature.

A check for $200,000, signed and dated.

Jez came in, fully clothed. Professional black slacks, a conservative gray sweater, and thick black glasses. No more bouncing tits. The spell of the night was broken. The enchanted castle with all its inhabitants clean and polished by first light.

"Kelly, we've got to go. Are you posting?"

Kelly nodded, grabbing her phone and flipping the screen around. She angled her face in the center, recording. "Rise and shine, KTroops. Today I used your letters as inspiration for a new song." She smiled, reaching for a piece of paper on the floor. "One letter in particular from @KTErica2, who's been going through a difficult time." Kelly fixed her hair, then looked into the camera with determined eyes. "Remember, when I returned from my own struggles last year, I promised that I would never abandon you again. Today I'm asking you to make the same promise, Erica. We are in this fight together. No one is left behind. Please pick her up, KTroops. Remember that our armor is forged in fire."

Kelly stopped recording and handed Jez the phone. "Post that in the car." Then she turned to me. "So what do you think?"

I was taking it all in. My eyes went back to the enormous painting in the room. The check was in my hands.

"Kaleb," she pressed. "The offer?"

"Kelly, I am truly intrigued. But—"

She stopped me before I could finish.

"Think about it. I'll text you later this week. Feel free to make yourself at home." She paused and followed my gaze back to the painting. "Do you like it? I commissioned it from a talented young artist I found. I'm a fan of Greek mythology. I'm sure you've noticed."

"It's impressive."

"Which character do you identify with? The monster, the damsel, or the hero?"

I didn't answer. Kelly already knew.

Before leaving the room, she paused and turned to me once more.

"Did he really do it?"

"Huh?"

"At the end of the book…AJ. Did he really do it?"

I smirked. "Do what?"

She giggled, then she left. I collapsed onto the couch. My gaze lingered on the painting. There was something about it. The green scales of the sea monster rising. Its sharp fangs preparing to dig into the soft flesh of the captured princess. I held the check up to the light. Bob was reading the newspaper on the couch. His legs were crossed, his dark eyes covered by the pages. He looked up, nodded. His eyes went back down.

"Think it over," he chuckled behind the newspaper.

Jez: Kaleb wasn't a morning person, I'll tell you that. It was cute watching them flirt. They were so playful. Kelly was upset that he didn't sign the contract right away. She was terrified that the paperwork might scare him. But she had to protect herself. Wouldn't anyone in her position?

Lizzy: No matter what he told you, that guy craved the fame. This was his golden ticket. He'd go from a no-name author to penning a Kelly Trozzo biography. Talk about a step up. But it's funny, the more I find out about him, I think it was more than that. He wanted other things. Much darker things. Call me crazy, but I think he always imagined this ending.

INSIDEJUICE: That story of your first audition is legendary. That's when you signed with your manager, Barry Monroe, correct?

TROZZO: Correct.

INSIDEJUICE: There's been a lot of controversy surrounding Barry, whom you've been with your entire career. Why have you been so loyal?

TROZZO: Signing with him was an easy choice. Barry Monroe was a legend in the industry. He was hard to miss in that first audition room—three hundred pounds and a smile that could haunt your dreams. He said it was my eyes that caught his attention. He recognized in me everything he saw in himself...strength and ambition. I wasn't like those other kids that auditioned day in and day out. He said that most of them were easy prey, mere sheep. But every so often, he found someone like me—a hunter, a wolf.

Those first billboards gave me chills. No matter how cheesy they were, even the one of my face bursting out of a cartoon heart. Every time I saw them, something inside me came alive. I was destined for this life. I can't say that it wasn't exciting, dressing up for the premieres, the parties, the private planes. I wasn't one of those coked-out Hollywood kids either—I never touched a drink or a drug back then. My purpose was too strong. My favorite part of the night was when Barry would see me mingling and schmoozing with investors, and in the middle of a conversation, our eyes would meet. I knew what he saw. He saw a partner.

I imagined I saw a father.

I haven't decided how I will end this. If I stay here, they'll find me. They will barricade me inside this motel room. It's last place I'll see as a free man. You would like that, wouldn't you? Don't think I don't see your videos. I read your tweets. I know what you think of me.

I know what I have to do. But I can't. I just can't. I'm not ready. I won't bother calling my lawyer. I'm on my own. This is what I do when I'm on my own. If someone needs me, if someone is counting on me, I'm better. I really am. When I have a purpose.

You don't believe me?

I hear my phone ringing. It's Nathan. I don't even have to look. He's the only one who would call. No one else would claim me. He'll tell me to surrender. To flush all the drugs and face this shit like a man. I don't pick up. I don't feel like hearing his stern voice. I smash the leg of a chair on top of the phone. It shatters. No more phone. No more interruptions. I feel like staying high.

Much better.

I do miss Nathan.

I met him at my first meeting, back when I ingested cocaine and pills like they were candy. He saw through my bullshit. During my introduction, I announced that I was a writer. What a joke. I hadn't written shit. One barely readable screenplay. A couple of half-assed short stories. I was twenty-five and full of it. Always loaded. A total amateur. Entirely self-indulgent. Still guilty. Nathan told me that writers didn't stand up in a meeting and announce that they were writers. They just fucking wrote.

I approached Nathan after meetings. He would grunt like some old bulldog declining a walk. Could I blame him? I was a mess. I used to get high every night, then go to NA with the same bullshit story. I blamed my family for cutting me off. My dad for being an unavailable asshole who hurt my mom. For abandoning her. For abandoning me. I blamed my friends for making drugs so available. But most of all, I blamed myself. For not protecting my kid brother. I've kept that guilt. Guarded it like it was sacred. Buried it deep in the shadows so I never had to look. I invested my time and energy into bullshit. Drugs. Distractions. I chose dulling and numbing instead of self-discovery and growth.

California was my answer. Who could go wrong in the Golden State? Manifest Destiny. I could outrun my problems. Leave my failures behind. Seemed logical. But my problems—all problems, all demons—they adore their owners. They follow them like shadows.

One NA meeting, I was getting coffee and Nathan looked at me and mumbled, "You're a fucking idiot."

I stood there, wounded. I knew he didn't like me, but c'mon. Thankfully, he was capable of remorse. At the next meeting, he sat down in a metal chair next to me. Handed me a coffee. A man of very few words.

"Want to stop doing drugs?"

I looked at him blankly.

He smacked me in the head with a newspaper.

"Be a man and start writing. Do that, and you won't care about your stupid pills anymore."

He stirred his coffee, tried to smile but his stubborn wrinkles were out of practice. He managed a half grin at best.

Our relationship developed slowly. We had…not a friendship, a non-committal sponsorship. He said that at the core of most addictions were people who were scared of their truth. Humans are petrified of God's will. God's plan. God's love. Scared of their potential. The universe rose and fell, expanded and contracted. But we clung to our tiny little worlds. We refused to fall into the unknown, into the mystery. According to Nathan, that was where real art took place. True transformation.

Where we faced God.

"Have you written anything?" he would ask every week.

"No," I would respond.

And he would reply, "Good luck with those bullshit problems."

The newspaper would unfold back over his face.

Nathan told me that everything in life came down to two choices: the right one or the easy one. Addiction was the easy choice—the impulse, the shadow. The right choice? Becoming an instrument of passion, of purpose, of spirit. Face the darkness in your heart. Face the rage. Face it with courage.

I got coffee with Nathan after I slept with Kelly.

I talked about our night together. Two hundred thousand dollars to write a book. I left out the drinking. And the sex. And all the cocaine on the glass table. I knew Kelly's lifestyle wasn't ideal for a recovering addict, but she was offering me a chance to take my writing to a real platform. That was a sound argument. Even Nathan couldn't disagree. She was the perfect subject. A public figure with a compelling story. She was relevant, mysterious, even inspiring in a way. She would push me as an artist. Wasn't that what professionals did? Push themselves? Evolve. Fall into the mystery. He couldn't argue with his own words.

I heard him chuckle behind the paper.

There was a long pause.

"You don't give a shit about the book," he said.

"What?"

He dropped the sports section. He was tough to look at. Worn-down, leathery skin. Wiry gray hair tucked underneath an Angels baseball cap. Fresh gray stubble on his chin. Massive brown eyes that scared the living shit out of me.

"You just want your rush. I can see your dick from here," he grunted. He laughed at himself, then held the paper up again, covering his face.

I haven't left the motel room all day. I can't stop watching my face on the television. *Authorities are calling for the immediate surrender of Kaleb Reed.* They found the murder weapon. I wonder if Jez offered some assistance.

The hunt begins.

I'm formally being charged.

Detective Donaldson finally got his moment on the podium. Well, almost. He is standing right behind the chief of police, looking sharp in a crisp gray suit. It's the best he's looked since the circus began. *Reed's fingerprints were on the knife, which matched the lacerations on Trozzo's arms and legs.* Cameras snapped in the background. *Reed's fingerprints were on the gun used to kill Barry Monroe.* Donaldson kept a somber expression as the chief spoke, but I saw the shrewd smirk twisting in the corner of the mouth. Don't worry. His elation won't last. Even if he tracks me down, even if he brings me to justice, he'll always have his doubts.

I turn the station.

The booze and drugs come back out.

The news station is broadcasting videos of Kelly's fans taken next to her star on Hollywood Boulevard. The hashtag *#KTroopsForever* is trending. On the screen, a skinny, acned teenager is crying hysterically. "All you haters need to shut your mouth! She wasn't fake like the rest of you. She was real! She actually gave a damn about us." He wipes the tears pouring down his cheeks. "Thanks to Kelly, nobody dims my light. No one drowns my voice. I face my haters head on. I rise and I shine, KTroops!" The crowd around him cheers. "You're an angel, Kelly. A goddess...Who is going to lead us now?" he cries. "She didn't deserve any of this."

I turn the television off.

Snort a line.

I take a pill for good measure.

I know it's bad. I know what I'm doing is wrong. It's been awhile since I've done this. You think I've given up, but it doesn't matter. I don't have to impress you. You need me. The reporters. The Internet. The comments. These videos. It's all the same shit. Imagine if there was no villain. No bad guy to tweet at. We despise the things we can't face in our own hearts.

I remember this next part of the story so clearly.

After I left Kelly's mansion, I returned to Santa Ana. At 2:00 a.m. I was still awake, listening to police sirens and my neighbor and her husband squabbling next door. I tossed left and right. Kelly's check was next to me on the nightstand. My stomach churned. Self-destruction circled like vultures in the desert. The way it always did before a setback. The storm was brewing. I'd go two weeks without drugs, and then I'd slip.

I hated being weak.

Five months prior, Sara and I were lying in bed. It was the eve of my brother's birthday. Typically, it was a tough day for me. But I had her. I had Sara. That was all I ever wanted. She was in her underwear and a long shirt. She looked over at me, and I saw such love in her eyes. She wanted to be with me. After everything we'd been through. All the shit. All the horrible things. I was terrified of losing her.

Then I saw a shadow standing in the doorway. My heart took off like a racehorse at the sound of the gun. It couldn't be him. Bob was gone. I convinced myself that I was seeing things. Imagining the worst. I kissed Sara and rolled over. But I couldn't sleep. Not with him standing there, whispering to me.

You're going to hurt her. Just like the guy before you. Just like your father hurt your mother. It's only a matter of time. That's what damaged people do. They hurt people. You can't protect her. You will never get rid of me.

I went to sleep with a stomachache. The next day, I slipped. I did the unthinkable.

It was the night Sara truly met my monsters.

We couldn't play house any longer.

I liked attaching myself to things. Losing myself to them. The easy choice. Drugs or people, it didn't matter. And when I burned out on the person or thing, I would just discard it and look for something else, something better, as soon as the thrill was over and the person or thing no longer served its purpose.

I didn't deserve Sara. She saw something in me that I couldn't. She believed deep down I was good, worthy. I was her protector. But I couldn't believe it. Not for a second. She could never understand. She couldn't stop me. No one could.

It was 2:15 a.m. when my phone finally beeped. As if Kelly knew I was lying awake, tortured by my thoughts.

Her message said: *Meet me in Philadelphia. We can hang before my concert* .

The easy choice or the right choice.

I could feel the desire growing, stretching. I wanted this. I needed this. There would be no mercy. Let the vultures feast.

I am your villain.

Lizzy: The turning point in their relationship? That's easy. It was Philadelphia—only a week into their little book arrangement. That's how quickly things unraveled. When Kelly saw him for the animal that he was. That's when everything should have ended.

Jez Philadelphia? That's the beginning of their fairy tale.

The Real Kelly Trozzo
TheInsideJuice.com Interview

INSIDEJUICE: Since your comeback, you've gotten quite a lot of tattoos. Do you have a favorite?

TROZZO: The first one…it hurt like hell. It's the stem of a flower, with thousands of dots covering the area where the petals should be. It was a sad day, watching the soft scar tissue being covered up with black ink. I didn't cry. I enjoyed every pinch and jab of the needle into my flesh. The tattoo is a reminder of pain. The stem leads to an array of black dots on my upper forearm, forming the cluster of stars that make up Andromeda, the chained lady.

Sometimes, when I'm in bed, I stare at it. The tattoo is rather abstract up close, but if you look at it from afar, you can see the constellation in its entirety. It's a reminder not to get caught up in the details, keep my distance, walk with purpose, never be chained again, never let the bloodsuckers close, never let them exploit you. The only difference in this story? Perseus is under *my* control. And I will free my fucking self.

Two days after Kelly's death. Detective Donaldson was grinning at me from across the metal table. He lit another cigarette. The flames ripped through the tobacco. The smoke swirled in slow motion, hovering between us. I was woozy, spinning. Trapped. My hands were trembling again. I hadn't slept since arriving at the station. Hunkered down in the interrogation room, the hours blurred together. I didn't know what they found. I didn't know what they knew.

Our lead detective was stronger than I gave him credit for. He wouldn't back off. His eyebrows were relentless. I saw all twenty-two signature moves. Phony empathy and condescending asshole were among my favorites.

This was all part of the game.

He was breaking me.

I had learned that Detective Donaldson is not a "gray area" kind of guy; he doesn't like to know the history of things, the true motivations. He wasn't patient enough. He only wanted my confession. By any means necessary. He pulled out all the stops. Jabbing. Poking. Prying. There was a text from Kelly on my phone. The last one she sent to me that night, telling me, *Read the obituaries.* Donaldson's face kept coming in and out of focus as he repeated the questions. *What does that mean? Why did she send you that? Was that some kind of code?* I didn't respond. He wouldn't believe me anyway.

He pulled out two photos and laid them in front of me, watching my reaction. He said he'd found them at the crime scene, next to my book. One was a picture of my brother. I kept it on me at all times. It used to help me with the cravings. Now? I don't know. It makes me feel like shit. The other was a picture of Kelly and me. Placed in a clear bag as evidence. Red blotches splattered the edges of the photo. You won't find it in a tabloid or posted on social media. It's not something you can Google, so don't bother trying to find it.

Kelly was in a tight black dress, and we were sitting on the couch. Her hair was tied up; her face wiped clean of makeup. Her smile was genuine. I liked that photo. I liked that she didn't share it with her followers. She didn't add a filter on it. Didn't turn it into something it wasn't. She gave me a hard copy of the photo on the night she died. She didn't email it to me or text it to me. She had it printed. Because pictures helped me get through tough times, and she knew that.

That picture was taken on Kelly's tour stop in Philadelphia. The chaos and kids tagged along. Loud beats pulsated inside a jam-packed hotel room. Lines were snorted. Smoke drifted. Kelly sat down next to me on the couch. She looked me in my eyes. I couldn't hide it. I was weak, pale. That twinge of eagerness. Tapping leg. Defenseless. The cravings clawed down my chest. Begging to be released. Screaming. Alcohol no longer sufficed. I knew she shared my symptoms. On the verge. Out of place. She grabbed my hand, squeezed. She turned over her forearm. The scar was covered up by tattoos, but I could still see the bubbles protruding from her soft skin. She cut herself. Cut with real intent. Not a cry for help. A scar that lasted forever.

"I know what it feels like," she said. "Which drugs are your favorites?"

"Anything that's white."

"Me too."

She avoided my gaze. "You think we'll ever be free?"

I reached for her hand. It wasn't in my nature to respond like that. I was raised to bury the pain. Never show your cards. Even with Sara, I guarded my wounds. I was scared of what she would think. Or what my demons would do.

I was right to be scared.

Kelly turned to face me, a tear trickling down her cheek. "I was free once."

"What happened?" I asked.

"It just went away." She wiped the second tear before it had a chance to run. "But I was free from it all, at least for a moment...at least I have that hope."

The moment was gone.

"Let's take a picture." She smiled, her guard again intact.

She extended her arm and snapped the picture. But I can never forget that moment. Everything that followed was an attempt to get it back.

Flickering shutters, neon lights.

The buzz of anticipation.

Cinematic war music thundered through the speakers.

Screams devoured the darkness.

"KTROOPS."

"KTROOPS."

"KTROOPS."

Kelly put her earpiece in, stepping into the spotlight. She was in a black camo leotard with shoulder tassels and combat boots. Her long hair flowed across her neckline, obscuring the silver sparrow medallion. On the projector behind her, an endless army of avatar fans appeared in formation. Her real fans cried out with tears pouring from their eyes.

Kelly sauntered across the stage, yelling.

"We are strong."

They chanted back: "Strong."

"We are bold."

They chanted back: "Bold."

"We will rise from the ashes."

They chanted back. "Rise."

"And then—"

The entire stadium stomped their feet against the ground.

"We will free our fucking selves."

The beat dropped.

Fire erupted.

Mayhem ensued.

Kelly's voice soared, captivating a sea of fanatics. She moved with grace and confidence, her hands gliding across outstretched fingers as she sang.

"We rise, we shine, we awaken to the beat."

They hung on every word, mouthed every lyric.

"We rise to the top of the penthouse suite."

Kelly rolled her body, gyrating her hips, stomping her boots with power. Raised fist, middle finger up. The crowd mimicked the gesture. She was their leader. Their goddess.

Song after song, the arena transformed in puffs of colorful smoke, entrancing us all. Kelly's mythical universe. With giant floats and animatronic dragons. Backup dancers dressed as scaly monsters and ancient Greek soldiers. Kelly commanded the stage in sparkly dresses and black leather bikinis, jean jackets and army green jumpsuits. Behind her, the projector flashed abstract, bizarre images. Disfigured faces. Affirmations. Evil creatures. Epic battle scenes.

And her fans sang.

They danced.

Their hands forever extended.

They were told to rise.

To fight against tormenters. Bloodsuckers. Bullies.

Kelly made them a promise: Accept my invitation and I will never abandon you again.

She glanced over to me on the side of the stage. I backed away. Farther and farther. The props. The colors. The lights. Her finger extended, beckoning me. *Come. Taste. Indulge. Whatever your heart desires. Your deepest wishes. I will provide.* I never stood a chance.

The stadium went dark, still.

Gray fog rolled onto the stage, hovering over the surface.

A moving spotlight broke the darkness.

A forest of black thorns appeared on the projector.

The song began, slow piano keys. The spotlight stopped when it reached Kelly. She was in a slip dress without a bra, her tattoos completely exposed. She sang the first words beautifully. The piano was gradual and harmonious, and I could feel the beat pick up as the chorus approached.

She fell to her knees as lit cell phones illuminated the stadium. She sang:

"I'm bare and tired
  Stripped and angry
  Scared and judged
  Tired and broken.
  Loved but not loved"

The beat picked up again. Her body slid across the stage and the spotlight followed. She held her scar up to the light. The song had taken everything out of her. She was on her knees, and one strap of her slip fell off her shoulder. Emotions lingered in her eyes. Dust motes floated around her as she belted out the final lyrics:

"I'm lying here naked
On a sea of pills
My life without you"

The stage went completely black. I saw shadows walk by me. I felt a kiss on my cheek, and when the lights came on, she was gone.

Lizzy: The drugs started during the final season of *Zoe Loves*. It was painkillers, mostly. A lot of things happened. Worst of all, she broke up with her costar, Noah Tash. He played my older brother on the show. Things fizzled out with them at the same time Barry broke the news that Kelly's contract wasn't being renewed. Then they offered me the spin-off, *Lizzy Loves*. Talk about the perfect storm of bad shit. It was a lot for her to handle.

Jez: Kelly used to make me watch Lizzy's stupid show every Tuesday. Ugh. I hated it. Lizzy's character wasn't believable. Plus, she didn't have half the singing voice Kelly did. But Kelly didn't have a jealous bone in her body. She was so happy for her friend. I wish I could say the same for Lizzy.

Lizzy: I told Kelly I wouldn't take the spin-off, but she insisted. Less than a month later, she was headlining every tabloid with her drunken antics. I imagine that's why she retreated to her mansion and barricaded herself in her room. Something happened inside that house . . . it was bad enough to leave that giant scar on her forearm. I'm sure drugs were involved. I didn't pry. I was just relieved she finally emerged, clean. And she was motivated. Probably the most creative and excited I've ever seen her. She got her shit together and went back to the studio. Everything was going well until she met Kaleb. He pushed her back onto the ledge. That guy was a black hole, sucking everything down with him.

THE REAL KELLY TROZZO
TheInsideJuice.com Interview

INSIDEJUICE: Recently, you tweeted in defense of a former costar diagnosed with a mental health disorder, alluding to your own battle with anxiety. Is that something you still deal with?

TROZZO: Yes, I still have episodes.

INSIDEJUICE: When did they first start?

TROZZO: My first one happened during a parade, smack dab in the middle of the happiest place on earth. I was dressed as Princess Jade, I mean, the whole nine yards white toga, golden sandals, wheeled out on some larger-than-life float, with my costar on my arm and animatronic animals at my feet. Thousands of screaming fans lined Main Street, holding out their hands and reaching out for their beloved princess.

We were rounding the last leg of the parade when I saw her. This pretty child, no older than five or six, with blonde hair and blue eyes. Just gorgeous. I remember she was wearing a sparkly dress and holding her mother's hand, just like every other little girl in the park. But it was the way she was gazing up at me, with such sadness, such hollowness. As if nothing in the world could bring her joy. That's when the cheers and screams vanished into nothingness, and the sunlight retreated behind dark clouds. And as I turned to smile and wave, this deep ache filled my stomach, and my vision blurred, and the girl's face—I don't know—it transformed. There were these green reptilian scales snaking up her cheeks. Her eyes turned yellow and wicked, and she had these razor-sharp fangs. Then I remember this voice hissing in my ear. "I see you."

I tried to tell myself that it wasn't real. Just an absurd figment of my imagination. But it was too late. It felt like a seal had been ripped open inside me, releasing fear across my soul. Then I collapsed onto the float with my music playing on repeat in the background.

Heat exhaustion was the official statement, but that couldn't be further from the truth. It was evil that crawled through my body that day. And the crowd never stopped smiling, never stopped taking pictures, never stopped reaching out their hands, because all they wanted was their beautiful princess. But my soul had been hijacked by a monster. I liked to imagine the horror on their faces if they saw what I felt.

I realize now the monster wasn't trying to kill me at all. No—he just wanted to show his face. He wanted me to know he was confined for now, but he was coming for me.

Two days after Kelly's death.

"You think I'm a monster, don't you?"

Detective Donaldson's eyebrows rose. This was it. I was backed into a corner. Moves and countermoves. He had his iPad out, replaying the video. You've seen the footage. Everyone's seen it. It spread like wildfire across the Internet. I almost killed that man in Philadelphia. I don't remember doing it. I don't remember anything. He was just a fan. The detective was right... I was...I am...a monster. I am capable of terrible things.

"Turn it off!" I yelled.

"Then talk," Detective Donaldson barked.

I turned away from the screen. I reached for the picture of my brother, still in the evidence bag on the table. My brother was the good one. Even-keeled, kind hearted. We had both attended an elite school in Massachusetts. It was full of pissed-off rich kids, desperate to project their own bullshit. So, they find the governor's youngest son. My brother. He was small and timid. Bullies like defenseless kids, and they beat him until he cried and begged for help. Never again.

On my final day of school there, I found him hoisted thirty feet in the air on a flagpole, crying, his eye swollen, nose bloodied. A group of kids huddled around the flagpole, laughing. I hoisted him down. Then I left. There was no decision. No right or wrong. Just rage.

I knew who they were. I found them at their usual lunch bench. Smoking cigarettes, snickering. I grabbed that bully's head and slammed it into the wooden bench. His skull cracked on the beams. Blood soaked his white polo, and I heard his screams and tears. Not so tough anymore. His friends shouted, *Stop! Leave him alone.* But I couldn't turn it off. I didn't know how. It was the same poison and rage that lived inside my father. But this was for good, for justice. This for my brother. I was his protector. No one would hurt him on my watch. I only remember bits and pieces. I don't remember taking it so far.

The ambulance roared into our school, and I drove away with my brother, my shirt stained with the bully's blood. The cops came to our home for statements. The boy had a fractured skull, two broken ribs. My father answered the questions. He didn't say a word when they left. Instead, he patted me on the head. A first time for everything.

He was proud of me that day.

This wasn't the first time my darkness had risen, and it wouldn't be the last. But if I hadn't gotten expelled, if I hadn't lost control, things would have been different.

My brother would still be alive.

After the concert, Kelly sat across from me in a limo, her knees pulled into her chest, her eyes fixed on mine. She dismissed her entourage and bodyguards. It was just us. She had on a white beanie covering her wet blonde hair, and tight black jeans with combat boots.

"What did you think of the concert?" she asked.

"Enthralling. Your fans…They worship you."

She put a bottle of tequila to her mouth, her loose-fitting sleeve falling down to reveal her tattoos. Tiny black dots and lines covered the scar on her forearm. I knew how she got it. A clash with demons. Tread lightly with that scar. Don't overstep.

"They don't worship me. They trust me to lead them. We are stronger together."

I nodded, reaching out for the bottle of tequila. "What's the tattoo on your arm?"

"A constellation," she explained. "Andromeda. Just like the painting you like so much. Chained to a rock and saved by the Greek god Perseus. It reminds me to stay true to myself, that there's something bigger out there."

"Wasn't that the same plot of that movie you were in—"

"*Castle Heart,*" she finished my thought. "But instead of Perseus, it was the humble knight, Percy, who saved the princess. But yes, same plot."

"You played the princess…betrayed by her father, and handed over to the sea witch…"

"And given an awful curse that penetrated her golden heart with fear." Kelly grinned, animating the fairy tale in her best narration. "And when fear infiltrated the heart of the beautiful princess, she would take the physical form of a monster, with thick claws, yellow eyes, and green scales." She grabbed the bottle of tequila back, took a swig. "And to rid himself of his guilt, the king sent his daughter to Castle Heart, the abandoned castle on the sea, where she was trapped in a lonely tower, waiting for her hero, her knight, to rescue her from the evil monster, from the curse."

"So who's your Perseus, or Percy? Who saves you?"

"I don't know." She took another swig. "Maybe it will be you?"

. . .

The bar got loud. Too loud. Packed to capacity. Overrun with drunks. They pointed, laughed, whispered, closed in. They were watching from everywhere. I couldn't stop them from pushing through to snap photos. They were reaching toward her.

"Kelly! Kelly!" they yelled.

I pulled her closer. She needed my protection. The patrons got bolder, friendlier. They shuffled over to take pictures with her. Three young guys in red Phillies jerseys held their cameras out. They smashed their faces to Kelly's cheeks without permission. They were slurring their words. I watched their hands. Spots of red. Flashes of rage. The transformation was beginning.

"You going to let them do that to her?" Bob was drinking at the bar; his back turned to me. "She needs you."

"No, she's used to this."

"Here we go again," Bob laughed. "Haven't you learned your lesson?"

The picture was snapped. They smiled and thanked her, lingering to talk. One of the guys playfully touched her arm, laughing, teasing. I stayed in the wings. Gulped my beer.

"She's fine."

"Don't be a coward, Kaleb."

I didn't have a response.

"Defend her," yelled Bob. "She needs you."

The guy put his arm around her. My body tensed. She was fucking mine. I grabbed Kelly's shoulder. She looked up at me, worried. She needed me. Of course she needed me.

Give us some space. He kept his arm around her and turned his back on me. I was slipping. Dark vibrations pulsed through my veins. My blood felt warm; my knuckles felt strong. I hated this feeling. I loved this feeling. I couldn't stop it. I didn't want to. The rage thrashed inside me. Oh, it felt good. I felt strong. Indestructible. They were all going to pay.

I blacked out.

I relied on the video online to put the pieces together.

I threw his hand off and pushed against his chest. He fell back with force. His face scrunched in anger. He took one drunken swing and missed. My knuckles pounded against his soft stomach and he fell back on the table.

I remember small flashes. My knuckles penetrated his face. One. Two. Three. Crack. Blood poured from his nose. My hands gripped the back of his head. His skull cracked against the table. The crowd shuffled to us. Blood covered my hands. *No. Stop. What are you doing?* My hands kept falling. His face softened like meat under a tenderizer. I couldn't stop.

I was there, kind of. I was watching myself. Everything was static. When the guy was on the floor in a puddle of blood, the rage retreated. The monster was fed, satisfied.

Kelly's bodyguards entered the bar. I grabbed her hand and led her toward the exit. She held on tightly and waved off the bodyguards. As we stepped out into the cold air, a smile played at the corner of her mouth.

"What?" I asked.

"Nothing."

"Tell me," I demanded.

She kissed me on the cheek. Still grinning.

"What?" I asked again.

"No. You're just . . ." She paused. "Thank you, Perseus."

She gave me one last smile before she lowered her head onto my shoulder.

"Why did you kill them?" Donaldson's nose was almost touching mine. My head stopped spinning, just for a second. The video was still playing. His aftershave made me sick.

"You took it too far, didn't you?" Donaldson seethed. "You lost control? You shot her manager. Then you attacked, Kelly.

You've done it before." He sat down. "What did she do to deserve this?"

I wondered, how many times he had gotten his confession? How many times had the killer given in, adorned in his filthy sin? They think it will make them feel better. Alleviate the guilt. Lighten the shame. How many times had Donaldson's eyes widened in anticipation? Eagerly awaiting. Oh no. He wouldn't get that satisfaction from me.

I started laughing hysterically. Laughing and laughing like a fucking madman. Staring at a video of myself doing something I don't remember doing. My rage and shadows on display for millions of viewers.

"You know what, detective?" I lifted up my Styrofoam cup. "I think I *will* take a refill."

Lizzy: It was his eyes in that video. There was nothing human left inside him. As if he was some feral animal. Kelly called me that night, crying. The pattern was so predictable. She claimed he was trying to protect her, and a bunch of other excuses. The truth was, he was out-of-control wasted. Did you know he vomited in the cab on the ride home? Bet he didn't tell you that. The bodyguards had to drag him to the airport and everything. He was a junkie.

Jez: Kelly crawled into my bed crying that night in Philadelphia. I used to love when she put her warm feet on top of mine. I loved her soft skin. The way she would tuck her little head into my shoulder. It was Lizzy who made her upset, not Kaleb. Lizzy was always reprimanding her, judging her. Kelly was quiet at breakfast, then out of nowhere she blurted, "I think Kaleb is going to move in."

Lizzy: I told her to watch the video. Just watch it! But no, of course not. Let's not be rational. *I'll never watch anything those gossip sites put up.* How naive can you be? I don't care who put the damn video up. Look at his eyes! Look at his rage! That shit was real. He was a psycho! But Kelly wouldn't hear it. Instead, she buried her head deeper in the sand.

Jez: Kelly and I watched that video a thousand times. He was her knight in shining armor.

Lizzy: Kelly and I stopped talking when he moved in with her. She tagged me and DM'd me a few times, trying to make contact. But I stood my ground. If she wanted to self-destruct, I couldn't watch. Not this time. But I should have. I really should have. I should have tried harder. I could have done more....I regret being so prideful. I left her to her band of merry misfits. All those so-called friends who gave her drugs and encouraged her obsession with an emotionally disturbed man. I hated them, especially her assistant. None of them were real friends. They told her what she wanted to hear, not what she needed. They weren't like me.

THE REAL KELLY TROZZO

TheInsideJuice.com Interview 2019

INSIDEJUICE: You have one of the largest and most loyal fan bases of any artist out there. What about your message do you think resonates with them?

TROZZO: When I get on that stage, nothing else matters. All the pain. All the suffering. None of it. My fans understand that it is our duty, our mission to spread our light, to resurrect ourselves into new beings. They bear witness to my rebirth, and in doing so, they become my disciples. More than that, they become my combatants. In the brokenness and evil that lives among us, my fans must be vigilant and resilient. They must stand up to the bullies in their lives. They must fight against the forces that wish to see them stay small. That's why I call them the KTroops. And I will do everything in my power to help them find theirs.

After Philadelphia, I moved into Kelly's mansion. Full of splendor, delight, a never-ending thrill ride. I became nocturnal in Kelly's castle. The days were for rest, cleansing. Weeks blurred together. I'd wake up, hungover in her bed. Find her meditating in her study. The house was always spotless in the morning. The sun was always shining.

 Everything changed at sundown.

 The fantasy began.

 Dancing.

 Singing.

 Jubilation.

 Every night, I watched Kelly dance and play around her packed house, full of Hollywood misfits and pleasure-seekers. It was hard not to stare, with her skimpy outfits, her subtle flirting, her playful smile, her bright eyes, always spinning and twirling with a red cup in hand. Everyone orbited around her like she was the sun. They all wanted something. A smile, a gesture, a picture they could share. Most of all, they wanted to be close enough to feel the great power that she wielded—

Fame. It was a special magic that made you feel worthy, significant. Loved by association.

I wanted something, too.

But what I wanted was far greater.

I never slept in the guest bedroom, always with her—at least in the beginning. Kelly wasn't a cuddler. Too intimate, I guess. Too sticky. Bad dreams pushed her toward me. I held her close because I missed having someone. I wished it was Sara. But I had Kelly, for now.

There were some mornings when she was mine. The few mornings she didn't slip out before dawn. She'd put her head on my chest, kiss my cheek. She snapped pictures of us, reaching her arm out so both our tired faces were in frame, her wild blonde hair, my matted brown hair. Her favorite silver pendant glued to her neckline. She stared at the images on her phone, smiling. I liked that.

Most days, I'd accompany her in the study while she wrote. For inspiration, she pulled out a box of memories from a safe hidden behind her favorite painting. The box was mostly filled with pictures from her years on *Zoe Loves*. Kelly and her former co-star, Lizzy, dancing in her trailer, blowing bubbles in oversized shirts. Playing their guitars together on set. Celebrating birthdays with cake covering their faces. Being kids.

She lingered on a postcard of the real *Castle Heart*, a picturesque château off the coast of France.

"Lizzy and I are going to go there someday." She beamed.

"What happened with you guys? Have you talked since she took over the show?"

She stared at me curiously.

"Lizzy and I are fine."

"But you miss the show, don't you?" I asked. "What happened?"

She didn't respond.

"I've read things…about your manager," I said. "He uses people."

She ran her fingers along the postcard. "You're not ready for that, Kaleb." Then she put the memories back into the safe.

My eyes lingered on the scar on her forearm. She pulled it away from view.

She kept her secrets. I kept mine.

Every night, I went downstairs into the strobe lights, into the darkness, into the abyss, into the swirling smoke. I surrendered to the night. The fantasy washed over me. There was no past, no sin in the madness. No rage. No guilt. No shame. Kelly's loyal subjects danced in the fog. They drank. They left behind their cares and worries.

I waited until Kelly was ready. She walked over to the couch and ran her fingers along my shoulders. My favorite part of the night. I would watch her ass as she walked up the stairs. She knew I would follow.

She led me to her bedroom.

She led me to her hot tub.

Her library.

She led me to her home theater.

Her movie had been cued. She shoved me against the wall, her hands clawing my back while larger-than-life animation flashed across the screen. I slid my hand beneath her underwear and rubbed my finger against her flesh. Pinned her arms against the wall. She bit my neck. She moaned and shoved me into the couch. I had a front-row view of the enchanted princess.

"The storm brings darkness, darkness brings fear," Kelly sang the opening number as she gyrated her hips. She closed her eyes. Thunder and lightning flashed across the movie screen.

A young Princess Jade fell overboard, deeper into dark waters, sinking into the shadows.

Kelly scratched my chest and screamed.

The head of a vicious monster rose from the depths of the dark sea, his jagged fangs extended. Before he could devour the princess, golden light poured out of her heart, into her hands.

Kelly screamed again. This time in pleasure.

The monster screeched in agony, then retreated to the depths from which he came.

Kelly sang:

> *"And my golden heart shall come alive*
> *And heal the shadows from inside"*

After we were done, we reclined into the couch. Jez brought in refreshments and we passed bottles of vodka and joints back and forth as we watched. The projector lights flashed across the smoke. The animation reflected off her pupils. Kelly curled deeper into the leather seat, waiting in childlike anticipation.

"Where are we going, Father?" said Princess Jade, running happily alongside him.

"Just a little further," said the king.

Kelly squeezed my hand as the sea witch lifted the beautiful princess off the ground.

The shadows of two serpents curled around her, penetrating her golden heart.

Kelly flinched as the bolts flashed. She hid her face in my shoulder.

With the curse in her veins, the princess was banished to the dark towers of Castle Heart—an abandoned rocky fortress on the sea, where cold, gray skies and violent waves never ceased. Every night, the monster came alive, spreading its shadows upon the castle. Until one day a hero washed ashore...

"Be my knight," Kelly whispered, climbing back on top of me.

She leaned back, closed her eyes. I closed mine. This was my fantasy. And in my fantasy, I would protect her. She was gifted, magical, and I was her loyal subject. I was strong and courageous. I would climb the shores of her castle. It was I who would battle the beast inside.

I would free her from her chains.

"I'm about to come," Kelly whispered. Dark clouds moved across the castle towers on the big screen. Thunder and lightning erupted through the speakers.

The knight moved through the cursed castle, a torch in hand.

Kelly slowed her hips and smiled in the dark as I watched the evil monster come alive on the screen.

The knight entered the princess's chambers, screaming her name. But she was no longer there. In her place was the monster, with piercing yellow eyes and sharp fangs. The knight drew his sword. Back and forth they fought, until the monster's power overwhelmed the weary knight. He fell against the wall, blood dripping from his mouth.

I was about to come.

"Don't close your eyes," Kelly panted as she slowed her pace on top. She shoved my head against her shoulder. "I want you to watch."

I opened my eyes.

The knight was beaten, his helmet tossed aside. The monster's fiery breath had scorched the metal of his sword. With fangs exposed, the beast was prepared to finish the job. But before he could do it, our hero saw her eyes. The princess was there, behind the darkness and rage. He whispered her name, "Jade." He held his hand to the monster's cheek. "Show me what is behind those eyes."

"Now look at me," Kelly said.

I put my hand on her cheek. Kelly bit my finger as I released inside of her.

The curse was dispelled. Light poured into the castle.

We fell back onto the leather couch. Kelly muted the

movie. Silence. Stillness. Only our breath and pounding heartbeats.

"Can I ask you something?" She turned toward me. "What really happened with you and Alice? Why are you guys not together?"

"You're not ready for that, Kelly," I teased.

She sighed. "C'mon."

"I imagine there's an evil voice inside me... the voice of fear," I said. "He laughs at the part of me that thinks happiness is even possible, and eventually, I fall for it. I take the bait. I hurt the people who love me. Then I hurt myself."

"I think I get that too," she mumbled, her breaths deepening.

I continued, "Usually, I find something that's bad for me, like you." I turned to her and smiled. "And boom, everything goes away. All the hard work. All the good things I've done. The progress. And once that evil voice is fed, they go back into hiding, but I'm always scared they will come back, and do it all over again. That something will trigger it when things get too good."

Her long lashes flickered back and forth as her eyelids slowly closed. "So I'm bad for you?" she asked with a grin.

"You're horrible for me," I said, and she chuckled.

We were silent for a moment, gazing at the screen.

"Maybe I'm just like the princess," she whispered. "There's a monster inside of me too."

She slid her underwear back on, shimmied her jeans over her legs. She fast-forwarded the movie to the next scene, unmuted the volume.

"I did what you asked," the king pleaded. "It is not my fault the knight broke the curse. Please let my daughter live."

"You think it will be that simple?" The sea witch cackled, her serpents slithering around the king's body, lifting the crown from his head. "Unless

you want to lose everything, you will tie her to the rock." She smiled. *"Let the sea claim her powers for their own. It is time for your daughter to die."*

The theater lights came on. A tear trickled down the length of Kelly's cheek.

"Are you—"

"You haven't signed the contract yet," Kelly interrupted.

"I know. Kelly, I don't…"

"No pressure." She got up to leave. "But time is running out. The offer won't last forever."

I pointed to the screen. "You don't want to finish the movie?" I asked, reclining in the seat with the bottle to my mouth. "You don't want to watch your happily ever after?"

She grinned, then opened the door and retreated into the fog.

She kept her secrets. I kept mine.

Lizzy: We were kids when we came to Hollywood. It took us a while to understand that happily ever after died when the director said cut. Kelly had a tender heart, a fragile heart. And what do assholes do with tender hearts? They break them. Kelly was always a hopeless romantic. That's not a good trait to have in Hollywood. I always told her she needed to toughen up. But she was determined to have her fairy-tale ending.

Jez: Kelly's voice was so beautiful. It makes me cry just thinking about it. She used to sing to me every night. Talk about a fairy tale coming true! Sometimes I was waiting for someone to pinch me.

Lizzy: When we were younger, Kelly and I made these grand plans to rent out this beautiful island in France, the location that the fortress in *Castle Heart* was based on. It was one of those bucket list dreams you make with friends, you know? Fun to talk about, but not something you *actually* put in the calendar. But Kelly never let it go. She always brought it up. . . You know that I played the voice of Mada, Princess Jade's trusty pelican sidekick? Kelly got me the part. Sometimes, she tried to convince me to use the voice when we talked on the phone. Honestly, it was a lot harder to do a squawky pelican voice than the beautiful princess. But that was always the case with us. I had to try harder. To get the attention. To get the sponsors. The followers. She was…well, her beauty and fame were effortless.

Two days after Kelly's death. Detective Donaldson extended the half-filled pack of cigarettes.

I refused.

"I'm trying to quit myself," he said as he lit the tip to the flame. "Wife hates it…though in all fairness, she used to smoke like a chimney." He blew the smoke in my face. "Got into the whole New Age yoga kick. Natural foods. Kale smoothies, I can't stand that shit. Like I should suffer because she gets all self-righteous." He leaned back. The chair grumbled under his fast food-induced gut.

He pulled out a copy of my book and slammed it on the table.

"You know, I've been reading your book at my desk." He took a drag. "Some of those scenes. . .Wow. Riveting stuff. That text message Kelly sent you, the one where she mentioned the obituaries. . . I think I'm finally starting to understand your relationship."

He flicked ash onto the tray. "Let me ask you a question, Kaleb. Was she real? Alice? Because if she wasn't, you sure do have a vivid imagination." When I didn't respond, he continued. "You know, it's easier to get these things off your chest. Why don't you tell me the truth? What really happened to Alice's husband?"

"It was fiction, detective."

We locked eyes.

I was thirty years old when I wrote it, holed up in a cabin in Oregon for three hundred and fifty dollars a month.

Two years before writing the book, I had fallen in love with a coworker. Sara. I did a variety of odd jobs during those first nine years in Orange County, including sales for the local weekly magazine, the rags that have more sex ads than articles. The plan was always to save enough money to rent a cabin in the mountains and finally write a novel. There was no subject in mind, just a vague notion that great novels came from isolation. Tucked away in a majestic forest with nothing but a typewriter and a few tins of strong coffee.

That sales job was like every shitty one I had before that— an excuse to avoid the blank page. Continue in the shadows. Pay bills. Afford drugs during my setbacks. That sort of thing. I was in love with the *idea* of writing but petrified of the work.

Instead, I cold-called, worked nine hours a day. Made 7 percent on print advertising. Just enough to pay rent, eat, and relapse once a month.

I liked Sara the moment I saw her. I'll never forget that first day. She was dancing in the middle of her cubicle, her arms flailing, her neck bobbing. She blushed when she saw me, but that didn't stop her. Never would. From that point on, I was smitten—with a married woman. Sara was beautiful and kind, unlike her husband. He was an asshole. No redeeming qualities. She married too young. As she grew up and shone brighter, he got meaner. And fatter. And violent.

As is the case with most forbidden relationships, I found ways to stay connected. I stole glances as often as I could, in between sales calls. At lunch. During meetings, our eyes lingered on each other from across the conference room table. Flirty smiles every morning and at the end of every day. Sara was a different kind of rush. Better than drugs. Nothing else mattered. Not my past. Not my failures. I got that side of her that her husband had shut out. The inside jokes. The warmth. The humor. I always thought she would leave him, or at least I hoped. She would love me someday, I dreamed. We could both go to Oregon. We'd be together. We'd be happy.

Sara wouldn't break her vows. Her husband would come into work once in a while like it was a chore. Nonchalantly standing over her desk. Everyone loved her playfulness, but not him. My obsession felt dark. It was my duty to blight their marriage. I needed to save her. Eventually, I told her how I felt.

We were driving back from lunch. I said, "You know I'm crazy about you, right?"

She didn't speak until the car was parked in front of the office.

She said, "No matter how I feel, no matter how unhappy things seem, I will not leave him."

She was adamant, and I got angry. I called him an asshole, and she said, "That's my fucking husband."

She stormed out of my car.

I kept pushing.

We kissed once. She told me it had to stop.

I wouldn't stop. I couldn't. My life revolved around Sara. I couldn't think of anything else. I went to work because of her. I'd come home to a blank computer screen. Fall asleep to a blank computer screen. Woke up for work. Repeat process. I was still using, but not as much. I didn't bottom out. I became a functional addict. I devoted my life to loving a married woman. Nothing else. I didn't give back. Or serve anyone. I maintained all my old addictions and I found new ones. I thought it was romantic. It was cowardly. My idea of love—one-sided, selfish, and full of shit. Just another distraction.

From writing, from evolving, from dealing with all the shit in my basement.

The grand finale came at a Christmas party. Everyone was drunk, including Sara's husband. I was itching for a confrontation, sneaking glances at them all night. She avoided my eyes. I was relentless. I cornered her when she left the bathroom. But her husband had been watching me too. Exactly what I wanted.

He grabbed my shirt and pushed me against the wall.

He said, "Did you tell my wife you were in love with her?"

I was happy she told him. Even happier to admit it.

Protect Sara. Kill him. Make him bleed.

We stumbled out into the street, drunk. We exchanged punches while Sara cried next to us. I found his jaw. He dropped. My hand fell faster, harder. My knuckles were covered in his blood. In my head, I thought, this was for Sara. I was helping her. She would thank me.

Bullshit. It was vengeance. For my mother. For my brother. For every fucked-up person in the world who did terrible things to good people. People shouted, and Sara stepped in front of her bloody husband, while I stood there with my fists still raised. My heart stopped. My vision returned. Everyone held their breath. My hand fell limp.

Her husband got up off the asphalt with his nose broken and his pride destroyed. Sara ran to him. He raised his fist. There was fear in her eyes. Precedent. He was more than just mean and apathetic in their marriage. He was violent.

What have I done? I had ignored all the signs. She suffered like my mother. I put my own needs ahead of hers. Like this was some game. Her husband was just like my father. She was trapped. I should have seen it. I should have known. I couldn't sleep that night. The guilt. The shame. My heartbeat pounded, ringing in my ears. I failed her.

I came to work the next day with my apology ready to go. I

was sorry for being selfish. For not seeing the truth. Not sorry for hurting him. He deserved more. But Sara never showed up that day. Or the next. She was gone. Her phone number changed.

I couldn't spend another moment staring at her empty cubicle. Staring at my failure. Instead, I stopped going into the office. I decided to numb myself into extinction. I nearly did it. Pissed pants. Vomit on the floor. Screaming for death to take me. It would have happened, too. But my sponsor found me in my darkest hour. He picked me up off the apartment floor. He got me coffee. He convinced me to leave town, do something worthwhile. To stop living a selfish life. I had two thousand dollars saved, and I searched for the cheapest place I could find, farthest away from a city. I spent the first week in the Oregon wilderness doing the same shit I've always done. Drugs and booze. Punishing myself. Avoiding the blank page. But in the stillness of the forest…something changed.

I woke up one morning and made my small twin bed in my 300-square-foot cabin. There were no longer any distractions. I was out of drugs. I prayed to my brother. I grabbed a pen. My hands shook from withdrawals. I didn't care. The story poured out of me. I wrote *Pay Me, Alice* in six months on a spiral bound notepad. Without a single pill, line, or drink. That's the story of my novel. How I got clean.

Donaldson smiled. He stamped out the cigarette in the already-filled ashtray. He didn't believe me. I didn't blame him.

"So what happened to Alice, I mean Sara? You never got closure?"

"That's correct."

"Never saw her again."

I shook my head.

He smiled.

He pulled out a Ziploc bag of photos and slid them in front of me.

Pictures of Sara and another man.

"Then why did we find these in Kelly's assistant's room?"

Jez: I don't know how those got there.

Lizzy: Kelly's assistant was sick in the head. She was obsessed with Kelly. If Kelly liked something, I guarantee Jez's fixation ran deeper. It would make sense that she became obsessed with the author and all the characters in his story. Ask her what happened on Kelly's birthday.

Jez: Her birthday? Oh my gosh! It was the best party ever. Kelly was in such a good mood, minus the little setback with Lizzy. You'd think she'd call to wish her a happy birthday. Instead, she called to scold Kelly. I was so tired of Lizzy's crap. Seriously. Just let us have fun.

Lizzy: I called to warn my best friend.

THE REAL KELLY TROZZO
TheInsideJuice.com Interview 2019

INSIDEJUICE: There have been lot of rumors floating around about your drug addiction leading to your exit from *Zoe Loves*.

TROZZO: It's true, drugs did play a role in my leaving the show. I consider my addiction to be genetic, passed down to me by my mother. I have early memories of her dragging me to rundown apartment buildings to score. That's how she silenced the voices in her head. If the pain was bad enough, she'd pull out her needles and shoot up right in front of me. Sadly, she was high the last time I saw her. She was screaming my name, running across the set with a dirty T-shirt hanging off her back. But it was her eyes that really killed me. She wasn't my mother any longer. There was no light left inside her. Security removed her before I could say goodbye.

That night, Barry came into my room and told me to make a choice—either shed the remains of my past life and start new or walk away from stardom. I'm sure you know what I chose. I thought about my mom a lot when I started down the same path. Like mother, like daughter. The only difference? I wasn't weak like her. I had a purpose.

INSIDEJUICE: Are you saying you overcame your addiction? When's the last time you used?

TROZZO: I haven't taken a pill in over a year.

INSIDEJUICE: How did you quit?

TROZZO. Sheer willpower. This might seem strange, but I kept buying pills long after I stopped using them. In fact, I keep a giant bucket of them in my room. There is something empowering about it—adding to this giant white mountain of prescription pills. I enjoy the temptation. This symbolic mountain that I clawed my way out of. I want to remember what I was up against. It is an everyday reminder of my inner strength. That the promise I made to my fans is far greater than a pathetic addiction. My mother would have chosen to dive into the numbness. Not me. I can't sleep through this part of the story. Not when I am finally myself. Not when there is so much work still left to do. Not when my fans are counting on me to lead them to victory.

Two days after Kelly's death.

"Are you finally ready to talk?" Detective Donaldson reentered the interrogation room with greasy stains dotting his grey button down. The smell of cheap fast food chicken lingered on his breath. He was getting impatient. The breaks were getting shorter. So was his fuse. His face was stiff and tense, his eyebrows raised.

I couldn't blame him for being upset with me. He had never met fans like Kelly's. They were trained to be persistent, unrelenting. The pressure was mounting for an arrest. The clock was ticking. Either charge me of the crime or release me back into the wild. I still didn't have a lawyer. Guilty people need lawyers. Hopeless people don't give a shit. I enjoyed our time together, the playful banter. The dramatic tension. It was therapeutic in a way. The detective couldn't say the same.

He sat down, wiping a napkin to his chin. "Why don't you help me make sense of this? I want to understand why Kelly hired you. Why her assistant would have pictures of Sara.

I didn't respond.

"Alright. Let's start small. What happened on Kelly's birthday?" Detective Donaldson dropped a stack of papers in front of me. He licked grease off his fingers, then rubbed the gray stubble on his round chin. He leaned forward, pointing to my signature on the top page.

"You know what this is, right?"

"A contract."

"For the completion of a book, love story, memoir, whatever you want to call it." Donaldson flipped through the pages, examining them. "A lot of interesting clauses in here." He scrolled his index finger down the page. "Oh, here's my favorite. 'Unless freed of contractual obligations, Mr. Reed agrees to finish the manuscript regardless of the following circumstances . . .' Hold on, let me find the good one." He wet his fingers, flipped to the next page. "Here it is, 'Mr. Reed's incarceration.'" He slid the paper over. "You see how all this looks? Almost sounds like Kelly knew you'd be here? Like she knew what you were capable of. Or maybe she knew you would betray her."

I didn't answer.

She knew me pretty well.

"You signed on Kelly's birthday. You were a busy man that night, weren't you? You attended a movie premiere with Kelly." He slid over pictures of us on the red carpet. "And we all know how that turned out…Then Long Beach PD received a 911 call from a neighbor of one Sara O'Conner. The man they reported on her lawn fits your description. Know anything about that? Or are we still pretending you never saw her after you wrote your book?"

I didn't respond.

Donaldson pointed to the contract. "And you also signed that." He studied me. "What the hell happened that night, Kaleb?"

I stared at my signature on the contract. The lines were jagged, crooked. My name was barely legible.

"You did something bad didn't you?"

He had no idea.

He turned to the two-way glass with an arrogant smirk. I hadn't seen him this confident since our first hours together. He had something to reveal. It was time for him to crack the big case. "Tell me what happened on Kelly's birthday."

I had been living at Kelly's for two weeks. Two weeks of pushing myself to the brink.

There was something satisfying about tiptoeing along the edge, staring into the abyss. Thus far, I had successfully avoided my favorite drugs. But I did everything else in large quantities. As a regular in Kelly's Hollywood court, I drank bottles of champagne that cost more than a month's rent at my apartment. I toasted with her entourage. I partied with singers, agents, producers, and actors.

I met a screenwriter named Kohl who was interested in adapting my book for the big screen. He was the best in the business. He was my age. He wore a leather jacket, tattoos on his fingers, slick black hair with gray streaks running through the sides. We were standing in the backyard, overlooking the Hollywood Hills. The pool area was filled to the brim with drunken kids. Skinny-dippers. People hooking up on reclined pool chairs.

"I fucking loved the book," Kohl said. "It was dark and gritty. I haven't written something that good in years. You could tell those chapters were crafted through pain."

"They were."

"You still talk to the girl?" He lit a joint, exhaled.

I caught Kelly's eye as she navigated around the mob of partygoers. She was wearing frayed jean shorts and a white tank top with her stomach showing. My eyes followed her everywhere.

"Huh?"

"The girl in the book. I assume she's real. I wrote my best shit about my ex-wife." He took another hit. "So, you and that Alice girl…you guys still talk?"

I took a sip of my drink. "Not anymore. But we lived together. For six months…we were happy."

He glanced down at my drink. "And then you fucked it up, didn't you?"

I nodded.

He understood. Maybe too well.

"Well," Kohl said, lifting up his glass, "At least you have a second chance." He stared at Kelly across the pool. "I can't wait to see what you're going to write for her. She's something else. I can't put my finger on it. But she has that thing, you know? Beyond beauty and talent."

"You guys ever—"

Kohl took a drag. "No," he exhaled a thick cloud of smoke. "She always turns me down. But I'm sure she'll make one hell of a muse. Maybe her story will be better than your book."

Kelly smiled at me from across the party.

I didn't smile back.

"That's impossible," I said.

Kohl eyed me curiously.

"Kelly is a fantasy. I'm using her. And she's using me too."

On cue, Kelly weaved in and out of the crowd, sauntering towards us. She put her arm around Kohl, taking a hit of the joint from his hand. A twinge of jealousy stung me. "So are you going to write the screenplay?" she asked him.

Kohl grinned, then glanced back to me. "I'd be honored to take a crack at it. But only if Kaleb trusts me with his characters." He laughed, throwing the joint down. "Now if you excuse me, love birds, I'm going to find some blow."

Kelly took a sip of her drink, bouncing her feet up and

down playfully. She reached for my hand. I withdrew. "What's wrong?" she asked.

"Nothing. I'm just—"

"You know it's my birthday tomorrow," she interrupted. "What did you get me?"

"I'm still thinking."

"How about you come with me to my friend Lizzy's premiere. And maybe a signature on the contract." She pressed her body into mine.

Chills ran down my arm.

I met her gaze.

Her eyes consumed, devoured, pulled me back in.

I chugged the rest of my drink. I grabbed her hand. I followed her back to my fantasy.

I remember flashes of the rest of the party.

Watching Jez and Kelly dance from room to room.

Jealousy. Longing.

Chugging a fifth of Vodka with Kohl.

Spinning. Fading.

Kelly's hand in mine, pulling me up the stairs, smiling back at me.

Lust. Hunger.

I remember seeing Sara. She was reaching out to me in bed, smiling beneath the covers. The dream played in slow motion. Her dirty blonde hair swept over her eyes. *Wake up, Kaleb.* She put her hand to my face. *Where are you?* she whispered. *Come back to me.* Then her smile glitched, eyes distorted. Shadows rolled across her body. Her face transformed. Kelly's sharp blue eyes came into focus. She mouthed, *Save me, Kaleb.*

I jolted awake in Kelly's oversized bed with my heart pounding. The sun poured in through the window. Head pounding. The sheets drenched in sweat. I took a deep breath, reaching to the other side of the pillow. Kelly was gone. In her place, the unsigned book contract and a ticket for the premiere. I knew what I had to do.

That night, I put on a crisp navy suit and polished brown leather shoes. I stood in front of the mirror, adjusting my tie, taking deep breaths.

Kelly was standing in the foyer, waiting. She was done up to perfection in a skin-tight sparkly dress, one shoulder exposed. Her shimmering blonde hair was parted to one side, flowing down her shoulders. Her eyes were smoky and beautiful, and for a second, my resolve weakened. What if I could have a second chance with Kelly? If I could break through the illusion. Perhaps in a different life. If our demons didn't have agendas. If neither of us had secrets.

"You look gorgeous," I said, helping her into the limo. "And happy birthday," I handed her a box.

"What's this?" She beamed, tearing through the present as the car took off. She lifted up a fountain pen.

"It's the pen I used to write the first draft of *Pay Me, Alice*. I'm hoping you can make better use of it," I laughed.

She didn't say a word.

"Sorry, I didn't know what—"

Kelly held up her hand, putting her fingers to her mouth. Emotions lingered in her eyes. "This is the best gift anyone has ever given me." She admired the pen, wiping a falling teardrop. "Thank you."

She reached for my hand.

I had prepared for this. "Kelly—"

"I know what you're going to say," she interrupted. "You miss her, don't you?

"I do."

"And you want to go back?

"Not yet. Eventually. Once I get clean."

125

She looked away so I couldn't witness her reaction. Then she turned back with a perfect smile. "I'm sorry for being so guarded, Kaleb. I should have let you in more. I have... trust issues." She crawled over to my side of the limo, nuzzling close. My body awakened.

"But I don't think it would have mattered, would it?"

She placed her hand on my knee. I shifted in my seat.

"You will never give yourself to this project when the real Alice is still lingering in the background."

"Kelly—"

"It's okay." She ran her fingers along my arm. My heartbeat pounded. I wanted her to kiss my neck and climb on top of me, straddle me. Convince me to stay. Convince me to sign the contract. But she pulled her hand away and my heartbeat calmed.

She leaned her head on my shoulder. "Just be with me tonight. I want you to meet my best friend."

The limo stopped and the uproar from the red carpet shook through the car. Angst tightened in my chest as a barrage of hands reached for the tinted windows, lights flashing. Flashbacks of the night in Philadelphia rattled through me. The stares. The whispers. The cameras. Kelly rubbed my back. "You look good." She fixed my collar, running her nails along my neck. "Just stay by my side, okay?"

I stood tall at her words.

They came at us from all directions, screaming her name. Flashes exploded. I gripped Kelly's arm, shuffling down the red carpet. I smiled and spun in the lights, ignoring the ringing in my ear and the unease in my gut. The fear building in the background. She stopped and posed for the cameras. *Over here, Kelly. Over here!* Her hand slipped from mine. I tried to keep smiling, nodding, spinning at their beck and call. But she kept getting further and further away. Bodies obstructed my view. I couldn't see her. The screams and shouts jumbled together.

The ringing in my ear amplified. I turned, scanning the line of reporters, cameras, fans.

Flash. Flash. Flash.

Bob's boater hat weaved in and out of the line.

Of course he fucking came.

Flash. Flash. Flash.

"What are you doing here?" I whispered. "Leave me alone,"

"You're really going to give up on her?" His voice rang in my head. "She believed in you, Kaleb."

Kelly came back into view. She was posing, a hand on her hip, the other on her thigh. They shouted and snapped their photos.

"She's fine." I whispered. "She belongs here. Look at her."

"I'm looking." Bob chuckled. "I'm looking at the scar on her arm…They did this to her."

"No."

"Here we go again. Go ahead. Ignore the signs. The bruises. The pain. The scars. But they were responsible, Kaleb. He was responsible." Bob directed me towards the theater entrance.

I recognized him from pictures, Kelly's manager—Barry Monroe. He was bald, with a thick manicured black beard and yellow framed glasses. Over six feet tall, at least three hundred pounds, mostly settled in his gut. His smile was wide and curved. He was taking a picture with a young, blonde girl in front of a movie poster—Lizzy Michaels.

Bob snickered. "And once again, you're going to try and run away. You're going to leave her to all these tormenters. You're going to leave her to me."

A shadowy hand reached for Kelly.

"Don't you fucking touch her," I seethed.

"Why?" Bob laughed. "What are you going to do about it?"

The rage fired like a gun inside me. I reacted. Everything went red. I shoved my way through. I reached, I grabbed. Two frightened eyes stared back. I was holding the shirt of an unknown man. I saw the microphone fall onto the ground. People were yelling, screaming.

Flash. Flash. Flash.

Whispers, murmurs.

I heard Kelly's voice through the static. "Kaleb. Let him go. Kaleb."

I released the man and fell backwards, spinning. I knocked over another celebrity on the carpet. More shouting, murmuring, confusion. I backed away, further and further. Until the carpet vanished into dirty sidewalk. Until the flashing cameras turned to dim street lights. Until the ringing in my ear faded into nothingness. Chaos settled into shame.

"I've been using again," I announced at the meeting. I was on a metal chair next to Nathan, still wearing my suit, my tie undone, heart still pounding.

"Not the stuff I really like, but it's only a matter of time. I've gotten myself into a bad situation. You wouldn't believe me if I told you. The truth is, I don't have a purpose. I can't seem to stay sober without one." I glanced at Nathan. "I know where this road ends." The brim of his Angels hat covered his eyes. "I know this ending. And yet, I can't resist it. It's all I want."

Thank you for sharing.

The meeting ended. Nathan handed me a small Styrofoam cup filled with coffee and sat down. Another grunt. He stared ahead. His leathery skin, big gray eyebrows, those chilling brown eyes. His gray hair flowing outside the confines of his greasy ball cap.

"Why did you come back?" he asked.

"There's still good inside me. Sara saw good inside me . . . you saw good inside me."

He scoffed. "You want some advice?" He gulped the last sip and handed me his empty cup. "Go write something, you fucking idiot. Go back to that cabin of yours!" he yelled. "There's your damn purpose. Do that and good things will find you again." The sports section landed with a thud on my head. I could hear him chuckle and grunt as he walked out, leaving me alone in the empty gymnasium. I leaned back on the cheap metal chair as the door slammed shut. The lights in the room flickered, dimmed.

A dark presence lingered.

The air turned cold and bitter.

He had followed me.

"Where are you?" I stood up. The legs of the metal chair screeched across the hardwood floor. "Show yourself, Bob."

He slithered in the darkness like the snake that he was.

Dark whispers rang from every direction.

"How did you find me?"

"Please," his voice strengthened. "I knew you'd run back to your little meetings."

Bob's boots echoed in the gymnasium. His silhouette materialized in the low light. He was walking toward me. My body shivered.

"I know everything about you, Kaleb," he said. "I know the real you. I know your darkest secrets. The stuff your precious sponsor doesn't know about. The stuff that would make anyone run for the hills."

"Why did you come back?" I pleaded.

"Because you need me."

"No," I slurred, "you're wrong."

"Oh please. Don't you remember what you did to your good life? Don't you remember what you did to Sara? You think you deserve to go back?"

I didn't respond.

"You asked for it."

Out of the darkness, Bob placed his hand on my shoulder, and I fell to my knees. A wave of terror throbbed inside my heart. My blood frosted over. Memories flashed—my fist going in and out of the plaster walls of the house. Sara crying, screaming. She begged for me to stop. But I couldn't. I couldn't stop. I lost control.

Bob pulled his hand away. "Not evil? Do you remember the look on her face? She was afraid of you."

"No," I slurred.

"Go back to the castle, Kaleb," Bob's voice boomed. "Sign the contract. Kelly needs us. She is trying to help us. She is giving us a purpose."

"You're wrong. I know that ending."

"Don't defy me, Kaleb. Look at me. Look at my face." He stepped into the light.

I put my head down, cowering in fear. "No!" I screamed. I wouldn't look at him. I couldn't. He was evil, and if I looked, I would become him.

I pulled out my cell from my pocket. Nathan was still close by. The phone trembled in my hand. A new message appeared—an unknown number. An image loaded. It was Sara with another man. He was older than me, scattered gray hair. Panic clawed through my insides. Who was this man? His arm wrapped around her shoulder as she washed dishes. That was our routine. That was our house. Her face went in and out of focus. They were smiling, cheeks touching. I was going to be sick.

"Who sent this?" I demanded. "Did you send this?"

Bob laughed. "It's been a while since you drove by Sara's house, hasn't it? I wonder if she's safe? You can't protect anyone, can you?"

My heart pounded.

"What do we know about this guy?" Bob asked. "Who's going to protect Sara now that you're gone?"

"Stop!" I yelled. "This isn't real. I don't believe you."

"Then go see for yourself."

Lizzy: I can't believe she brought him to my premiere. She knew how important that night was to me.

Jez: Oh please. It was a cheesy horror film. Lizzy had like three speaking lines total. She was just the token blonde girl who got slashed halfway through the movie. And she couldn't even get that right. Talk about bad acting. My six-year-old niece screams better than her.

Lizzy: I should have known Kelly would find a way to make the night about her. Barry was livid after the red-carpet incident. He swore to make sure that the author never came to another event with Kelly again.

Jez: I don't know what the big deal was. Kaleb barely touched that reporter. Everyone should have thanked him. That was the most entertainment the crowd got all night.

Lizzy: After everything that happened, there was no way I was going to go to her birthday party.

Jez: Lizzy missed out. The party was so amazing. We rented sixty smoke machines and $20,000 worth of lights. It was epic.

Lizzy: You think Jez really cared about my best friend? How well can you trust a diehard fan that scored an all-inclusive ticket to the Kelly Trozzo show? She was nothing more than a groupie. I don't know exactly what happened that night of Kelly's birthday, but things got dark.

Jez: I'm not going to apologize for getting a little wild. It was a party! I would do anything Kelly told me. Anything.

THE REAL KELLY TROZZO
TheInsideJuice.com Interview 2019

INSIDEJUICE: Let's go back to your departure from *Zoe Loves*. What happened? Walk me through the events leading up to your exit from the show.

TROZZO: That's a complicated story.

INSIDEJUICE: Isn't that why I'm here?

TROZZO: You might remember my sixteenth birthday—MTV made sure of that. The highest-rated *Sweet 16* episode of all time. To Barry, it was the perfect opportunity to demonstrate his power and wealth. Every big name on his roster performed that night, just for me. He rented tigers, elephants, and the biggest house in Malibu. He even bought me a dress that had more bling than the crown jewels. When I look back at the footage, I'm amazed how well the producers painted the fairy tale: Kelly Trozzo's enchanted life, full of glitz, glamour, and eternal happiness. But re-watch that episode, and you'll notice very few clips of me. Because what the camera didn't see that night was me leaving the party in haste. They didn't see me wade into the ocean by myself, still wearing that $50,000 dress.

It's funny—I thought about Princess Jade when I was paddling into the waves. How many times she must have imagined leaping from the tower, crashing into the violent sea. How could she not? That fucking monster…it came every damn night. What hope did she have? She knew her golden heart was cursed with evil. But who could she turn to for help? What if no one was coming to save her? What if she stopped believing in her happily ever after?

So there I was, neck deep in the waves, shaking in the cold water, ready to plunge, when I heard his voice. Noah Tash was screaming at me from the beach. We'd met a week prior when he was written into the script as Lizzy's older brother, and Zoe's first crush. And there he was, wading into the ocean, begging me to return to shore. I was angry at first—no one had ever seen me like that, consumed in my state of madness. But there was nothing I could do. He had come in my darkest hour.

Noah reached for my hand as the waves crashed down over us. I resisted at first, but he put his arms around me and pulled me back to the beach. Then, with my sparkly dress covered in sand, and the tears streaming down my cheeks, I let him comfort me. I was tired of fighting this thing on my own. I wanted someone to rescue me from this life. Maybe I wanted the singing montage and the happily ever after. I needed to believe.

At the end of the MTV episode, you can see me cutting the cake in front of all my fake friends and hired hands. But my eyes were on one person. My knight in shining armor. If only I had known.

My father makes an appearance on television today. He's on
the steps of the New Haven courthouse. Seagulls soar in the
background. His gray hair is parted neatly to the side; a red tie
pulled tightly into a crisp white collar. He has his sleeves rolled
up. The town of New Haven polls better with rolled-up sleeves.
As if he could still run for office after the things he's done.

On the bottom of the screen, the ticker reads: *Former
Governor Begs Son to Surrender.*

My father tells the reporters that he's concerned, and if I
can hear him, I need to turn myself in. Do the right thing.

Oh please. Concerned? That's rich. He doesn't give a shit.
He wants one last moment in the spotlight, no matter the
circumstances. He'll call his old campaign manager on the ride
home. How did I look? He'll pretend your career isn't over. We
haven't spoken since I headed west. A year after my brother
died. After the felonies. The drugs. He didn't have the guts to
say it to my face. He left a voicemail. *You failed me. Leave your
mother alone. Both her sons are gone.* Now he's playing eighteen
holes of golf in the morning, a crossword puzzle, and scotch by

dusk. His next wife got a few fists to the face as well. Can't say I'm surprised.

The truth is, I want to believe in you, Detective Donaldson. I don't want to surrender. I want you to find me. I want the spectacle. I imagine you are staring at a map, colorful pins pushed in around my location. You are prepping for the finale. You'll have your man. No more mishaps. No more blunders. And yet, I wonder if I've given you too much credit. You're still clinging to the evidence in front of you. You still can't see the bigger picture.

Detective Donaldson strode confidently around the interrogation room. His palms slammed onto the table. "What made you drive back to Kelly's and sign the contract that night?" His eyebrows raised in excitement. "What do you remember most about that night?" He couldn't wait any longer. Whatever he had, the surprise was about to be delivered.

"It seems like you already know."

Glossy photos slid across the table.

Donaldson stared at me with contempt. "Did Kelly know?"

I peeked down at the picture of Jez and I having sex. The picture was blurry, taken through the window. The time stamp said 3:00 a.m. The morning after Kelly's birthday. You could barely tell it's me in the corner, standing behind Jez. But that picture didn't tell the entire story.

"That's it? That was your big reveal?" I chuckled. "You think that's what I remember most about that night?"

Donaldson dropped his fist on the table, "Don't fucking play games with me." He shook his head. "You're going to tell me there's something *more* memorable than this?"

Seeing Sara, for starters. That first line of cocaine was close behind. Let me rephrase that—my first line after abstaining for five months. Jez poured it on the glass table. I remembered that. Kelly came to join us with a birthday tiara on her head. My heart trembled with the bass of the music. It was just what I needed. Just how I remembered. How could I ever forget that feeling?

It made me feel indestructible, strong. Not pathetic. The beats pounded through the house, shaking paintings and mirrors on the wall. Not broken. Kids waved glow sticks and danced with their eyes barely open. Not cowardly. Not someone who gave up. I bumped into a guy, and he turned to me, eyes opened wide. His pupils were oversized and grotesque. His black hair was soaked. His smile was crooked and frozen. I smiled back. Not someone who couldn't protect the people he loved.

I saw Sara's face in the fog. She was reaching for me, smiling. She vanished. Her voice echoed, reverberating through the speakers.

"Stop it, Kaleb. You're scaring me. Stop it."

I had slipped. On the eve of my brother's birthday, Bob's shadow appeared in the hallway. I wasn't sure at first. I didn't get a good look. But deep down, I knew. He had returned. And the next day, I left the house. And I got my fix. I welcomed fear. I welcomed pain. I destroyed over two years of sobriety. I returned home as the monster. I destroyed Sara's house. Lamps. Holes in the wall. Anger. Rage. I fucking destroyed it all. I ruined my good life. I was protecting her.

Get rid of me. I'm no good. Don't you see? He will never leave me. I did what I had to do. I can't trust myself.

"Who will never leave you?" Sara kept saying. "What are you doing? Don't do this." She reached out for my arm while I was punching the walls. "Stop it!"

I knocked her over. She screamed. No! What had I done? I hurt her. Just like my father hurt my mother. Just like her ex-husband. I did it. I did it. I collapsed to the floor. I touched her arm. She cringed, turned away. She had finally seen me for what I was.

I destroyed everything.

I deserve everything.

Bob smiled from across Kelly's mansion. The memory turned and twisted in the dark fog. He was showing off. More images swirled through the mist.

"What the fuck are you doing here?" Sara shouted from her front lawn. The man from the picture had come out with her. He was holding her hand.

I am protecting you. Don't you see? He is going to hurt you.

My gaze turned to Sara, then back to the man.

Sara wasn't scared of him.

She was scared of me.

"What are you doing, Kaleb? I'm calling the police."

I pleaded, "If I could just . . ."

She stopped me, mid-sentence. "It's over," she said firmly. "You need to get help. You need to stop. We have to move on with our lives."

Another line.

"Stop driving by the house."

Another swig.

"I don't want to go to the police. But I will."

Another pill.

"I am no longer yours."

The voice changed. Sara smiled in the fog of Kelly's castle. Her voice still echoed through the speakers. She reached out to me, "I love you, Kaleb. Thank you for protecting me. Do you miss me?"

"Yes."

"We had a good life, once."

"I know."

"You saved me."

"I know."

"Come back."

"I can't."

"Protect me."

"Alice."

"Protect me."

"I'm so sorry."

She reached her hand lower and lower, till I could almost touch it. I could feel her warmth and her love. I could see her smile...

"Come back, Kaleb."

The image of her swirled away in the fog.

I stumbled through the party, a bottle to my mouth, my other hand reaching into the mist. She was gone. The smoke rolled across my shoulders. Lights beamed across the shadows. I saw Kelly. The birthday girl.

Oh, my beautiful fantasy. She was mine. She was dancing from room to room. Neon green bracelets jangled around her wrist. There was a lollipop in her mouth. Pupils enlarged. Sweat coated her brow. Jez was with her, her large breasts held in a tiny bikini top. Colors swirled across their bodies. They both turned to me, giggling.

Bob tipped his hat from across the room, "This is for the best."

I raised my glass. This was a fine fate.

"Cheers, motherfucker."

Jez passed me the dollar bill. I sat back on the couch and closed my eyes. Kelly climbed on my lap. *I'll follow you anywhere.* She placed a pill on my tongue, and I swallowed. She kissed my cheek and then my mouth. Our lips moved back and forth, my teeth softly biting her bottom lip. Her lips felt good. Her tongue felt better.

Anything you ask. I am yours.

The pill kicked in. The euphoria was never-ending. We danced in a dark room with neon lights. Where she went, I followed. I felt her body, and I wanted every part of her. She was wearing a silky black dress, and her hair was up in a bun. She turned her backside to me to dance. I touched every curve. I felt someone watching us—a kid with buzzed hair standing in the corner, drinking.

Lights flashed across Kelly's face. I looked back over at the kid. In between the strobes and darkness. It wasn't a clear look. But I remember that scar on his left eye. A deep scowl. I can't forget that face. Kelly directed my attention toward her. I rubbed my hands on her thighs.

She led me down a hallway. People were hooking up against the wall, their bodies propped against one another. She turned back to me, laughing, her hair stuck to her forehead with sweat. She slipped into a dark room, illuminated by a neon sign and one strobe light. She pushed me against the wall, wrapping her fingers around my head. I pulled off her slinky dress. She was wearing a glow-in-the-dark thong. My hands gripped her tiny bare cheeks, and my momentum carried her toward the bed.

She fell flat onto the mattress and I lowered my head to her crotch. She arched her back to accommodate. I began licking away at her soft flesh, enjoying every taste, extending my tongue and repeating the process. She tasted so good. The high never stopped. I heard the door open.

A petite redhead entered the room. Jez. She was holding a stack of papers and smiling nervously. Kelly opened her eyes and grinned. Jez came over to the bed and lay down next to Kelly. They started kissing.

Jez let down her hair, mid-kiss. Long, red hair. Soft freckles scattered over her ample ass and enormous chest. She was gorgeous. She pulled her panties off effortlessly. Kelly kissed her freckly white skin. They had done this before.

I didn't like that she was kissing Kelly.

I tried to curb my craving by going back down to Kelly's soft skin below, but she stopped me. She pushed me back and pointed down to the stack of papers. The pen I had given Kelly entered my hands.

"Let's write a new story, Kaleb."

I grabbed the pen that once saved my life. I stared into Kelly's eyes.

I didn't back down.

I wanted more. I wanted everything. I signed my name. Take me away. I kissed Kelly's soft lips. She directed me toward Jez. I kissed her soft lips.

I went to lay Kelly down on the bed, but she turned away and arched her back up to me. I saw the opening from behind. I slipped my penis inside of her. My entire body shook with pleasure. Pure ecstasy. The strobe lights cascaded bright colors all over her backside. Kelly did all the work, moving her ass up and down. I wanted the feeling to last forever. Jez followed suit and arched her ass alongside Kelly's. Kelly pulled away and directed me toward Jez.

I did what I was told. My leader. Jez's ass jiggled back and forth; her soft skin wrapped tightly around me. My eyes lingered on Kelly as she watched us in the darkness. Our gazes met. The strobe light flashed. I saw Sara's face. My stomach tightened. Her innocent, sweet, beautiful, perfect, face. My breath was shallow. I reached for her.

The light flashed again, and Sara vanished.

My heartbeat pounded. Breath panicked. What was happening? I was still inside Jez, her backside clapping together. I pushed harder and harder, thrusting with rage. But nothing calmed me. Fear slithered through my veins.

Bob was in the corner, pointing, laughing. *You finally get it, don't you? I took her away. I win. I win. I win.* What the fuck? Anger. More rage. Harder and harder into Jez. My jaw clenched.

My vision blurred. I knew I was about to come. I didn't want to—not with Jez. I pulled out and moved toward Kelly. *I win. I win. I win.* I felt myself go inside Kelly and I looked straight into her eyes, hoping to see Sara. *Where is she?*

Colorful lights flashed across her face. *Take me away.* Cobalt blue. It was Kelly. We stared at each other intensely. I didn't back down. The rage in my heart exploded. She bit her lip, gliding the sides of her thumb near my mouth. I bit down on her fingers.

Jez was nowhere to be seen as I came inside of Kelly.

I woke up naked in Kelly's bed. Alone. The sun peered into the room and blinded me. I walked downstairs through a spotless house. No sign of the night, as usual. Kelly wasn't in the study. Her bags were gone. There was no note. I looked out the window and saw a black truck pull out of the driveway. An old pickup truck, cracked windshield, unwashed. The same truck I saw again on the night she died.

"And that, detective, is what I remember most about that night."

LIZZY: Pardon my language, but that house was fucking cursed.

JEZ: To be honest, Kaleb scared me a little. I didn't mind, as long as Kelly was there.

LIZZY: I've never seen that truck before in my life.

JEZ: That truck belonged to Noah Tash.

THE REAL KELLY TROZZO
TheInsideJuice.com Interview 2019

INSIDEJUICE: Tell me about your relationship with Noah Tash.

TROZZO: Noah was my first love. After my sixteenth birthday party, my heart belonged to him. I laugh thinking about it now. This giddy little teenybopper, skipping around the set, conjuring fantasies of a happily ever after. But in my defense, Noah played the part. He replaced my darkness with cute text messages and secret glances. He did little things, like bringing flowers to set and leaving notes in my trailer. Our first time was on set—right on the Claireborn family's old red leather couch. If that couch could talk! Filled with memories of young Zoe learning how to play the guitar or writing her first ballad with Lizzy. Then memories of me getting fingers shoved down my pants, then my bra, and then my cherry popped.

I took a pregnancy test on the night before my seventeenth birthday. I was in my trailer with Lizzy. She was just a kid at the time, fifteen years old. She told me it was going to be okay as I cried on her shoulder. I wanted to believe her, I did. But deep down, I knew that the fairy tale was over. Underage princesses don't get pregnant.

I need you here
My courageous knight
Destroy this fear
This heart of mine
Is all I hold dear.
—*Princess Jade (From the theme of* Castle Heart*)*

That song haunts me. That annoyingly whimsical ballad, with its overdramatic piano riffs and sappy lyrics, played on repeat in minivans. I got a little carried away last night in the motel. I'm almost out of drugs.

Another bout of swirling images and nightmares. It was a doozy. Perseus made an appearance, holding a shield with the head of Medusa carved into the bronze. The venomous snakes on her head came to life, slithering toward me. Her glowing eyes opened. She hissed, "You'll never save her."

Cold air swept across my face. I was paddling a small rowboat as choppy waves crashed over the side. Kelly was tied to a rock in the middle of the sea, struggling to break free.

White foam cascaded over her naked body. She was screaming for me. I paddled and paddled as fast as I could.

A monster rose up from the darkness, its fangs extended. The monster devoured her in one gulp.

A powerful wave swept across my boat, knocking me into the depths of the dark water.

I was drowning.

Sinking.

Deeper and deeper.

Reaching up to the fading light.

I was in Kelly's bedroom. A silhouette of the theme park mouse with a dagger in hand appeared on her wall. Animated bluebirds floated over her bed. White pills showered down upon me. I screamed, digging through the mountain of prescription pills. I couldn't find her. Then I realized...

We were outside.

I stared at her stunning white gown soaked with blood, dripping across the driveway. Her song pulsated in my ears. I pulled her in my arms. What have I done? The princess is dead. What have I done? I was rocking her body back and forth. I'm sorry.

I open my eyes.

I'm in the motel. Among stale sheets and bloody pillowcases.

There is no air in my lungs.

I'm sweating, panicking.

I reach for the nightstand next to the bed. Pills, lines, vodka. Anything.

I hear Nathan's voice.

Face this.

Face this.

I take a swig.

Snort a line.

Swallow a pill.

Take a deep breath.

That's better.

I lay my head back on the pillow. The television is still on. The picture comes back into focus. A panel of experts discussing the only event that America wants to hear about. I don't mind. I'm starting to enjoy seeing my face on the screen. America's Most Wanted. It has a nice ring to it. The Hunt for Kaleb Reed Continues. Perhaps this was the ending I'd always imagined. The ending I always wanted. Right here. In this very motel. It's a very special place.

"Did you read the novel, Kim? It's essentially a stalker handbook. We're looking into the mind of a very psychologically disturbed person."

"Yes. I read it. Granted, there were a few disturbing scenes. But on a whole, I don't think we can judge a man by the fiction he's written."

"Martin, can you weigh in here? Will Kaleb Reed have a fair trial with a book like this? What jury in their right mind wouldn't read see the blueprints of a killer in these pages?"

They do have a point. I'm capable of dreadful things. Do you want to know my favorite section of my book? I think it's appropriate to share. It's the chapter where AJ had just rented a house in St. Charles, Missouri. He had discovered the whereabouts of Alice, after a year of searching.

It was a humble place, a one-bedroom with an old brick fireplace. He didn't need much. He had no furniture, no belongings. Only a mattress. On his second day there, he was driving to the grocery store. That's when he saw her, walking, crying, rain matting down her long blonde hair. In AJ's head, it was fate. He stopped his car, opened the door.

"AJ? What the hell are you doing here?" Alice yelled, angrily.

He didn't have a choice. He had to tell her. "I came to find you."

It was a lot to take in for Alice. But she was vulnerable, scared. Soaking wet. She had run out in the cold after a fight with her husband. It was complicated. She was complicated. In real life and fiction. She went home with AJ that night. They were together for the first time. He finally got a taste. A woman he had been chasing for ten years. And it was everything he'd imagined.

She felt it too. She had to. Because they were destined to be together. This was surely the start of their new life. A good life. The life that AJ had always dreamed of.

In the morning, he woke to find the other side of his bed was empty. He heard her footsteps on the creaky staircase. He ran and caught her just before she went out the door.

AJ yelled, "You're not going back to him, are you?"

Alice looked up at him. "I didn't ask you to come here, AJ."

"But why?" He was shocked, hurt, disappointed.

She hesitated. "Please go home."

Then she walked out the door. AJ had given everything to this girl. For what? Would she ever be his? His thoughts felt poisoned. He was angry. He got a taste. It wasn't enough. It was never enough. He needed her attention. She needed to know he wasn't going away. He showed up at the post office. Her gym. He drove by her house. It didn't work. She was hiding.

He was forced to do something bold.

It all sounds so familiar.

Two weeks after her birthday, Kelly went back on tour. After the incidents in Philadelphia and at the movie premiere, Barry banned me from all public appearances. I couldn't join Kelly on tour. I was a liability. I was bad for her image. The cuddling, the sex, the drugs, the fantasy, the parties—gone.

Poof. I was already hanging by a thread. She was the only thing that I had left to cling to.

My apartment became a prison. Self-induced quarantine. Kelly was everywhere. The computer. The television. My dreams. The grocery store tabloids. The odds were in her favor. I wanted to be in her bed, just one more night, one more moment. I wanted to fuck her on the dresser. I wanted to shove her head on the pillow and put my head against hers and bite her ear and fuck as hard as I could.

Sobriety was no longer an option. I scored whatever was available. Used without restraint. No more meetings. No more Sara. No more routine. I threw it all away. For what? A pop star? A book? What did you think would happen when she left me? I can hear Nathan's grunt from here. Yes, it was my choice.

I vanished into the digital landscape. A never-ending pit of online trash. I said it was research. Laughable. It was an obsession. Googling. Clicking. Watching. Staring. Consuming. I read every comment. I watched every video. A clip of a fan on stage in Houston, sobbing into her hands. Kelly pinned a brass KT logo on the girl's jacket and she collapsed onto the stage, overwhelmed with emotions.

They were all seeking a greater purpose.

A tribe to belong to.

A place to feel safe.

I kept clicking. I wanted more. The fantasy wasn't enough. I had a taste of the real thing. Hours, days would go by. I didn't write a thing. The sun rose and set from my worn-down mattress. I drank bottle after bottle. I needed something more than a pin on my shirt.

I needed a chance at redemption.

I browsed images of Barry Monroe. His enormous stature always lingered in the background. At concerts. Hollywood sets. Red carpets. With his oversized suits, his dark beard and yellow glasses. Monitoring from afar. He was the one responsible for keeping me from Kelly. I didn't need to read the articles, or the horrible lawsuits. I didn't need to watch the depressing testimonies of his former artists. He was an evil man.

I wondered what he did to Kelly? How he hurt her?

He knew that I would protect her.

That's why he kept us apart.

I revisited my favorite bar. Did drugs in the bathroom. Blacked out.

One week became two. Two became three. Kelly's messages were casual and short, excessive emoticons, abbreviated words. I couldn't communicate like that.

She texted me the picture she took of us in bed together. She was leaning into my chest, grinning. The bed sheets barely covered her chest. My face was slightly turned into the pillow. It was intimate. But more importantly, it was proof. We were more than friends. I liked that. I needed that. I craved more. But there were other things too. The fame. It gave me a rush.

I wanted people to know.

I was sunken into the couch. Cartons of takeout and bottles of booze spread out before me. *Late Night with Jimmy Kimmel* was on. Kelly was the guest. That meant she was in Los Angeles and she didn't call me. She should have reached out. I grabbed a bottle of vodka and took a long, slow swig. She was wearing tiny black shorts and a white blouse, her long, skinny legs perched in patent leather heels. Jimmy did a double-take and made a face to the audience like *Wow!*

She was good on camera. Her gestures and facial expressions were instinctive. She could turn an audience in seconds. She was mature, fun, witty. Bantering back and forth. Delivering a punch line at the precise moment.

Kimmel insinuated that her activities hadn't been so sweet and innocent as of late.

She said it was part of her spiritual path and told him not to worry, that she'd be home by curfew. The audience laughed on cue. Jimmy had this shtick where he showed flashcards of paparazzi pictures of stars.

"Look at this one," Kimmel said. "TMZ caught you eating a corn dog at 4:00 a.m. Is it safe to say you like gas station corn dogs?"

She shook her head. "No. I don't like corn dogs, Jimmy." She paused. "I freakin' *love* corn dogs." The audience laughed.

"We also have a picture of you with a couple of handsome guys," said Kimmel. Then he pulled out a picture of Kelly and me on the red carpet.

I sat up on the couch. I took a swig.

"This is the author of your favorite novel, correct? Kaleb Reed, right? Will you be having beautiful babies with him?" asked Jimmy.

She smiled. "No, Kaleb and I are good friends. When I read his book, I had to meet him. It was that good."

"So, nothing there? Does he know that? I've seen the video of him pummeling one of your fans. He must have missed the memo."

"Nope, just friends. But if he ever decides he wants a career as my maniac bodyguard, I would be happy to consider him."

The audience chuckled.

My hands clenched around the bottle of booze.

Kelly crossed her legs, placed her hands in her lap, and her blue eyes turned toward Kimmel, intensely.

Fuck you.

"Fuck you!" I screamed.

The bottle smashed against the wall.

A carton of old Chinese food was next, splattering alongside the vodka dripping down the cheap plaster. *I want you to fall in love with me.* I flipped the coffee table over. She didn't get to do that.

"What do you want from me?" I screamed.
She couldn't claim me and then run away.
I signed my services over to her
She couldn't discard me at will.
She needed to come back for me.
She was mine.
And I was hers.

I paced, took a deep breath. The show had gone to commercial. I stared down at my book on the carpet. I wiped away sauce from the cover. A twisted thought. As an author, it's a joy to watch your characters come to life, seeing them react and respond on the page. It's a thing of beauty. It really is.

A good writer understands his characters like his children. He doesn't have to manipulate the action or force the dialogue. I didn't outline a single chapter of *Pay Me, Alice*. Everything AJ did was on his own accord. Or real. I'll let you decide. Like when he took out an ad in the local newspaper five weeks after he slept with Alice. It was a full-page ad in the only section she ever read: the obituaries. Alice told him it put life into perspective. Our lives are small. Just a few brief lines in the paper. Focus on what is important. So, AJ's ad said, *I have always focused on what is most important. I'll be waiting when you're ready. —AJ*

What a grand, romantic, gesture. I was proud of AJ for doing that. Not stalkeresque in the slightest. That was love. You do what you must. Why not take a cue from my own character? I was staring at the picture of me and Kelly lying in bed. A wicked thought…I typed in the email to the *Huffington Post* reporter I had been talking to the day before. *This would show her.* He had asked me in an interview if I had a romantic relationship with Kelly and I said no. I always said no. I was trained to say no. Section II of the contract I signed required it. But things were different that night. I wanted her attention. *She deserves this.*

I attached the picture of Kelly and me in the email. In the subject I wrote, "Does this answer your question?"

Three days after he bought the ad, Alice came to AJ's door, holding the newspaper, crying. Their affair began.

It worked for AJ.

It would work for me.

Lizzy: What a pathetic cry for attention. Listen, Kelly could spill spaghetti on her shirt and make the front page of the tabloids. Now imagine what a damaging photo like that could do? The guy showed his true colors. She finally understood how dangerous he was.

Jez: Oh please. Kelly was flattered. It made her feel like the real-life Alice. She thought it was hot. She would never tell Lizzy that, of course. Plus, she looked so sexy in that photo.

Lizzy: I have no problem talking about the trip to New York. It was three days after the author leaked that little cuddling photo. I went because I needed my best friend. Not sure if you know, but my show didn't get picked up for a third season. The thought of life after television terrified me. What was I going to do? I could barely land a horror movie with ten speaking lines. I didn't have the following Kelly had. I couldn't just steal headlines like her. So, yeah, I accepted her invitation to New York. I wanted to make up with her. I wanted my best friend back.

Jez: Please. She didn't come to New York to be Kelly's friend.

She came to save her own skin. She needed Kelly's publicity to survive.

Lizzy: He wasn't supposed to be there. Kelly swore to me she'd break up with him after the leaked photo. That was the last straw. I knew she would be upset, but that's fine. It would be just the two of us, watching movies and eating ice cream. Making our dream vacation plans to France. Venting about boys, shooting our YouTube movies, all of it. It was going to be the perfect weekend.

Jez: Surprisingly, the first night went well...I knew it wouldn't last. It was only a matter of time before Lizzy snapped. Such an ungrateful bitch. It makes me angry just thinking about the things she said.

Lizzy: I tried to play nice. I really did.

Jez: If that's nice, I'd hate to see what mean is.

Lizzy: Did I say things I regretted? Absolutely. But Kelly needed to hear the truth. She needed to know how this was going to end.

Jez: Things with Kelly and Kaleb changed after New York. They were...closer. Guess it's true what they say—the heart wants what the heart wants. Sometimes, I think Kelly did things just to spite Lizzy. That isn't gossip; that's just the truth.

Lizzy was jealous. I mean, she got the spin-off, she got Barry's attention, she got everything she wanted, and she still wasn't as popular as Kelly. Then the network doesn't renew her show? Oh my gosh. She had nothing left but Kelly's coattails to ride on.

Lizzy: Sex tape? No. Not Kelly. No matter what the media portrays, Kelly was prudish off camera. She didn't do things like that. Unless she was under some emotional spell, or some horrible influence. He was the one who wanted the attention. And trust me, he would have done anything to get it. The more fame, the higher the stakes. The higher the stakes, the greater the fall. And that man was all about the fall.

Jez: Yeah, I know they did some filming. I watched some of the clips. It was hot.

The Real Kelly Trozzo
TheInsideJuice.com Interview 2019

INSIDEJUICE: Just to confirm, you're saying that your costar, Noah Tash, got you pregnant?

TROZZO: That's correct.

INSIDEJUICE: What did you do?

TROZZO: I had to do the hardest thing I've ever done—tell my manager. Barry had two sides. When I obeyed him and the money was flowing, he played the doting father. There wasn't a jewel or a present he wouldn't buy me. But when things didn't go according to his plan, when he didn't have control, it was an entirely different story. He hated tears, hated weakness. And there I was, sniveling at his desk, blowing snot into a rag, basically begging him to let me take a break from the show. I wanted to have my baby. I can't tell you why. Do I think I would have been a good mother? I don't know. But I wanted a way out. I wanted to find my mother. Use my influence for good.

When Barry finally spoke, his face was red and he was practically foaming at the mouth. *You're going to take care of it. How the fuck could you let this happen? This would ruin everything we've built. Do you want to end up like your screwed-up junkie mother?* Then he grabbed my wrist and slammed it down on the table. He made sure I looked him dead in the eye as tears poured down my face. *You don't get to leave. I own you. I made you. And I can fucking destroy you.*

The St. Regis Hotel, New York.

"Turn it off." I covered my face. Kelly had on a black bra and panties underneath her robe. She was holding her phone, recording. It was the night before her concert at Madison Square Garden.

I smiled with the camera still pointed at me.

"C'mon, don't you want to show people you're fucking me? Don't you want Sara to know? Isn't that why you sent the photo to that reporter?"

"Turn it off."

"You know how many headlines you would get with this? How much attention? That's what you want, right?"

She crawled across the large hotel bed. She pulled out a bag of coke from her bra, emptied it on a small mirror. Sniffed. Exhaled, then sat up. She turned her face to the phone. "This is Kelly Trozzo, live from New York. Here with best-selling author, Kaleb Reed," she handed me the mirror and dollar bill, "who wants everyone to know that we are fucking. Isn't that right?"

I snorted, relaxed, exhaled. Yes, I did. She was right. I

wanted everything. I wanted her. That flat stomach. Those enchanting eyes. I missed those small, perky tits and perfect ass. I snickered and averted my eyes back to the TV, acting for the camera. *Look at me. Disgusting.* Feigning apathy. Oh, I wanted this. I wanted it bad. C'mon, feed me. Give me the attention. I loved headlines. *Former Governor's Son Arrested for Cocaine. Former Governor's Son Arrested for Assault.* Look what you created. Look what I've become.

She slithered closer.

"How bad do you want me?"

Bad.

She pointed the camera at me. "Here's your chance. Tell the world about us. Tell Sara. Do you love me, Kaleb?"

My penis thickened and she kissed my neck, still recording.

"You'll do anything for me, won't you?" she whispered in my ear. "You have no one else left?"

My stomach lurched.

"What did you say?"

"Isn't that right, Kaleb? You scared them all off." She laughed.

"Turn it off." I got off the bed. "Stop it."

I couldn't breathe.

The camera was still on me. She was pushing me. Why was she pushing me?

"Broken beyond repair. Who would want you now?" She got up and moved toward me. She touched my arm.

I shoved her off. "Enough."

"Oh c'mon. You love this. Why resist? It's almost sad how helpless you are. How easily I can suck you in."

The rage pulsed. It flowed through my veins, throbbing. My body felt cold. Knees wavered. Hands trembled. Breath hitched, convulsed. What the fuck? Vision blurred in the corners. I couldn't lose control. I had to stay in control.

"Turn it off!" I shouted, pacing the room. "I'm not helpless. This shit is over. Turn it the fuck off."

"Oh no, Kaleb. It's just beginning. I want the world to see you for what you truly are. I want them to see your demons. That infamous Kaleb Reed rage. Did Sara finally see your monsters? Is that why she left you? Is that why no one wants you? Is that why I found you in that tiny apartment all by yourself?"

It was happening. I couldn't stop it.

Clenched fists.

Tunnel vision.

Red in the corners.

"Why are you doing this?" I yelled.

"Because you're fucking weak," she cackled. "Because you fell right into my trap. Like a little insect crawling into my web. You're stuck." She pointed her finger at my chest, "Stuck. Stuck."

"No. I'm not." I mumbled. "I can make the right choice. Nathan believes in me."

"Who's Nathan?" Kelly sneered "I made you, Kaleb. I can return you. You think I'm Alice, don't you? Isn't that what this is all about? You wanted my attention? Isn't this how it worked in your precious book, with the precious love of your life? Who is it? Sara, Alice, or me? Who are you trying to protect now? Who are you going to fail this time?"

"Shut up! Shut up! Shut up!"

"Uh-oh, here he comes. Angry Kaleb is coming out. Now the whole world will know what you're capable of." The phone was still recording.

"Stop!" I pleaded. "Please. Stop. Stop. Stop."

"Why, what are you going to do? Are you going to hit me? Isn't that what your father did to your mother? Don't think I didn't read about him. Are you the one who tattled?"

She slapped me in the face.

Again.

Again.

I didn't want to hurt her. Stop. I could see my father's fists. I hated those fists. My body went limp. Pulsing fear. Pulsing rage. My eyes rolled into the back of my head. I shoved Kelly against the wall. The phone fell from her hands. I gripped her arms. She couldn't escape.

The rage overflowed.

My fist went into the wall.

Right next to her face.

Again.

Again.

She moved away.

Blood spilled from my knuckles.

Over and over.

I collapsed on the floor.

She picked up the camera.

Laughed.

Still recording.

Her hand came to my back. I turned with my fist raised. She didn't cower. She leaned in. Pulled me to my feet. My heart pumped with madness.

"Shhh," she whispered in my ear. She kissed my neck. She rubbed my back.

My heartbeat slowed.

My jaw and fists loosened.

Consciousness resumed.

What was happening?

She touched my face.

"I'm sorry," she whispered.

I closed my eyes and buried my head in her neck and shoulder.

I wanted to dull.

Stay numb.

Do what felt good.

Avoid pain.

Stay broken.

Make it go away.

"I'm sorry," she said, stroking my back. "You just make me so crazy." She put her hand on my pounding heart. "I took it too far." She kissed my neck, then my collarbone. She kissed my lips. "I missed you."

I closed my eyes.

Emotions swelled.

I was broken.

"You are mine, Kaleb. I don't like it when you disobey me...I'm sorry."

My breath slowed, deepened.

"You forced me to punish you."

"I'm sorry."

"Like when you wouldn't sign the contract." She unbuttoned my pants, her teeth pulling at the skin on my neck. "I had to send you that picture of Sara and her new boyfriend."

Chills ran along my arms.

"I don't like sharing," she whispered.

She kept kissing.

"Because you are mine. Not hers. Say it. Say it!"

"I'm yours."

"Good." She pushed me down on the bed.

"You are *my* soldier. Not hers."

The phone was in her right hand. I closed my eyes.

"And soldiers obey their leaders, don't they?"

She pulled my penis out of my shorts and put her tongue around the tip. I reached for the phone. Her lips felt good.

"Yes."

She licked her way up to my chest and slowly passed the camera into my hand. She grinded her body on me, kissing my neck. Our hands intertwined. She released. I was holding the camera as I flipped her tiny body underneath me and pushed her underwear to the side. I put it in. The glow of the camera shined on her.

I relished in the warmth and the sensation. I pushed harder. In and out. Her legs wrapped around me. I panned to her face. Her eyes closed in pleasure. She was acting—of course, she was acting—but it was so natural, and that scared me. She opened her eyes and looked straight into the camera.

I threw the phone on the side of the bed, and it landed on the carpet. She reached out in protest, but I grabbed her face and kissed her mouth.

Afterward, she watched the footage, naked in bed, giggling.

"What do you think Sara will think when she sees it? Here, take a look."

I didn't want to see it.

"You ready for me to post it?" She laughed.

"You wouldn't," I said.

She laughed again, "Oh, now you don't want people to know?"

"I shouldn't have disobeyed. I'm sorry."

She smirked and got off the bed. She flipped her hair in the mirror and started to wash off her makeup. "Then your atonement is finished. I'd like you to meet my best friend, Lizzy and come to my concert tomorrow."

"I thought I was banned."

"I'll worry about that."

I leaned back on the headboard and closed my eyes.

"But next time you pull a stunt like this," she said. "We are done."

I saw her eyes in the mirror, an expression I'd never seen. Cruelty.

"I'm sorry for being harsh," she said. "But I can't have any loose ends."

"And what about the video?"

She glanced over at the bed and smiled.

"I'll wait till you're ready. Or when you act out again. Or when you decide you've had enough."

I swallowed.

"And then I'll post it." Her face twisted into a sadistic smile. "Now wouldn't that be a fucking headline?"

Lizzy: I'll tell you what happened. I was there. She gave him a second chance, a third chance, a fourth chance…who could count at that point? That's just who she was. Kelly always saw the best in people. All it took was one sob story. The author had a million of those. But deep down, it still came back to the same thing. She wanted the abuse. She wanted the knife to dig a little deeper. I guess it's proof that no amount of fans, money, attention—none of it could fill that void.

Jez: Don't you see? She was the princess with the golden heart. She was healing his wounds. She was making him whole. One day you'll understand. Everything Kelly did was for a reason. She had to strengthen his armor. The final battle was nearing.

The Real Kelly Trozzo
TheInsideJuice.com Interview 2019

INSIDEJUICE: Did you have an abortion?

TROZZO: I did.

INSIDEJUICE: How did Noah react?

TROZZO: Oh please. Not a day after I broke the news to Barry, Noah tried to save his career by breaking up with me in my trailer. He said we needed to cool things down. A little late for that. But it didn't matter, Noah was written out of the show. We had a dramatic goodbye on set, surrounded by a studio audience, saying our farewells on the same couch he fucked me on. My tears in the episode were real, though I was too doped up to truly feel them.

The cast and crew tried their best to help me, but the darkness came on with a vengeance. I lived in this constant state of fear. I was sick. And just like my mother, I found solace in things that numb, specifically opiates. Toward the end, I couldn't get through my lines, or make any public appearances. That's when the producers decided to change direction.

Lizzy Loves . . . I understood why they did it. I was a liability. I get it. Things were bad. On the last day of filming, I was the pathetic girl who took enough pills to fall asleep behind a prop on set. And when I woke up, I heard the voices of the two most important men in my life. I can hear them so clearly.

First, Noah: "I've done everything you've asked."

Then Barry: "No. I asked you to get close to her so we could control her, not make things more difficult. I didn't ask you to get her fucking pregnant."

Noah tried to interject and convince Barry that he could bring me back from oblivion, but he wasn't hearing it. Barry said: "The show is done. Maybe I pushed her too far, but I have to get rid of her now. She's weak." He paused for a second as if he knew I was listening. "Just like her druggie mother."

The driver who killed my brother was a tattoo artist. He got a measly one-year sentence for involuntary manslaughter. His blood alcohol content was right at the legal limit. The DA said his hands were tied. My dad couldn't use his influence to keep him behind bars.

I was eager for his release.

It was a cold day in February, and I was waiting for him in the parking lot outside his tattoo parlor. Bob was sitting next to me in the passenger seat. He had led me down a dark road that ended here. Raindrops fell on my windshield. I saw the man exit the building. His face was pudgy, and he had a scar on the top of his shaved head.

Bob tapped my shoulder. *Do it.* My black hood went up, my steps quickened. I approached the man, wearing all the pain of my past. He turned around when I was only feet from him. A look of dread plastered his face.

He must have known.

I was there to kill him.

On that cold, rainy day, the man who killed my brother turned to me with fear in his eyes. He looked around for help, but there was no one there to save him. I pulled my hood down. I wanted him to see my face.

My first punch hit his throat. He fell to the ground. My kneecap split his lip open. He tried to swing back, but I grabbed his hand and bent his wrist back. He cried and whimpered in pain.

"Justin Reed. Remember that name?"

He looked up in in agony, shock.

"That was the kid you killed." I twisted his wrist harder. "That was my brother."

Another punch. And another. And another.

Nothing calmed the anger. It scared me that I couldn't stop. I didn't know where this darkness came from. But it was there. Pouring out. And it made me powerful. Another punch. And another. My wrist snapped. The bone broke.

I dropped to the ground, screaming. The man gasped for air, his face battered, soaked in blood.

"I'm sorry. I'm sorry," he yelled as blood poured from his open wounds. He leaned up against the brick building, shaking his head. Red blood mixed with rain on the pavement.

I picked myself up and glared at him. The anger had deflated, but it was still there. Maybe if I'd finished the job, the shadows would have released me. I ran to the car. I pounded the steering wheel and cried for my brother, for the life I wanted to leave behind. I didn't flee. I waited for my fate in the parking lot. Bob stared at me with disappointment.

The police arrived ten minutes later. A crowd had gathered around the tattoo parlor. They pulled me out of the car and took me away in handcuffs. I had gone there to take his life. I had only managed to commit assault.

But I was capable of that type of darkness.

I could kill.

The Real Kelly Trozzo
TheInsideJuice.com Interview 2019

INSIDEJUICE: What happened after you were fired from the show?

TROZZO: Haven't you seen the tabloids? I partied every night. My pain became a public spectacle.

INSIDEJUICE: But then you disappeared from the public eye for the better part of a year. Did you go to rehab?

TROZZO: No.

INSIDEJUICE: Then where?

TROZZO: I was holed up in my house.

INSIDEJUICE: For all that time?

TROZZO: Pretty much.

INSIDEJUICE: Did anyone visit you, try to help you? Your friends, co-stars, Barry Monroe?

TROZZO: Lizzy tried to get me out of that house. My manager also came by…once.

INSIDEJUICE: How did that go?

TROZZO: I was in my tower when he came. You have no idea how happy I was to hear him shout my name from the entrance. Even after everything that happened—even after he destroyed my will to live and made me get rid of my baby—I wanted to forgive him. I wanted him to reach out and be a father, a mentor, anything. At least acknowledge everything I did for him. Or pretend to care. Instead, he said: "Pull your shit together." And he looked me in the eye and said harshly, "I didn't raise you to be a fucking quitter like your mom."

I can only imagine what he saw. My hair matted in knots, my eyes swollen and red. Trust me, I wanted to be strong. But he was right. I *was* my mother. I was weak. Because as soon as he said it, I burst into tears. I should have known what would happen next. The more I cried, the more disgusted he became. Finally, he got up off the couch and headed for the door. "I'm sorry I came." Then right before he walked out, he said, "Hopefully, your friend Lizzy can pick up the slack."

I wouldn't see the light of day for another six months. I would have to die and be reborn. But I'll never forget those words. I'll never forgive him for what he did. He sent me to that tower to die.

We were lying in bed, still breathing heavily, the hotel sheets in disarray. It was the morning of Kelly's concert at Madison Square Garden.

Kelly was quiet, and I pinned her arms against the pillows and kissed her. I ran my fingers along the scar, feeling the protruded skin on her lower forearm. I put my lips to it, and I felt her shudder. When I looked up, a tear rolled down her cheek. I flinched. My dad used to show me his hand when there were tears. He showed anger when I showed weakness. Even at the hospital, next to my brother's lifeless body. He glared at me. *Don't you dare cry. This was your fault.*

I tapped the scar. "What happened here?"

I met Kelly's frightened gaze. I wanted to be better.

She wrapped her arms tightly around me, and I whispered, "You can tell me."

She kissed me back but didn't respond.

I added, "You don't have to."

"Is this for the book, or do you want to know?"

I didn't hesitate. "I want to know."

I rubbed her hands, her forearms, her neckline. She stared up at the ceiling.

"I tried to kill myself...after my TV show ended...after I was betrayed. I locked myself inside my tower. Just like the princess. And every night, evil came to devour my soul. That's when I realized that none of it mattered—the fame, attention, nothing. For the first time in years, there was no concert to play, no role to act, no sense of self. Just darkness. And I was alone. Every night, I would scream and scream, and no one heard me, Kaleb. I became the monster I feared, and I wanted to die...

"I woke up and took pills. Slept, then took more. I hoped each day would be my last. I prayed for someone to save me. But no one came. All the screenplays, all the roles I had been promised, they were all lies. There was no Prince Charming to climb the tower and rescue me. There was no humble knight, no dashing Greek god. I stopped believing in fairy tales.

"Then one night, I picked myself up out of the tub. I walked naked through the house, with water dripping on the marble floors. I went to the kitchen and got a knife. I remember the moonlight shooting through the window and reflecting off the blade. I hacked away at one side of my hair, watching the wet locks fall onto the kitchen tile. I had given up. I fell on my knees, screaming to God, with the knife still in my grip. I let my demons take the reins. I had made the decision to kill myself."

I was fixated on her every word.

She rolled over and looked me straight in the eyes.

"But God gave me three gifts that night. The first was my reflection—my blue eyes shimmering in the metal blade of the knife. The gift was in the form of light, this last piece of my old self being stripped away. I was no longer the girl staring back. And when it happened, I can't explain, but there was this final sense of dread, and then it all melted away into nothingness.

"I remember screaming and laughing, surrounded by this overwhelming bliss…But just when I thought I was free, my shadows made one last stand, and that moment of peace vanished as quickly as it came. The monster was fighting for his life. He was angry because he was exposed. So I made one cut down my arm with the knife. I had cut deep, and I knew it.

"But then came the second gift. As blood dripped down my arm, the darkness stopped in its tracks. Somehow the pain had restored my connection, like the veil had been lifted in its entirety, transmuting every ounce of fear to pure joy, all the fog and darkness in my mind, poof, gone."

I put my hand on Kelly's cheek. She leaned in.

"Don't you see? The blood was a reminder. Everything good flowed through my veins, like rays of light reconnecting to its source. I fell to my knees, completely naked, with blood smeared all over, and I laughed. The demons were gone. The monster had been slain. I was free, Kaleb. My soul had been cleansed. I had been reborn.

My hands went back to rubbing the scar. "What happened next?"

"It's all so fuzzy, but I remember lying on the floor in peace, blood flowing across the tile. I remember feeling tired and weak and my vision fading. But right before I closed my eyes, a great burst of white light jolted me awake, and then God's final gift emerged—an angel was with me that night, Kaleb. She held my hand and told me it was all going to be okay. I woke up to sun shining through the hospital window.

"It was a miracle. Two days later, I came back home with bandages on my arm and my chopped hair tied in a ponytail. I was myself for the first time in my life. I was ready to return the three gifts that were bestowed upon me. I wanted to give back to my fans. I wanted to lead them. I remember smiling a lot that day."

"But how. . ."

"An angel, Kaleb." She smiled, and her eyes met mine.

We were quiet after that.

Before she drifted off to sleep, she asked, "Will you put that story in our book?"

I kissed her forehead. "Of course."

A sea of shrieking fans devoured Madison Square Garden. Their screams vibrated through concrete walls. The stadium shook.

The war cries of her devoted.

They chanted.

"KTROOPS."

"KTROOPS."

"KTROOPS."

Bright lights illuminated an empty stage as Kelly's voice reverberated through the speakers.

"You shall never dim our light.
You shall never hide our strength.
You shall never steal our worth.
You shall never drown our voice.
But if you do. . ."

The arena chanted back: "Then we're coming for you!"

"Coming for you."

"Coming for you."

"Coming for you."

Darkness.

Screams.

A spotlight of the K and T logo zipped across the stage. Kelly was still nowhere to be seen. The projector behind the stage came alive with animation: a disfigured man. He had very little skin. Patches of tendons and muscle covered his skull.

A crown of gold sat atop his head. The dark and twisted voice of the floating head pulsed across the stadium:

"CHAIN ME TO A ROCK
BABY, THROW AWAY THE KEY
THE MONSTER'S ON THE LOOSE
AND HE'S COMING FOR ME
HE'S COMING FOR ME
HE'S COMING FOR ME
THE MONSTER'S ON THE LOOSE
AND HE'S COMING FOR ME"

The beat dropped.

A circular door on the stage opened, and Kelly rose up, chained to an artificial rock. Pandemonium. She was dressed like a princess turned hostage, wearing a linen toga, ripped and burned, a gold belt fastened around her waist and glittery gold sandals strapped to her feet. Her hair was tousled and wavy. Backup dancers dressed in green scaly costumes funneled across the stage. The swarm of sea monsters danced in unison, slithering toward Kelly. They fell to their hands and knees, crawling toward the rock, clawing up her body, hissing.

At center stage, Kelly fought the restraints. The screen behind her displayed a battle scene. Perseus flew across the horizon. A pixelated monster rose up from the sea, blowing fire across the screen. Real flames erupted from the stage, illuminating the faces of her enamored fans.

Then, darkness.

"He's coming for me," Kelly whispered. "He's coming for me."

The spotlight shone on her. The stadium hailed. She sauntered away from the rock, chains still encircling her wrists. Cell phones hit the sky.

"You can stab me in the back
   You can push me back to sin
   Use me till there's nothing left
   Serve me to the sea again."

The choreographed monsters danced behind her. The evil king's face returned to the screen. He had reclaimed his former glory. He had a thick beard covering his fat cheeks and dark beady eyes that followed Kelly as she sang.

"You can never let me go
   You can never break my chains
   Bring me joy, bring me pain
   Bring me hope and private planes."

The king faded.

The sea monster's fiery eyes appeared on the projector. Screams ripped through the crowd. Kelly fell to her knees in the glow of the monster's eyes.

"So burn me to the ground
   Baby, torch me with your lies
   'Cuz I'm rising from the ashes
   And I'm coming for the prize."

The emotions poured out of her. She screamed:

"'Cuz I do it all for you
   I will face the night for you."

She pointed to the crowd and they chanted back:

"I will give my life for you.
   I will break my chains for you."

Kelly sang:

"I will fight the beast for you
I will shine my light for you."

Kelly got up from her knees, the yellow eyes of the monster still fixed on her. Audio of sinister laughter rolled across the stadium. Then the animation faded to darkness. As the beat played on, a life-size animatronic monster rolled out onto the stage. A dragon-like beast with green scales. Glowing eyes. Horns atop its head. The monster craned its neck toward the crowd and then turned to face Kelly.

"Chain me to the rock, baby
Throw away my key
The monster's on the loose
And I will slay that fucking beast."

She snapped the chains off the rock and flames devoured the entire stage, whipping wildly across the beast. The fire reflected off her pupils. She looked out at the crowd and belted out the words like a battle cry:
"Don't you know that I'm coming for you?"
The beat faded into the night. The projector went black. The spotlight fell on Kelly in the middle of the stage. Her chest was rising up and down in exertion. Tears ran down her cheeks. She closed her eyes.

I looked across the stage. Lizzy Anne Michaels was staring at me, unblinking. Cold and callous. She was wearing a crew neck sweatshirt bearing the KT logo. There was something else in her expression. Sadness, pain. I wasn't sure. My gaze gravitated back to Kelly. She opened her eyes, turned to me. She mouthed two words that gave me chills.
Save me.

Lizzy: Kelly left me a voicemail on the night she died. I thought it was a pocket dial at first. She was sobbing, trying to catch her breath. She kept whispering scattered phrases over and over. *He is coming. I need you to be strong. Atonement is near.* Bizarre stuff like that. I didn't know what to make of it. But then she said one last thing before she hung up. She used the voice of the princess when she said it. Her words are so clear in my mind. *I need to hear your voice...*I'm sorry, can you give me a second?

Jez: She tried to send me away on the night she died. It would have been my first day off in a year. Obviously, I would never leave Kelly's side. I made sure to stick around and watch.

Lizzy: That was our code, detective. *I need to hear your voice.* We both had busy schedules, so if either of us said that, we made time. I should have gone to her. Not a day goes by that I don't think about that. She must have understood what was about to happen. I was just...I was mad, okay? She had made her choice. She chose him. By the time I called her back...I'm sorry, I told myself I wouldn't cry.

Jez: Yes. I recognize that book. It's Kelly's copy. I'm not surprised it was found in a pool of blood. Whoever left it was leaving a trail for you. You must know the truth by now, detective. Kelly and Kaleb rewrote the ending. In fact, they made it better. They made it magical. One day, it will go down as the greatest fairy tale ever written.

Lizzy: Get that book out of my goddamned face. I will never forgive him. I will say his name. Kaleb Reed. He is a monster. Please, detective. Make him pay for what he did.

Jez: I think it's time for Lizzy Michaels to tell the truth. It's time for her atonement.

The Real Kelly Trozzo
TheInsideJuice.com Interview 2019

INSIDEJUICE: So, after everything you've been through, what motivated you to climb out of that hole?

TROZZO: My art. My fans. I don't know exactly what it is, but something happens to me when I perform for them. I feel invincible, powerful, and I sing till the veins feel they will burst in my neck, because they are *my* words, and it is *my* story and *my* act and *my* life and *my* fans. No one else's. Not my mother's, not Barry's, not Zoe's, not the princess's—mine.

Before this is all over, the world will know the real Kelly Trozzo. They will never see me or my fans as weak, or naïve, or vulnerable. They will never use us, manipulate us, or control us again. With every move I make, I go deeper into this liberating image I created with my power of will. It's invigorating. And I am free.

I want you to know…I didn't return for my own glory. I returned to lead my fans. I came to give them power. I came to give them the headline they all deserve.

Two days after Kelly's death.

"I'd like you to take a look at these again," Detective Donaldson said, pointing to the pictures in front of me. He lit another cigarette, exhaled. His grin widened behind the cloud of smoke.

"The infamous Sara O'Conner," he paused. "Would you mind if I call her by the other name? I mean, I can't believe I'm looking at pictures of the real-life Alice. It's nice to put a face with the story."

I glanced down at the picture. Gray shirt, hair up, a trifling smile in the corner of her mouth.

"Why did you lie to me, Kaleb? You knew I would find out. She's all over your phone records. You guys even lived together for a short period of time, didn't you?"

I nodded, sliding the pictures back.

"Wow. AJ almost got his happy ending."

I couldn't help but smirk.

"See? Telling the truth isn't so hard." Detective Donaldson scanned me up and down, considering my reaction.

"Are you ready to tell me the truth?"

"About what?"

"About what…" He snickered. "About everything."

ACT II

I leave the motel for the last time today. The diner is right next door. A final pit stop before the home stretch. I take my seat in a cozy booth and set my laptop over the leftover crumbs on the table. There is something very nostalgic about this diner.

I order toast with a side of avocado. The waitress brought coffee, but she hasn't come back to refill. I don't blame her. I can't imagine how I look. Swollen eyes. Sunken cheeks. An overall faintness. A three-day drug binge will do that.

I want to thank you all for reading, for being patient. For taking the time to comment and tweet. Listening to my ramblings. Dare I say indulging the pleasures of a wanted man? At your request, I will continue onward.

Our finale is near.

I have paced my recreational intake. I need to concentrate if I'm going to get it right. It won't be easy, but I promise it will be worth it. Who doesn't love the classics? The myths of old. The princess locked in the tower. The damsel in distress. Evil lurking in the shadows. Happily ever after? Depends on whom you ask. Still, I think you'll enjoy it.

There are things you don't know.

Things we must discover together.

To our admirable Detective Donaldson: It's the wee hours of the morning, but I suspect you are still at your desk, overrun with cups of cold coffee and an ashtray filled with cigarette butts. I'm sure you're going over the files, wondering what you've missed. I've seen you on television, standing in the background as the police chief reports your mishaps. You look dreadful. The stress is wearing you down. New expressions are appearing on your brow. Unease. Disappointment.

This is a complicated case. I don't envy you. You didn't realize how much backstory you'd need. How much conflicting testimony you'd receive. Things aren't so black and white, are they? I do owe you an apology. There are a few lapses, a few minor fabrications. Omissions. Time gaps. Things I withheld before requesting my lawyer. As you and I both know, I'm an unreliable narrator. Nothing I say will hold up in a court of law.

I have nothing left to hide. You will all bear witness to the finale. I don't think Kelly imagined this ending. But she entrusted me to write her story. I'll take some liberties. This is my story, too. For better or worse. Without further ado. No more lies. No more speculating.

Welcome to our final act.

LIZZY MICHAELS SPOTTED AT POLICE STATION!

JULY 24, 2019

It seems like the Los Angeles Police aren't done with teen star Lizzy Michaels quite yet! Yesterday, the 19-year-old was spotted walking into the Los Angeles Police station wearing a black hoodie and dark sunglasses. Kelly Trozzo's fan club, @KTroopsOffical, broke the news, posting the photo on Instagram with the caption, *"It looks like @LizzyAnneMichaels has been under a lot of stress lately. Maybe she's feeling guilty about something."*

The person responsible for the @KTroopsOfficial handle did not respond directly to questions regarding the post, though they did comment that justice was coming for everyone involved with Kelly's death.

THE REAL ALICE
NEW MEXICO, 2015

SILVER CREEK, NEW MEXICO was a ten-hour drive, seven hundred miles of barren desert. It was an impulsive mission on my way home from work. I was thinking about Sara. It had been three months since the Christmas party. Three months since she went missing. Each day, I was reminded of my failure. I was using again. Anything I could get my hands on. It was the only thing I had to look forward to. I was pushing myself to the brink.

A change of scenery was needed.

I missed the first exit. Then the next one. There was no reason to turn back. A life in shambles. A job I despised. There was something therapeutic about the open highway. The starry night sky in front of me. The warm air felt good. I didn't have a specific address, just a town, courtesy of Caroline in HR.

Maybe my mission wasn't so impulsive after all.

I awoke to the hot sun pouring through my car window. Silver Creek was a sleepy town—almost cliché, with its wild tumbleweeds and old brick buildings. Faded signs swung on rusty chains.

I sipped coffee and gazed drowsily out the car window. The momentum from the drive had all but deflated. The thrill was gone. The only clothes I had were the ones on my back. Baggy slacks, a stained button down. What did I expect? I'd bump into Sara running errands in town. She'd be grateful that I'd followed her. What if Caroline in HR was lying to me? She knew how I felt about Sara and that I'd beaten her husband. Why would she give me the real address?

One more hour. Two hours went by. I needed a sign. Anything. This was a fool's mission. My hands were shaking. Empty prescription bottles filled the glove box. The withdrawals were coming, ready to consume. I'll call my boss, I thought. Make up a story. I'll head home. I put the key in the ignition.

And then suddenly, there he was.

Sara's husband stuck out like a sore thumb—two hundred pounds of flab and flannel bolting across the street. My sign. My precious sign. Yes. God agreed with my bold actions. I was doing the right thing. I grabbed a hat from the trunk and followed him into O'Keefe's bookstore.

A quaint bell chimed as I entered.

A bookstore wasn't where I expected to find him. But there he was, among the racks of used books, thumbing through a novel he had no interest in buying. I weaved in and out of the bookshelves, watching, waiting. It was risky. It was a small store. He seemed distracted. I stared at his chubby face, his sparse beard and stained shirt. I despised him.

He flagged down a female employee working behind the counter. She was pretty, but life, maybe this town, something had worn her down. Her hair was in a ratty ponytail. Her nails were chipped. Her brow was tense. Her expression was somber. Sara's husband and the woman exchanged pleasantries, but there were things unspoken. She fixed her hair, fidgeted. She looked uneasy. She stared at the ring on his hand. The same hands he hit Sara with.

He reached for her elbow and then leaned in, whispering something. A strained smile moved across her face. He had struck a chord. A good memory submerged beneath a pile of shitty ones. High school sweetheart? Silver Creek must have been his hometown.

The woman grabbed her notepad and jotted down her number. Infidelity? Add it to the list. I knocked a book off the rack. They both glanced back. I ducked, pulling down the brim of my hat. I exited the bookstore before he saw me.

I was in the front seat of my car waiting for him. All I could think about was his hands. His callused fingers. Knuckles. I pictured him pushing Sara. Hitting Sara. The same way my father hit my mother. Those fucking hands. I wanted him to suffer for what he did. I wanted to get high. I didn't want to face my anger. I would need a fix soon.

A decision needed to be made. I'd come all this way. If Sara wanted me gone, she needed to tell me. At least I could apologize. I should have been better for her. Stronger. I should have seen what was happening.

I should have protected her.

Sara's husband was smiling as he got into his truck. He must have proven his high school buddies wrong. He got the number. After everything he must have put that girl through. I pulled out onto Main Street, following him through the town, onto the highway.

I didn't have a plan. I needed a plan. There was a fork in the road. Follow him or hit the highway home. A chill ran down my spine. I knew the right decision.

Leave.

Get out of here.

Go as far away from this place as possible.

Nothing good will come of this.

Turn right at the fork.

Do it.

Just do it.

Count to three and do it.

"Stop."

I swallowed hard. It was him. I didn't have to look. I could feel his cold breath next to me in the front seat. I hated when he was that close. He had more control. He had this way of making my breath shallow. Making my heart pound and rattle. I was scared of him. He knew it. I always cowered. My voice always stammered. "What are you doing here?"

"Just thought you needed a visit," Bob said. "I haven't seen you since you let your brother's killer go."

"I…"

"Tell me you're not thinking about going home?"

I didn't answer.

Bob chuckled. "You finally have the chance to make amends."

"But…"

"Don't be a coward, Kaleb. Follow that asshole."

He reached for my shoulder. "Aren't you tired of being a coward?"

THE REAL KELLY TROZZO
TheInsideJuice.com Interview 2019

INSIDEJUICE: Rumor is, the network offered you your old job back when you returned to the public eye.

TROZZO: They did. As long as I was clean and ready to work.

INSIDEJUICE: Why didn't you take it?

TROZZO: That role belonged to Lizzy. I wouldn't steal it from her.

INSIDEJUICE: Speaking of Lizzy Michaels, your fans have been very critical of her.

TROZZO: My fans have always been protective of me. They thought Lizzy was trying to dethrone me. But they don't know her like I do. I can't blame her for doing the spin-off. She had an opportunity and she took it. I didn't get along with many of the cast members, they were small minded and gossipy, but Lizzy—she was my first *real* friend. She brought light to my life when there was so much darkness. Even if we were just watching movies in my trailer. She'll never know how much those little moments meant to me.

She might not know this, but she kept me alive during my darkest days. Alone in my room, I would stare at this old post-card of the real *Castle Heart*. I fantasized about this trip that Lizzy and I planned on taking to France, skipping down cobbled streets with gelato in hand, laughing, dancing, just being kids again. That hope pulled me out of the darkness. I'll never stop loving that girl. I'm terrified that Hollywood will take her innocence. She still has a chance because she's still pure, still guiltless. I just hope it's not too late.

Jez: I never understood Kelly's infatuation with her. What could she possibly get out of that one-sided relationship? Lizzy was vindictive. Do you want to know what she said in New York? She told Kelly that she should just retire and do us all a favor. That the world was better off when she was alone in her tower. The nerve of her! It makes me so mad. She was supposed to be her best friend. But Kelly knew the truth in the end. That's all that matters.

The lights went on in Madison Square Garden. Abandoned signs, wrappers and confetti filled the aisles. Kelly's team paraded past security and stadium staff, through the cement tunnels beneath the historic arena. She was wearing the ripped linen toga with a boxing-type robe over the top. Her sweaty, matted hair was covered by a large red hood. As we entered her dressing room, her friends raised their red cups and hollered in celebration. Kelly gave a half smile, scanning the crowd. Jez approached, whispered in her ear. Kelly nodded, then disappeared into another room.

"Everyone get the fuck out," yelled Jez. "Party is back at the hotel." She motioned everyone to the door, then grabbed my arm. "Not you."

I took a seat on the couch as the room emptied. Stale blunts and half-filled liquor bottles littered the table in front of me. Something had happened to darken Kelly's mood. Playtime was over. I grabbed a half-filled whiskey bottle. Down the hatch. Twenty minutes later, Kelly returned wearing a loose-fitting T-shirt, baggy sweatpants, her wet hair tied back. She was distraught, tapping wildly on her phone.

Finally, she sat down across from me. Legs crossed. Her eyes were somber.

I broke the silence. "Great show."

She pulled out a mirror and emptied a bag of cocaine on top.

"Where's Lizzy?" I asked.

"She left," Kelly murmured, chopping the fine powder into neat lines.

"Everything okay?"

"Can we stop playing these little games, Kaleb? I'd like to ask you a serious question."

She snorted, wiped her nose. Offered me the straw.

I refrained.

I was craving something else.

The anticipation of a bigger purpose.

Our eyes met. "I need you to tell me the truth about something," she said.

I nodded.

"What happened to Sara's husband?"

I took a deep breath.

Anything but that.

"It's not that simple."

"Isn't it?" She chopped up another line. "I've sacrificed a lot for you to be here, Kaleb. The least you can do is level with me."

I didn't say a word.

She snorted the next line.

She smiled. "Fine. How about we look at the pictures of Alice again? Your precious Sara." She handed me the phone.

I took the bait.

"I never asked how you found her." I scrolled through the pictures, staring at the strange man putting his arms around her. Pictures of him kissing her cheek. Sara looked happy. "How did you know where she was...who she was?"

"I have my ways." Kelly wiped her nose and reached for her phone.

I didn't give it to her.

She was taken aback.

"You know, when your fans read my book, they all want to know what happens after. What happens to AJ? What happens to Alice? But you never asked. All you want to know is about Alice's husband. Why is that?"

Kelly smiled. "Because I know the other stuff."

"I don't think you do," I said harshly. "Whatever relationship I had with Alice died on those pages. There was no ending, Kelly. It was fiction. Alice and AJ were personas, characters. *My* characters. Based on real people. But characters, Kelly. The same will happen if I write our story. I'll let you go when it's over," I said. "Because you are a fucking character."

Her brow furrowed.

"But I will tell you one thing," I continued.

I had her full attention.

"I made a pact with God before I wrote a single page of that book. I was walking in the forest. It had rained the night before, and I remember the smells of the trees and wet grass, the sounds of renewed life. Just perfect. And I was thinking about Sara. I was always thinking about Sara back then. But I hadn't written a damned thing. I was still terrified of facing the shit in my basement.

"But I looked up to heaven that day, and I felt—" I paused. "I felt something. Something like that moment you had on your kitchen floor—that open space you talked about. An open line to God. And I started talking, and I said, 'I will never look for her again. I promise you. I will never text her, call her, anything. Just let her be happy.' Those were the words I prayed.

"When I got back from my walk, I sat down with a notepad, closed my eyes and wrote the first six words that opened the floodgates—*AJ Daniels was a persistent man.*"

Kelly looked off into the distance. "What if that wasn't enough? What if she was still being mistreated or beaten or abused?"

I didn't say a word. I stared at the pictures on her phone.

"Would you drive by her house and check on her then?" she asked.

I avoided her gaze.

She took a deep breath, grabbing her phone back. "Fine. Keep your secrets. Either way," she said, preparing the next line on the mirror. "I made a pact too." She snorted. "But I'm not going to bother God with it. Now get the fuck out."

THE REAL KELLY TROZZO
TheInsideJuice.com Interview 2019

INSIDEJUICE: There's one thing I don't understand. Why did you return to Barry's management company after everything that he put you through?

TROZZO: It was liberating to return. I knew he would stare at the bandages on my wrist. I knew he would see my suicide attempt as a sign of weakness. In fact, I knew exactly what he was thinking. *How could some frail little girl be a threat to me? She's harmless.* But I played that to my advantage. Barry forgot how much he taught me over the years. He had no idea what happened to me in that house, and because of that, he welcomed me back with open arms. His prizefighter had returned to restore his empire. Nothing could have been further from the truth.

―――――

Lizzy: Trust me, nobody was happier than I was—my best friend was back. Except she wasn't the same person. It was all so strange. Take our first meeting, for example. Kelly told me to drive out to some crappy café in the middle of the desert, just because it reminded her of this great scene from a book she was reading. Had I only known. You should have heard her talk that day. *Spread light on evil. Build an army. Bring down the empire.* Blah, blah, blah. But what she didn't seem to realize was that I was part of that empire she wanted to destroy.

Jez: Kelly's fans saw right through Lizzy's fake blonde hair and whiny pitch. Of course, that didn't stop Lizzy from getting a big head. But Lizzy always knew in the back of her mind that Kelly could destroy her career with the push of a button. She needed Kelly's support. Deep down, that drove her crazy.

Lizzy: She wanted to destroy everything I had built.

Jez: Oh please, Lizzy didn't build anything!

Lizzy: I worked hard on my show. I did. They never gave me a chance.

THE REAL ALICE
NEW MEXICO, 2015

THREE DAYS SOBER. I steadied my trembling hands on the sink. I wiped vomit from my mouth. My face was swollen, my eyes bloodshot, my body weak. How could I let her see me like this? Sara agreed to meet me at a ratty diner near my motel. I was lucky to get that. It was wrong of me to show up outside her gym, but I was desperate. It was the only way to get her attention.

I spotted her through the window, running on the line of old treadmills. Sweat poured down her forehead as she pumped her fists. Just the sight of her was worth the ten-hour drive. I loved her high cheekbones, scattered freckles, dirty blonde hair. I loved everything about her.

Blood drained from her face when she spotted me. She ripped the headphones out of her ears, leaping off the treadmill. She burst through the front door, grabbing my arm and shoving me into a nearby alleyway. She pushed me against the brick wall, glancing around suspiciously.

"What the hell are you doing here?"

I didn't have an answer.

"Where are you staying?" She spoke through gritted teeth.

As soon as I told her, she whispered, "I'll meet you at the Hopper Café at six."

She put her headphones in and left.

The entrance bell rang, and ceramic plates stacked.

I spotted her in the booth with a beanie on, a cup of steaming coffee in her hands. She wasn't smiling. No eye contact. I made her uncomfortable. I couldn't blame her. I'd followed her seven hundred miles. I looked like shit. Three days in a motel room without drugs brought me to a scary place. Without the drugs, there was nothing to impede the darkness that seeped through the cracks in my soul.

The thoughts were coming on stronger. I couldn't stop picturing her husband hitting her. Then my father's cold and angry fists. The visions wouldn't stop. They kept circulating. Kept pushing. It wasn't my fault. Bob's reflection stared back at me in the motel mirror. His dark, sinister eyes. His power was strengthening within me. He placed his hand on my shoulder, and I didn't shove him away.

I was giving him more control.

"Do you remember the beach house?" Bob yelled at me through the mirror. "Do you remember your brother pleading with you to come play as you listened to your father's rage? But you just sat there, didn't you? You were only eleven, but you knew." He squeezed my shoulder and another wave of cold fear pulsed through me. I remembered my dad's silhouette through the window. His fist landed on my mother's shadow. She begged for mercy. My brother pulled on my arm, begging me to play. He was too young to understand, but he knew something was happening.

"You did nothing, Kaleb!" yelled Bob. "You should have done something. Your family needed you. Your brother looked up to you. You were their protector."

I crawled into the booth across from Sara, reminded of my purpose. I had come to save her. I was here to make things right. I was here to made amends for what I couldn't do before.

"Why are you here?" she whispered, crossly. "I can't believe you came to my fucking gym. What were you thinking? Have you lost your damn mind? How did you even find me?"

My eyes scanned her face, then her shoulders, then her arms. I stared at the tattoo on her forearm. A black sparrow facing left. Her husband had the other one, facing right. A reminder of their bond. She wouldn't leave without a fight. She caught me staring at the yellow and blue bruises that speckled her collar like freckles.

"Are you okay?" I asked.

She pulled up her shirt in annoyance. "Oh, don't be a fucking hero, Kaleb. You're the one who needs help. Look at you. You can't even hold the fork. You're literally shaking. You're a junkie. How are you going to help me?"

I dropped the fork, placed my hands over my face. My eyes swelled with emotion. She was right. I was a mess. This wasn't how I wanted her to see me.

"Listen, I'm sorry." She reached for my hand. "He and I needed a fresh start." She squeezed my fingers. "Whatever you thought this was, it's over. This isn't a game. Just let me go. And please, get help. You do know you need help?"

"I do. I just—I'm so sorry." Without the drugs, my body and mind were failing me, crumbling. I didn't want to be weak. Sara needed me to be strong. I was tired of being weak.

"I know you're sorry," she said. "But promise me you'll go back. You'll go get help."

I finally looked up to meet her gaze. "And you?"

"I'm tough, Kaleb. It's nothing I can't handle."

She watched me from the window of the diner. She wore a

brave smile as the waitress filled her coffee. Her gaze never left my car. She wanted to make sure I left. I took a deep breath, waved. I pulled out of the gravel parking lot and onto the interstate. At least I saw her. That had to be enough. For now. It had to. I needed to get clean. I needed help. If it was fate, our paths would cross again.

I had just reached for the radio when I felt his cold breath on my neck.

"You were so pathetic in there. Letting her see you cry. What the fuck is wrong with you?"

"She doesn't want me here."

"Are you really that stupid?" he yelled. "That was a cry for help."

"She said she was fine."

"Was your mom fine?" Bob screamed, and the fear trembled in my chest. "Protect her, you fucking coward. She needs you to be strong."

"No. No. I need...I need...I need to get clean."

"That's what you're doing."

"There must be another way."

"There's not."

"Please."

"Don't be pathetic."

"I'm not pathetic. I'm not."

"Who would ever love you? You can't protect anyone."

"Yes. I. can."

Bob's put his hand on my shoulders, and I saw my mom coming out on the porch with black-and-blue bruises. She put on a fearless smile as my brother played in the yard. Just like Sara did in that diner. But in the middle of the night, I heard my mother get out of bed. I followed. She went back to the porch. This time, there was no brave smile. I watched the tears stream down her cheeks. She was hurting. She was trapped.

I imagined Sara after the brave face wore off. The tears

would follow. She would look out onto the parking lot of the diner knowing her protector was gone. He gave up without a fight. Her fate was sealed. She would die in this sleepy old town.

Bob pulled his hand away. "Then fucking prove it."

The Real Kelly Trozzo
TheInsideJuice.com Interview 2019

INSIDEJUICE: I'll just ask the question. Did you come back to bring down Barry's empire?

TROZZO: His empire? No. It was *our* empire.

INSIDEJUICE: Explain.

TROZZO: I was the one who stood next to Barry at his fundraisers. We were Hollywood, and they were the investors with big pockets and empty lives. Money-hungry parents eager to exploit their children. His management business was the great illusion. Would precious Princess Jade really steal your money? I was tangible—something investors and parents had seen on television, the star on the big screen. Barry taught me how to sell the fantasy. "Take them on a ride, baby, strap them in, paint the picture, give them a taste, but never the whole thing." It was almost too easy, getting them to write checks and sign contracts.

INSIDEJUICE: So you're admitting that Barry's company is one big scam?

TROZZO: Yes. The investors, the parents, they all paid for the illusion. They paid for the production company, the vacation homes, his eccentric, perverted parties. It was all about appearance for Barry—the suits, the venue, the cars, and especially me. I was his best illusionist. The reason they all bought into Barry's Hollywood hit factory long after the hits stopped coming. I was the face of his elaborate scheme. He needed me. I helped him build his empire.

INSIDEJUICE: Why blow the whistle now?

TROZZO: I did things I'm not proud of—things I hate myself for. I used anything at my disposal to help lure and seduce the investors. Even my body.

INSIDEJUICE: How old were you?

TROZZO: Too young.

INSIDEJUICE: Kelly…I'm sorry.

TROZZO: I'm not telling you this for sympathy. I need my fans to understand. It wasn't Kelly Trozzo doing any of it. It was the weak little girl inside me that wanted to please a father whose heart was black as the night sky. I tell you all this because I need my fans to know the truth. They need to understand why the old me had to die. Why everything has to be destroyed. Why I returned to Barry Monroe. Because the best way to destroy an empire is from the inside.

Lizzy: I'm not stupid. I knew that Barry was a ruthless businessman. I knew what kind of person he was. Or at least I thought so. Sometimes, Kelly would make these little comments, implying I had no idea what she had been through. Maybe she was trying to protect me from the truth. Either way, she had no right to deliberately sabotage her best friend's career. Barry was *my* manager too. My fate was in his hands.

Jez: I never talked about Barry with Kelly. No way. She hated talking about him.

Lizzy: After Kelly left, I was the biggest name on Barry's roster. I should have been the new face. I should have been the one at the fancy dinners. But whenever I asked, he would tell me I wasn't ready. I knew what he was really thinking. He wished I was Kelly. That I had the same charisma and allure as she did. He never gave me a shot. I could never escape Kelly's shadow.

Alas, our story is coming to an end. So are the drugs. From the motel balcony, I watch the dark clouds rush in like an enemy attack. Thunder splits through the warm desert air. This will be my final night. I can feel it. I am ready. No more running. No more hiding. Lightning flares behind the clouds. There's a certain peace inside me. This is a fitting end. The storm will add to the theatrics. The scene is set.

I take inventory of what is left. Two bottles: one booze, one prescription. A bag of psychedelics. Both of the Ziplocs are close to finished. Less than a gram of cocaine and PCP. It should do the trick. What else? I have three pictures left. The rest have been burned.

I hold the picture of my brother one last time. Detective Donaldson gave it back to me, a good-cop-routine souvenir. It's crumpled and damaged. Creased from holding it during my darkest hours, my rock bottoms. I was holding it on the night of Kelly's death. The police pried it from my bloody hands.

I do love that picture.

My brother is holding a baseball bat on his shoulder, outside our old beach house. His hair is all messy, his shirt covered in sand and water. I like to think there was a piece of his soul inside of it. Watching his big brother. Wanting to be proud of me. Wanting to forgive me. I place my lighter to the corner of the picture. I watch the flames move up his body, around his smiling face, charring the laminated paper. It had to be done. He can't be here for this ending.

What else do I have left?

My first copy of *Pay Me, Alice*.

Two more photos.

One wrecked cell phone.

One silver sparrow necklace.

I twirl the jewelry in my fingers. Kelly's most treasured piece. It's not much to look at. It's lightweight, a sterling silver chain. The ruby jewels inside the sparrow's eyes are corroded, faded. I can still see her grasping that necklace. Now it's in my hands. My lady's favor.

Given to her loyal knight.

Our last few months together.

The parties never stopped after New York.

The mansion never emptied. Kelly slipped into darkness. There was no more cleansing. No more morning routines, meditation. No more writing. Just madness. She stopped talking to her fans. She stopped leading them, uplifting them. When she did post, they were pictures of herself. All provocative and shocking. Either naked covering her chest or lying down with her ass exposed. Those got the most attention. After she would post, she would obsess over her body. Over the number of likes and views. She would read every comment. If she spotted something negative, she required constant validation. *You are so beautiful. You are the hottest thing out there right now.*

I didn't say anything.

She never wanted her entourage to leave. Night after night

of drugs and chaos. She became distant, aloof. There were nights I barely saw her at all. Brief moments amongst the strobe lights. I watched blood drip from her nose. Fog rolled across through her enlarged pupils. The bass of the music swayed her dazed body. I could feel her demons soaking through her heart, running out the pores of her skin.

I stayed in the castle, watching, waiting. Using just enough to stay lucid. I slept in the guest bedroom by myself. Kelly never slept. At least not with me. Sometimes, she would sneak into my room early in the morning, still high from the night before. She would pin me down, bite my lip. Her blue eyes gone. Lost in the madness. It wasn't her.

Most nights, I withdrew to her favorite room, the study. I laid on the couch staring at the painting. I pitied the chained beauty. Despised the monster. Envied the hero in the sky with his determined eyes and sharp bronze spear in hand.

Why did she choose me?

I looked down at my own hands, gripping a bottle of booze. This wasn't a hero's weapon. I poured the remains out onto the carpet. Jez came into the room, disheveled and sweaty. She could barely stand. Her pupils the size of quarters.

"Your presence is requested," she slurred. "Kelly awaits you in her tower."

Wind rolled through the window, rustling the curtains. The room was dark and cold. You could feel the shadows lingering in the air. Kelly's phone was on the bed, unlocked. Bait taken. I clicked on a red notification in the upper right-hand side. A conversation with @LizzyAnnMichaels.

@KellyTrozzo: Please call me.

@KellyTrozzo: I need to explain.

@LizzyAnnMichaels: There's nothing to explain.

I clicked on Lizzy's profile. Singer. Songwriter. Actress. I scrolled through her feed. Most of her photos were pictures of herself or posting with other famous people. She was pretty, but the photos were all alike. Perfect makeup, fancy clothes, selfies in the mirror. All her fan comments were identical. *Gorgeous. Beautiful. Stunning.* She had a fraction of the followers that Kelly had. I clicked on a picture she posted with Barry Monroe at her movie premiere. *Happy birthday to this legend. Thank you for giving me my start.*

I clicked back to Kelly's inbox. Another conversation with a user named @NoahTash.

@NoahTash: We need to talk.

@NoahTash: Now.

I clicked on Noah's profile. Music producer. Promoter. Los Angeles. He had a leather jacket. Shaved head. Tattoos on his neck. I scrolled through the thumbnail images. Some of Kelly's friends were in his pictures. The same kids that partied at her mansion. But he wasn't a regular. I tapped a close-up of him. I had seen him before. That scar…

"What the fuck are you doing?" Kelly stood in her bathroom doorway, swaying. She was naked, only the sparrow necklace dangling from her neck.

I dropped the phone.

"I'm glad you're here." She stumbled toward me, her eyes wavering. "Get your book." She grabbed my hand, leading me toward the bed. I fetched a worn copy of *Pay Me, Alice* from her nightstand. She took it and flipped through the pages, pacing the room.

"Here it is," Kelly beamed. She pointed to a page, squealing with excitement, "It's just, this is so good…right here." She took a deep breath. Blood pooled in the corners of her nose.

"AJ stares at his phone resting on the coffee table," she read. "He hears the vibrations of the incoming messages, but he can't look. He can't do it anymore." Kelly pumped her fist like she was acting out a movie script. "He just can't!" She screamed. "His bags are packed, and there is nothing left in this abandoned home but pain. Goodbye, St. Charles, Missouri. Goodbye forever."

She sat on the bed, cross-legged, concentrating on the page.

"He has a job interview lined up in New York. It could be a fresh start. He could leave this shithole of a town. His days have been squandered—no job, and no purpose, other than waiting for her to call or text." She flipped to the next page. "No more. Because no matter what he said or did, no matter how long the affair lasted, she always returned to her husband. AJ is helpless, and that's what hurts the most. It isn't his problem anymore. Alice made her choice. Now he must make his." Kelly paused, her face scrunched in pain. Another trickle of blood flowed from her nostril. She dabbed her finger to the trail.

"Kelly..." I interjected. "Please..."

"Wait, here's the best part." She pointed to the page. "Another text message comes through. He looks. Old habits die hard. Let's just see what she wants, he thinks to himself. Of course, he already knows."

"Kelly..."

She held up her hand in protest. "Alice wants him, needs him, and his stomach moves and shifts with each text. Because he can picture her face, bruised, bloodied by that coward." Kelly's lip curled. She sucks in air, struggling to get through the words.

"But if he stays," she whimpers. "These moments would never end. She made her choice. She made her fucking choice," she yelled. "She chose his fist. His rage. There is nothing left here. He must start over. Stop living off hope. Stop avoiding reality. But reality is her tears, her bruises—she needs him, and it breaks his fucking heart. He must be stronger. Why can he not be stronger? He is trapped. Whether it is love, or infatuation, or just insanity at this point, he doesn't know. But when she needs him, he is helpless to her pleas. Helpless to her pain. Helpless altogether."

Kelly smiled at me like she was gazing at the real hero.

I wasn't who she thought I was.

She slammed the book shut. "This is…this is just so brilliant, Kaleb. It's brilliant. How you capture that magnetic pull, that insane, impossible, emotional fucking attraction that forces you to come back…*Ugghh*." She let the book fall and then kissed me on the mouth. "It's so fucking good."

She fell back on the pillow and turned to me, her bright blue eyes flashing. Her true self beneath the madness. A tear trickled down her cheek. "You know, I…" She stopped midsentence, biting the inside of her lip. She stared at me like she was staring at someone important, someone she admired. She was beaming with pride.

She was going to reveal something. I put my hand on hers. I touched her scar. What do you want from me? Why did you find me? She closed her eyes at my touch, letting the tears run. I didn't flinch. Her tears didn't scare me. I was stronger with her. She believed in me. She opened her eyes. Her blue pupils were gone. Overrun by swirling darkness.

"*Ughhh*. So fucking good." She fell flat on the bed, her body shutting down. "So good," she mumbled, closing her eyes, my book nestled into her chest.

The Real Kelly Trozzo
TheInsideJuice.com Interview 2019

INSIDEJUICE: Did anyone know about your plan to topple the empire you helped build?

TROZZO: My ex did, Noah Tash.

INSIDEJUICE: When did he come back into the picture?

TROZZO: We reconnected this past year. Noah was working as a server at an investment dinner, a week after I returned. I hardly recognized him. The pretty boy look was long gone, replaced with a shaved head and fifteen pounds of new muscle. Even more noticeable was a scar beneath his eye. He looked like hell. Truthfully, I thought Barry had hired him as a welcome back present. Like, look where your ex is now—serving us shrimp cocktails. I was wrong.

Noah lost everything after he got fired from the show, everything. Even his confidence and good looks. Toward the end of the night, I summoned him to the balcony, and he confessed that he came to the party to find me. He wanted to apologize and tell me that the feelings were real, despite everything that happened. Two years ago, I might have eaten that shit up.

But all I saw was anger in his fierce, hazelnut eyes. He hated Barry for what he took from him. He told me he would do anything to make it up to me. I had to smile. Anything?

Lizzy: I was overjoyed they reconnected. It gave me hope. Maybe someone could talk some sense into her—pull her back to the real world.

Jez: I've known Noah for a long time. He was my brother's drug dealer. I think he used to have a thing for me. He used to come in my room and stare at all my posters of Kelly, bragging that he used to work with her. It was annoying, really. I never forgot what the tabloids said about him. He broke Kelly's heart. But then one day he waltzes into my room and says he was going to a party at Kelly's mansion and asks me if I want to come. Noah was the one who handed me the invitation to my fairy tale.

Lizzy: Kelly claimed that Noah was a different person now—a determined person. That he had fallen from grace and had been redeemed, purified. How did she put it? Atoned. She believed he could develop into "a worthy soldier." Classic Kelly talk. But it might have been the one thing we agreed upon. Noah had changed. He wanted to do right by her.

Jez: Trust me, Noah is no solider. I tried to warn Kelly. Noah looks out for Noah.

Lizzy: Did you know how Noah got that scar under his eye? A group of college kids were gossiping about Kelly at a club. One of the guys called her a slut and Noah lost his temper. He ended up taking a bottle across the head and getting thirty-six stitches. He would do anything for her.

Jez: Are you kidding? Noah got that scar at my brother's house. He got high and fell through a glass table.

THE REAL ALICE
NEW MEXICO, 2015

TEN DAYS SOBER. The poison had left my body. I woke up stronger, more lucid. Sara's husband's routine was consistent. In his scratched up pickup truck by 7:00, at Buster's Donuts & Bagels by 7:15. Coffee and a bear claw, back on the road by 7:30. On the construction site before 8:00. He wore the same thing every day, blue jeans and a hooded Carhartt sweatshirt. A greasy baseball cap. A giant wad of tobacco stuffed in his left cheek. He packed up at 4:00 every day, shooting down the gravel road.

He always made the same stop on his way home. The woman from the bookstore. She lived in a rundown one-story house with knee-high weeds that swayed over the cement walkway. Sometimes, she would come out and watch him leave, hovering at the door in tiny blue shorts and an oversized V-neck. She held a cigarette to her mouth, taking long drags as she watched him pull out of the driveway. I never saw bruises. This was a different kind of abuse.

He always returned to the construction site before going home to Sara. That was the part I didn't understand. He wasn't there to work. His entire team had already packed up.

Instead, he walked to the edge of the cliff and gazed out across the valley. I wondered what he thought about. Perhaps he imagined the view from the dining room of the future house being built there. Maybe he had dreams and hopes. Maybe he had regrets. Maybe he didn't like the horrible man he had become. I didn't care. Those were the thoughts of a weak man. Sara needed me to be strong. He smoked one cigarette and watched the sun fade from the New Mexico sky. Then he returned home to the woman I loved.

Each day, I ended the night in front of their house. I parked the car, turned the headlights off. Binoculars in hand. Detox was painful. But she gave me the strength to fight. I wasn't using at all. Not a single beer to ease the withdrawals. She gave me purpose. That was my plan. Continue watching, waiting. Maintain the routine. Stay sober and wait till she needed me.

I lingered until midnight before turning the engine on again. I had just put the car in drive when I heard a scream from upstairs. Something crashed into the wall. I imagined the worst. Her beautiful body tossed against the plaster. Knocking down hanging photos. My ears perked up like a dog. My heart-beat had never thrashed so hard in my chest. There was shouting. If there was a chance to protect her, this was it.

No. No. No. I couldn't just barge in. It would make things worse. He would punish her. I looked over to the passenger seat. Where was Bob? I needed him.

Sara ran through the front door in a panic. I exhaled five minutes' worth of anxious breath. She got in her car and whizzed out of the driveway, tires screeching.

I followed at a safe distance. My heart wouldn't stop pounding.

I couldn't help but smile when she veered off to the diner next to my motel.

From the front seat of my car, I watched her through the

diner window. She ordered coffee, but she didn't touch it. The steam stopped rising. She was biting her lip, tapping her fingers against the porcelain. There was a reason she chose this place. There must be. It was time to cross over. To be her true strength. To be her everything. Why else did I come? Why else was I sober?

I walked into the diner a new man, a determined man. This time, I was sober and healthy. I was strong and brave. I was a protector. We locked eyes. I pretended to be surprised to see her. She did the same. Her nails stopped tapping.

A tiny smile moved across her mouth.

Rain has begun to fall. First light, then heavy. It's perfect. I open the blinds. Imagine the scene. It's almost exhilarating now. The sirens. The helicopters. The bloodsuckers outside with their vans and cameras. Yes, it will be our masterpiece. This is what you wanted, Kelly. It's what your fans deserve. It's what you deserve. I look over to the chair in the corner of the room. Bob isn't here yet. I suspect he'll come once he discovers my intentions. He'll want a front-row view.

But that's neither here nor there.

Rituals must be performed. I pull out the photo of Nathan and me at my first book signing. He isn't smiling. It looks like I held him at gunpoint to be there. But he was proud in his own way. He witnessed a glimmer of my potential.

I hold the flame to the photo and watch it burn. The flames move up Nathan's body and then dim at his weathered face. The flames are scared to touch him. I don't blame them. He's terrifying. I blow and blow until the fire overtakes him, consuming the photo.

My fate is sealed.

What's next?

I thumb through my copy of *Pay Me, Alice*. Often, I dream about a life that could have been. I recall the day I pulled the advance copy out of the box. That was a good feeling, rubbing my fingers along the cover, feeling the skull and crossbones embossed on the smooth matte finish. I'm proud of this book. It was the first thing I ever finished. Trust me, I wanted to turn back. But every day, I faced that blank page. Every day, I heard Nathan's voice ringing in my head. *Face this. Face this shit.* I did. And I didn't stop till it was done. Till I bled and poured it all out. Till there was nothing left inside me.

I want people to know that version of myself. I wrote AJ to be the type of person who stood and fought for what he believed in. Who fought for the people he loved. My best self. Strong. Steadfast. Sober. AJ didn't run when things got hard.

The last picture I have left is hidden on page 345. It's Kelly's favorite scene in the book. I call it AJ's true motive. In the picture, Kelly is wearing an oversized T-shirt, nothing else. Her long blonde hair matted and uncombed. Her eyes are puffy and red. She looks so beautiful. At her worst. At her best. Our backs are pressed against the bathroom wall. It wasn't an appropriate time for a picture. Then again, it was Kelly. Document it all. Share the parts you want. I imagined this picture would be on the cover of our book. At the very least, it would go in the middle section, the glossy pages that readers flip to first. It would be captioned *The Night We Fell in Love*.

She went missing the night we took this picture.

That morning, Jez was frantic, pacing the mansion— leaving voicemails on Lizzy's phone. Kelly had a show that night and they needed her at rehearsals. I stayed in her bedroom, staring at my book, flipping through the pages. I was thinking about AJ. What made him special? He was a persistent man. I was thinking about the scenes that Kelly loved so much. What did she see in those pages? What did she really want from me?

Jez ran up the stairs in tears, screaming, "Where is she, Kaleb? Do you know where she is?"

I shook my head.

But I did know.

She had ventured into the shadows. We were all accessories. We watched her tread along the edge of the black hole. Pushing and pushing until she lost her footing and plummeted into darkness. If she survived the fall, she would return. When she was ready. Then she would need someone to help her climb out.

As usual, Kelly's show was sold out. Twenty thousand-plus fans would fill the Staples Center in Los Angeles. The final stop of her Reborn Tour. The arena would host all of Hollywood's elite. Celebrities. Actors. Influencers.

She missed sound check that afternoon. Her phone remained off as the hours ticked away and the sun descended on Tinsel Town. The stadium lights beamed. Fans began to funnel in with their signs and their costumes.

Backstage, I couldn't take my eyes off of Barry Monroe. I wanted him to say something to me. I wanted him to address my presence. But he never gave me the satisfaction. He was wearing a black suit, white shirt, no tie. A gold chain glued to his thick, hairy chest. I stared at his fat fists. I wondered if those hands ever hit Kelly…Maybe he didn't need to. Psychological warfare was just as powerful. I watched promoters and assistants tiptoe around him. None of them would meet his gaze. They were terrified. I never understood Kelly's loyalty to him. It was one secret she had left to play. Only a matter of time.

The screams of the sold-out arena hummed backstage. The openers went on. Thirty minutes until showtime. Ten minutes. Kelly's backup dancers paced in their tiny, colorful outfits. Her entourage drank and smoked in silence. The roars got louder and louder in anticipation of their leader's presence.

"KTROOPS."

"KTROOPS."

"KTROOPS."

First, there were murmurs, then whispers. A slow applause followed. Kelly was being escorted backstage by two security guards. My body recoiled at the sight of her. Her face was bright red, her hair a mangled nest. Sunglasses covered her eyes. She could barely stand. She had on pajama bottoms and Ugg boots with an oversized *Zoe Loves* sweatshirt. The team turned to Barry for instructions. He tapped on his phone, then looked up, nonchalantly. "What are we waiting for? Clean her the fuck up."

Stylists swarmed her dazed body, combing out her knotted hair, plastering makeup around her puffy, glassy eyes. They draped Kelly's boxing-style robe over her. They handed her an energy drink and a solo cup filled with the worst kind of poison. The elixir of life. Barry Monroe oversaw the assembly line, watching his product shined for the big stage. My blood boiled beneath the surface. He shut the door when he saw me staring.

And the stadium rumbled.

"KTROOPS."

"KTROOPS."

"KTROOPS."

I took my place to the right of the stage. Kelly was wrong about me. I wasn't her soldier. This was bigger than me.

A colorful spotlight beamed down, and Kelly's silhouette appeared in the center. She squinted in the bright lights, adjusting her earpiece. Screams erupted from the sea of fans. She was everything they expected. Cleaned and polished, with shiny hair and perfect skin. The chained beauty, ready to lead her fans into battle.

"Reborn" was the opening number. The beat detonated through the stadium and her silk boxing robe fell to the ground. She took one step forward, letting her glittery black crop top shimmer in the spotlight. The poison in her drink kicked in and somehow, she moved around the stage in unison with her dancers.

Somehow, she sang:

"This ain't no act
This ain't no game.
This is my show.
Say my name."

They chanted. "Kelly! Kelly!"

"Bitch, I'm reborn.
I'm reborn.
I have risen from the dead.
Say my name. Say my name.
My ego has been shed."

She swayed like a branch in the wind. Her voice wavered, off-key. My stomach lurched every time her footing slipped. She always recovered. Back in formation. Like a fighter in the ring, holding on for dear life. No one noticed. Her fans held their signs and chanted her name. They saw what they wanted to see.

Her entourage was no different. Promoters were glued to their phones. Her friends were bobbing their heads to the music. Jez was beaming with tears streaming down her cheeks. But there was one exception. Barry. Our eyes met, and a crooked smirk twisted across his bloated face. He nodded his head, gloating. He was enjoying this. He was evil. He was a bully like my father. A creator of pain. Rage throbbed into my clenched fists. Kelly didn't have to share her secrets with me. I knew he was responsible for the scar on her arm. For the wounds in her heart. He would suffer for what he did.

She made it to the second song, third song. She changed outfits. She made it to "My Life Without You."

The blue spotlight fell on stage as the piano keys played. She started in her usual position, standing upright in her black slip. She closed her eyes in the blue beams, clutching her favorite silver chain. Her eyes remained closed as the first cue passed. The pianist replayed the notes. She missed the second cue. Finally, she sang:

"Baby, when you say help me,
you mean break me.
When you say love me,
you mean numb…"

She stopped, mid-lyric, face scrunched in distress. "My life with you," she stammered through her tears before kneeling on the ground. The piano kept playing, but she stopped singing.

"I'm sorry," she whispered. "I'm sorry." Kelly's body collapsed. She turned to the side of the stage, scanning with urgency. She was looking for me. She needed me. Yes. My heartbeat thrashed wildly. She needed me to transform. To become the man she believed in.

I was about to run onstage when a hand grabbed my arm. Barry's fat fingers tightened around my wrist.

"Don't fucking do it," he commanded.

The rage seared beneath the surface, seeping into my bloodstream.

The music kept playing.

"Don't fuck with my business," he growled.

Power radiated through my body. The familiar red flashes came.

"Or else."

The rage exploded.

I grabbed him by his fat neck and I shoved him against the wall. I squeezed the soft flesh as hard as I could until his sweaty bald head swelled with blood. Until his yellow framed glasses fell from his face. Veins burst from his forehead. I wanted him to feel the pain that Kelly felt. "Fuck you," I spit. I wanted to keep squeezing until he had no more air in his pathetic lungs.

I felt Jez's hand on my back. "Kaleb, stop."

I let go.

Barry fell to the ground, choking, smirking. "You have no idea what you just did," he exhaled, shaking his head, chuckling.

I turned back to the stage. *Kelly.* She was still on the ground, fighting her way back up. Still trying to perform. I rushed towards her, shielding my eyes from the blinding spotlight. The crowd whispered nervously as I knelt beside her, prying the microphone from her grip. Her face was drenched with sweat, her eyelids at half-mast. I could feel the stares, the cameras, the whispers. They wouldn't stop me this time. Kelly flinched at my touch, mumbling, "Go away. Go away."

The crowd booed and shouted in confusion as I picked her up in one quick swoop. She fought my restraints, trying to return. But I wouldn't falter. I carried her past the wall of shocked faces, through the cement tunnels. As we got further from the stage, Kelly softened in my arms. She stopped resisting. She put her arms around my neck, leaned into my body. I took her to her dressing room and laid her down on the couch. Her teeth chattered, her body trembled.

"I went to find her Kaleb," she cried. "I needed to find her."

"Who?" I put my hand to Kelly's face.

"My mom," she closed her eyes in pain. "I drove for hours looking for her. I couldn't find her."

A knock on the door.

Kelly opened her eyes in fright.

I stood up, clenching my knuckles. I was excited for the confrontation. I opened the door to find Barry standing in the doorway with his chest puffed out, grinning arrogantly. He stared me up and down, sizing up his opponent.

"She's not going back out," I stated.

"Is that right?" he snorted. "What's your name again... Kaleb Reed. The penniless author she found in the box of broken toys. The one she decided to pick up and play with. You have no idea what you've gotten yourself into."

"She's done for the night," I said through gritted teeth.

He grinned. "I know."

I was about to close the door when his hand jammed it back open. He was surprisingly strong. "Listen, you pissant," he frothed. "You have my permission to leave. But if you ever interfere again, I *will* destroy you both. Do you hear me? I will never let her leave."

Is that so?

"She will always return to me."

You're wrong.

"I can break her."

Not if I destroy you first.

I slammed the door.

I escorted Kelly out of the building, into flashing lights. I held her close as we made our way past the mobs of fans that were waiting outside the arena. They held out their hands. They screamed her name. She kept her face buried in my chest. She was no longer performing. She was letting me protect her.

She didn't want to go back to her castle, so I took her to my apartment.

She was silent as we climbed the stairs. She came out of the bathroom in my clothes, her head down. She closed her eyes when we kissed. Gentle, not assertive. I could feel her letting go, surrendering. Part of me wanted her to take control like she always did. Her face looked innocent, and her kiss felt real. Her moves weren't calculated. She buried her forehead into my chest. I felt tears. I wanted to take away every pain, every burden. Everything that hurt her. I wrapped my arms around her tiny frame and held her as tightly as I could.

I didn't want to lose her.

Her body moved slowly, waiting for me to lead. She wanted me on top. She closed her eyes when I was inside. With every thrust, she clenched tighter. She wanted this. She was giving me everything. Tears rolled down her cheeks. I put my forehead on hers. I felt her warm, salty tears on my cheeks. Her nails lingered on my neck. Her lips lingered on my mouth. Her eyes remained shut. Her moans were whispers, not theatrical. I glided my thumbs across her cheek.

Then it was over.

Stillness.

Pounding hearts.

She reached over to my nightstand and grabbed my book. She opened up to a page and nuzzled closer. "Read to me."

"Kelly—"

"Please."

I took a deep sigh, then read: "It is a thirty-minute drive to the dirt parking lot outside Old James Frosty. The night falls on the landmark restaurant that serves cold drinks and ice cream to overheated locals. Alice is sitting on a bench, her hands on her face, and only the sounds of crickets and passing trucks fill the night sky. She has been crying. Her cheek is bruised, her eyes are swollen. There is nothing worse for AJ. It tears and pulls at everything inside of him. The most beautiful girl in the world, bruised and beaten by a coward. How could she let him do this to her?"

I stopped.

"Keep going," Kelly pleaded.

"AJ and Alice don't speak. There is nothing left to say. AJ places his hand on hers, and she allows herself to cry even harder. They are both trapped. AJ is forced to watch the girl he loves cry with bruises on her face while he does nothing. She cries because she isn't strong enough to leave him. Both are stuck. Both are exhausted. AJ keeps his arms around her and just holds her, because that's all he can do now—hold her as tightly as possible and pray that he can strip the pain away— for the moment at least. He may not save her, but he can be there. She cries on his sleeve, lifts her head, puts her lips to his.

'I'm going to leave him,' she says through the tears.

AJ smiles as she burrows her head deeper into his shoulder. He knows it isn't true, but there is no point in arguing. No point in pushing her.

'I know you don't believe me,' she says, looking off into the abyss, 'but I'll prove you wrong this time. I promise I will.'

AJ holds her even tighter, and he knows right then. He will never be with Alice. And she will never be free. Unless her husband somehow went away."

I closed the book and turned over to face Kelly. She had rolled away, sobbing.

"Kelly? Are you okay?"

She ran into the bathroom. I gazed down at the book. I never fully understood. Not until the very end. I knocked on the bathroom door. It slowly opened. Kelly was leaning against the wall, tissues in hand. I dropped down next to her. We stared at the cheap eggshell-painted wall in my bathroom.

"Please don't quit on me, Kaleb," she sobbed.

"I won't."

"I need you now," she whispered.

Then I held her too long because she was the only person I had left.

"I need you, too," I said.

She smiled through the tears.

"I love you," I said. Whether I was talking to Sara, my brother, or Kelly, I didn't know. I didn't care. Because I said it, and I didn't regret it. It was real. This wasn't an obsession on a computer screen. Not a quick fix. I cared about her. I was hopeful.

She took a deep breath and laughed—not the reaction I was looking for. She weakly mumbled, "See? I was right."

"What?" I snapped out of my sentiment.

"I said you were going to fall in love with me."

I pulled my head from hers. She squeezed my hand.

"But I love you too." She closed her eyes.

A smile broke out on my face.

"Will you come with me tomorrow? I want to see Barry," she said. "I'm going to fire him. I want to start over. I want to take a break and get healthy. I want to find my mother. Do you think you can be there?"

"Yes," I said.

She pulled out her phone. "Let's take a picture so we can remember this moment."

An hour later, she was in my bed, eyes closed. She looked so beautiful, peaceful. I glanced over to the silver sparrow on my nightstand. I had never seen her take it off. Her voice was so clear in my mind.

I want you to fall in love with me...

But then those other words—

And in the end, I'm going to break your fucking heart.

Lizzy: That concert was a disaster. They had to refund everyone's tickets. I've never seen Barry so upset. To be honest, I think it was all part of her act. Maybe a cry for attention. I don't know. I told Barry that Kelly wasn't ready. But he didn't want to listen.

Jez: I would have done something sooner. But she wanted Kaleb to rescue her.

Lizzy: He was no match for Barry.

THE REAL ALICE
NEW MEXICO, 2015

SIXTY-SEVEN DAYS SOBER. Sara was sitting on a park bench, a black scarf protecting her bruised neck from the cold. A half smile played in the corner of her mouth as she watched the sun rise behind dull gray clouds. Then she bit her lip, a sure tell that she was returning to her daydreams. It was her way of avoiding pain.

Her body sank deeper into the bench as her mind drifted into the fantasy. I knew exactly where she was going. She called it the perfect sunrise. With it, her smile grew wide. She imagined blue skies and fluffy, white clouds. She imagined the sun illuminating the morning sky. She imagined herself as a free woman.

In this fantasy, she had no husband. The day was full of possibility. Free of bondage. No pain, no fear. Sometimes her fantasy included children running around, playing as she watched the day commence. She would never have kids with her husband. If she was too afraid to leave him, she would be too afraid to protect her children.

I looked off into the distance.

Just like Sara, I was good at fabricating stories.

Like fantasizing about my life with her. I imagined our house, kids, everything. But for the first time since we met, I knew for certain that the fantasy would never be real. She would always be trapped. She would never have that sunrise. And I would always be on the sidelines, ensnared. Rapt in my obsession, thinking about her, waiting.

A new fantasy sparked in my head. One much darker. It started as a thought, but my stomach didn't twist. In fact, my body felt euphoric, almost light. This wasn't a daydream. This wasn't a fantasy. No. For the first time, I was starting to understand the difference. This was my destiny. I was here to protect. I knew what I must do.

Bob's cold hand clasped my shoulder.

I didn't flinch. Not this time.

I must kill her husband.

INSIDEJUICE: Walk me through those first months back in the spotlight. How did you decide on the new image you would present to the world?

TROZZO: If I wanted to move forward, I knew I would have to kill the personas from my past. I had to destroy all the memorabilia—the clothes, the awards, the photos, all evidence of my vulnerability. My ex, Noah, turned out to be very useful in my comeback. He helped me build my new image by recruiting his band of merry misfits—artists, writers, hip-hop heads, and dancers—ready to come party at my command. He even found me the perfect assistant. I saw them as a buffer, the moat in my castle's defense. Perfect accessories for the new life-style I created.

INSIDEJUICE: What did Barry think of this new image?

TROZZO: I remember the day Barry and his team heard the first single off my album, as well as the storyboard for the video. It was a little shocking for everyone. I'll put it this way. My very first music video had four horses, a fake family, a blond-haired boy in a charming log cabin. This new one had two lesbian hookup scenes, three whips, and one scene where I go down on a tattooed guy in a bathroom. But Barry had to agree. I had already gone too far. There was no turning back.

After that meeting, we had a celebratory party at my mansion. I remember catching Noah's gaze as I moved through the mass of kids. I could feel my new image start to seep into my thoughts. I wasn't the weak little girl he remembered. This time, I was leading. He was following. I loved how strong that made me feel. How easily I ripped off his shirt and shoved him against the wall. He needed to know. This time around, I did the fucking.

Lizzy: She had this incredible life. This great guy who adored her. Her music career was taking off. She was so ungrateful. All she cared about was recruiting soldiers for this make-believe "spiritual war." The whole thing was so absurd. I couldn't believe her fans bought into that madness. And Noah was caught right in the middle. He wanted to please her. But at what cost? Kelly and all her "troops" were living in a freakin' fantasy!

Jez: Noah was as weak as Lizzy.

Lizzy: Do you really think Kelly trusted Jez with her secrets? Please. She meant nothing to Kelly. She was a pawn. Just another fanatical KTroop that Kelly could manipulate. Jez didn't know a damn thing. But I did. I knew everything. She told me everything in New York. Why do you think I left?

Jez: Where was Lizzy on the day Kelly died? Ask her! Ask her!

"Today, we have obtained pictures of the murder scene. I warn you ahead of time, these images are incredibly graphic and disturbing."

I fill another coffee mug with vodka. Pour out the last of the cocaine on the motel dresser. I smash up the last of the pills. Dump out the psychedelics for good measure. This should be fun. One last hurrah. One final fantasy. It's time to finish the story I was paid to write. I can't tell you I'm not nervous. I am. I'm frightened of what comes next.

"I realize these photos are very difficult to look at," says the anchorman.

There's nothing I haven't seen.

Donaldson once laid the same pictures in front of me. He was confident recreating the murder scene with his photos strung together like puzzle pieces on the table. He made me stare at Barry's bloated body in the foyer. He waited for my reaction. He showed me the pools of blood atop the marble. Then a picture of my footprints clearly marked next to the body. My bloody handprints smeared on the railing. Then a picture of Kelly, her body strewn across the driveway. A close-up of the knife wounds. I couldn't look.

I turn the television off.

Not tonight.

The drugs will assist me with the fantasies, not the night-mares. Not the tragedy. Not the blood. Give me the bluebirds. Our beloved leading lady. I want the good stuff. I want the stuff that numbs. I know Bob will come for me. But not now. Not when I'm high. Not till the very end. The drugs will hold him off for a while. This will just take a second...

Ahhh, much better.

When I close my eyes, the blood in the mansion washes away. The marble is white and polished. The darkness is penetrated by rays of white light. Outside, puffy, animated clouds float gently across blue skies. It is all so beautiful. Kelly appears in her paja-mas. I see a breakfast spread on the dining room table. Every box of cereal you can imagine. Everyone is there: Jez, all the regulars. Kelly beams and passes me a bowl. The sun gleams brightly through every window. I hold her hand underneath the table.

We were driving to Barry's office. I watched her in the passenger seat. She whispered, "Thank you."

The end was in sight.

It would be a fresh start for both of us. We could get clean together. We could go somewhere tropical and warm. Far away from Hollywood. Away from fame. She squeezed my hand, gazing up at the blue skies. She took a deep inhale, closing her eyes, letting the sunlight drip across her face. She was remark-able that day. There was something underneath it all. This still-ness. Something I wanted to capture. The best version of herself. I kept watching. Even if I knew deep down that the impending storm was on the horizon. I held on just a little longer. Before the blue faded. Before the sun retreated behind the black clouds. Before singing birds turned to circling crows.

"Do you believe in fairy tales, Kaleb?"

"Huh?" I snapped out of my daze. "What do you mean?"

"Do you believe in happily ever after?"

I smirked. "Whatever helps you get up in the morning."

"That's not what I'm asking." She smacked my arm playfully. "I'm not talking about hope. I'm asking about the reality of everlasting love. Complete freedom from pain. Do you think that's possible?"

Her energy was infectious.

"Could be."

"Your book and my movie, you know, they might seem very different, but they share a common theme," she continued. "Just like the princess and AJ, people like you and me, humanity in general, we're cursed. There is darkness inside us all. Sometimes, it makes us want to go into a tower, alone, and drown in that despair and shame. But the darkness can be defeated. Every curse was meant to be broken."

I looked at her, puzzled. "Where is this coming from?"

"Don't you see?" she insisted. "The darkness isn't real. The humble knight broke the curse because love was the only thing that could show fear's true nature. It was just a curse. It wasn't who she was. Just like it's not who we are. Love can dispel our darkness. Isn't that why AJ did what he did? His love for Alice surpassed his greatest fears."

She looked forward, grinned. "He wanted Alice to have a happily ever after." She turned toward me. "But why didn't you give AJ a happily ever after?"

She squeezed my hand. "You do deserve it, Kaleb."

We were walking on the street, heading toward Barry's office building.

A young girl skipped toward us. "Kelly, Kelly, can I have your autograph?"

Kelly bent down so she was eye level with the girl. "Of course, sweetie. What's your name?"

"It's Tiffany."

"And what do you want to be when you grow up, Tiffany?"

"I want to be a star like you."

Kelly laughed and then looked up at the girl's mother, who shrugged, smiled.

Kelly stared back at the girl. "You are a star," she said. "Because you're full of the greatest characteristic of any star... light. You are perfect as you are." She signed and handed the piece of paper to the girl. She reached for the girl's hand. Both of them were beaming.

The tall office building cast shadows across our faces.

Kelly took a deep breath. "Now we ask for the evil king's blessing."

Lizzy: You don't just fire Barry Monroe. Kelly knew better. He wasn't going to make it easy.

Jez: That was supposed to be the day that Kaleb and Kelly rode off into the sunset. Instead, it became the night that Kaleb truly battled her monster.

Lizzy: Barry had pictures. Horrifying pictures.

Jez: I don't know anything about Kelly's mom.

Lizzy: It was an overdose that killed Kelly's mother. They didn't find her body for three days. She was pale and bruised with track marks covering her arms. I knew those photos would break her.

Jez: Kelly didn't say anything about pictures.

Lizzy: I imagine she withdrew to her tower after the meeting. And once she retreated, nobody could enter that room. I tried. I really did, back during those months she went missing, I knocked on that door. I screamed. I tried to get in. But that was the birthplace of her madness. That was where the sickness overtook her. If I couldn't get her out of that tower, no one could.

Jez: Kaleb did. He climbed that tower. And because of his efforts, he solidified his role in our story. They had an agreement. Forged by love. What was the agreement? I'll let him tell you that.

I've ingested it all. The last of the drugs. It was a bit excessive. I'm not sure my psyche will survive the madness. It doesn't take long to start feeling the effects. The colors. The light. The vibrations. My hands are bigger, stronger. I feel powerful. The carpet is moving. Everything is starting to burst into life. I've cued Kelly's movie on my laptop. The enchantment is coming. The whimsical music. The joy. The happiness. The magic. The animation swirls out of the screen. It takes on a life of its own. The characters frolic around the motel room, spinning, singing, laughing. I dance. I float.

Everything is alive.

It's all so beautiful.

The walls of the motel room are melting away. My world is transforming. I can't help but laugh. I open the curtains. Water is rising behind the glass. The last bit of sanity is being swept away. I keep laughing and laughing. It doesn't matter. Let the visions come. Ocean waves crash against the motel windows. I look in the mirror. My eyes and face blur. Distort. Animate. I am wearing a full suit of armor, shield and sword in hand. Her silver sparrow necklace is around my neck. My lady's favor. A token of love.

I will fight for you, Kelly. Yes, I believe. Do you hear me, Kelly?

"I'm coming for you," I sing.

"He's coming for me," my princess sings back.

I will find you.

I will protect you.

The window can't hold the water. Cracks shoot across the glass.

BOOM. The water bursts through. Sweeping through the room. Rising up the walls. I swim...

My head emerges into gray skies. The waves are thick and choppy, devouring me, drowning me. I cough out saltwater, keel over in the wet sand. Gasping. I'm alive.

The dark towers of Castle Heart loom above me. Shadows move across my face. She is in there, my princess. I rise and begin my ascent up the winding stone steps, through the castle archway. Hideous carvings of gargoyles and beasts stare down upon me. Crows circle overhead, cackling at my intrusion.

"Hello," I call out as I enter the cold and rocky fortress. My words echo back.

The last remaining rays of light withdraw from the stained-glass windows as shadows stir across the stone floors like jungle vines in a ruin. I light a torch, moving slowly through the desolate halls. A strange mist rolls across the cold stone. The curse brings the castle to life. The gargoyle fixtures hiss. Snakes slither along the walls. Blood drips down the oil paintings. My sword is drawn. Black vines with thorns grow and twist across the floor. I chop frantically, fighting through the barbs, as I stride through the darkness.

The curse will end at first light. It is not real. The princess warned me. I would find her. No matter how dangerous the quest. It was the promise I made.

I am a defender of the weak.

I climb the narrow steps to her tower. The air turns bitterly cold, snuffing out my torch. The monster is inside; its powers grow stronger in the darkness. My breath moves in and out in puffs of cold air. I arrive at her tower door. A serpent doorknocker spins and swirls, its eyes aglow in the darkness.

"Who goes there?" the voice hisses.

"It is I, the humble knight."

The serpent cackles. "You dare enter the monster's lair. You will die! You will die!" A wicked smile twists across the snake's face. "You may enter, Sir Reed."

The flame on my torch reignites.

The door creaks open, and a wave of frigid air strikes my face. It makes me sick. Pure evil resides inside these chambers. I take careful steps, my sword extended. The canopy bed is empty. The princess's beautiful voice rings from a small box where her golden heart rests.

I need him here
  My humble knight
  Help me destroy my fear
  This heart of mine
  Is all I hold dear.
  He is coming for me.
  He is coming for me.

I can feel the monster's dark presence, its wicked soul, the source of evil. The window is open, and the curtains rip in the stormy winds. I peek into the next chamber, and my knees buckle under the weight of my armor. A powerful vibration barrels into my heart, and darkness and fear grip my body. I hold the shaky torch, imagining the carnage. Imagining the monster standing over the princess in victory, his fangs dripping with her blood.

"Princess," I whisper.

No answer.

"Princess," I whisper again, creeping a little closer.

"Kelly," I murmured in horror.

She appeared on a sea of white that spread across the floor. She was naked, rocking back and forth. Her knees pulled to her chest. She was perched on a mountain of white pills. They were everywhere, hundreds and thousands of pills, spread out on the carpet. Her hair was uncombed, her eyes swollen and lost. Overrun with shadows. Her face was bright red, her teeth chattered.

I said her name softly. "Kelly."

Her head turned. Her eyes narrowed. Her body convulsed with fury.

She screamed, "Get the fuck out!"

I walked backward. Her naked body lunged toward me at full force.

"I'm the biggest fucking star in the world," she seethed. "Everyone will fucking love me! You're a nobody. I will kill you quicker than I made you. Fuck you—get the fuck out of my house. Fuck you. Fuck you."

She pushed me, and I didn't fight back. It wasn't Kelly. It was the darkest part of her soul. Its wicked fangs. Its horrible eyes. All the brokenness. All the malevolent fear and shame. Fighting. Breathing. Enjoying its time in power. Draining its host. I grabbed her shoulders and shook her. I needed to catch a glimpse. *Give me those blue eyes. Let me see the real you. Come back to me.*

She collapsed, struggling in my arms. I squeezed her body. *Come back to the light.* Another surge of rage pulsed from her body. She kept pushing, clawing, fighting. I would protect her. I put my hand to her cheek. She slapped it off and scratched my face. "Fuck you. You piece of shit."

I shoved her naked body onto the bed, and she pounded her fists and screamed. "You druggie fucking loser, you're a nobody. You're pathetic. You're weak! I am Kelly Trozzo. I am Kelly Trozzo." Her energy was waning. "I will be bigger and better than everyone," she cried and curled back into herself.

"Get the fuck out," she whispered.

She sobbed.

"Get out." Even softer.

I stepped into the bathroom and shut the door. I pushed down the lock. There was a large plastic container overturned in the corner. The mound of prescription pills had spread across the tile.

The song kept playing.

The humble knight sang.

We shall fight this curse together

She pounded on the bathroom door.

The monster cannot be real

"Let me in! Let me in!"

For love will overcome all odds

Her pounding subsided.

Your golden heart shall heal

"Let me in…" I could barely hear her.

I'm coming for you. I'm coming for you.

And then she stopped.

I collapsed and rested my head against the door. I heard her go back to the bed. More screams. I listened closely. The music stopped. An hour went by. The house was muted. Stillness. My eyes went heavy. I was jolted awake at 6:00 a.m. to the sound of a dying phone battery in my pocket. I poked my head out the bathroom door. Fresh rays of morning sun seeped through the closed blinds. Kelly wasn't on her bed. I hurried down the stairs. Tiptoed into the kitchen. The tile was white and clean. I knew where she was.

I lingered in the doorway of her study. She was perched in

a meditation pose. As if the curse ended at first light. As if she could be cleansed and start over. But I knew the truth. The monster had retreated, but it would return. Each time, it struck harder. We shoved it deeper into our souls. Suppressed it. Covered it. Hid. Dulled. We pretended that we would never have to face that dark entity again. The root of our pain and destruction.

If we wanted it to end—one day, we would have to look. We would have to face the worst fears inside our hearts. These trapped shadows. This energy that fights and claws to get out. This living, breathing thing that has taken residency inside us. This broken world created it. We buried it. Only light and love and God can destroy it.

I stood in the doorway. Kelly turned toward me. Her face was still pale, exhausted, maybe scared. So was I. She didn't say anything, but her eyes were asking for something. *Save me. Help me. Rescue me.*

I nodded. Then a weak smile.

I was her loyal soldier. Until the very end.

I walked out of the mansion that day. The morning was crisp. The sun was bright. Fresh dew shimmered on her perfectly manicured lawn. My hands were shaking. My mind was tired. Still, I felt strong. Powerful. I was a new man. Redemption was coming.

One day sober.

THE REAL KELLY TROZZO

TheInsideJuice.com Interview 2019

INSIDEJUICE: Your performance at the VMAs shocked the world.

TROZZO: I knew it had to be memorable—something that would send shockwaves across the internet. Something my fans could rally behind. I have to say, it was everything I imagined. I can still feel the heat of the spotlight on me as I came out in that leather bikini. Then, as the beat awakened, so did the greatness inside of me. I enjoyed the power coursing through me as I climbed on top of the dark male dancer, scratching my nails into his chest. I knew this wasn't in rehearsal, and the network would pay the price, but I couldn't care less.

When it was over, the stage went dark, and the crowd roared. My lungs were throbbing, and my heart pounded like it had never pounded before. It was the greatest feeling in the world. When the last pulse of the beat faded, I knew everything had changed. I saw the shock and intrigue on everyone's faces—the whispers of "slut" and "whore." Exactly what I wanted—the world witnessing my rebirth.

Then I looked over to Barry. It was a look I will always cherish —pure bewilderment. He finally understood how strong I had become.

———

Lizzy: It's true. The performance *did* shock the world. But that wasn't all Kelly had planned. That wasn't enough for her.

Jez: Kissing her on stage was one of the greatest moments of my life. I will cherish that kiss forever.

Lizzy: Kelly summoned Noah into the dressing room an hour before the performance. She handed him a knife.

Jez: I don't know what you are talking about.

Lizzy: It was that book. That ridiculous book. It twisted her damn mind. She thought true love was some sort of ultimate sacrifice. She asked Noah to put a dagger in Barry's back. Kill for the girl he loved. Some bullshit like that. I don't care how much Noah loved her. Look at what she was asking!

Jez: I was with Kelly the entire time. I know, because I had to calm her down in the dressing room. Oh my gosh, she was so nervous. It was so cute, pacing around in her little bikini, blowing into a paper bag. No, I never saw Noah. Why do you keep asking that?

Lizzy: Think about it. It was the perfect ending—Kelly gazes into Barry's eyes as the performance ends, and the knife is thrust into his back. Then he would know the truth. That Kelly orchestrated all of it. Don't you see? This wasn't my best friend anymore. I didn't betray her. She betrayed me.

Jez: That sounds like something Lizzy would make up.

Anything to alleviate her guilt. You'll see, detective. You'll see. Ask her where she was on the night Kelly died. Ask her!

"It's been a tough month," I confessed, three days after leaving Kelly's mansion. *Three days sober.* I was sitting in a circle with my NA group. "I've done it all. Ecstasy. Coke. Pills. Probably some other shit I don't remember."

I could feel the eagerness of my fellow participants.

"But I'm sober now." I looked over to Nathan. He didn't glance up. "I have a purpose now. It's been three days. The cravings are settling."

The meeting ended. I went to get coffee. I expected his presence, his grunt, his patronizing remarks. Instead, I glanced back over my shoulder to see the gymnasium door shut. He left without a word. *Good riddance.*

At home, I turned the hot water on in the kitchen and let the warm water run over my hands. The water felt good. I scrubbed each dish, slowly, carefully, until the sink was empty. I dumped every last bit of alcohol out. I cleaned the entire apartment. I opened the windows; fresh air rolled in, along with the sun. By late afternoon, the place was spotless. I took my laptop to the kitchen table and poured myself coffee.

I found a routine. I woke up at 6:00 a.m. and drove north. I stopped at a coffee shop near LAX. A croissant and a medium black drip. I took the same spot near the window. I powered up my computer. My hands moved slowly at first, but eventually, the words came. My fingers glided across the keyboard.

After a few hours, I took a breather. I looked out the window and stared at an old billboard for Kelly's album. Her beautiful face, blonde hair and sharp blue eyes on a black background. Light and shadows. Blurred but clear. Just like the Kelly I knew.

One week became two. Two weeks became three. *Twenty-one days sober.*

It wasn't easy. But I had a purpose. A job to do.

I stopped by a rundown gun shop in downtown Los Angeles.

I drove and wrote at the coffee shop every day.

I checked Kelly's social media accounts every hour. She was talking to her fans again. She spoke of grit, strength and purpose. She was talking about me. Then I drove home, back to my apartment. She always posted goodnight on her feed. She was talking to me.

I woke up each day a determined man. I turned in new pages to my publisher. The screenwriter I met at Kelly's mansion sent me a script for the movie adaptation of *Pay Me, Alice*. It was good. It was darker than the book. I liked it. He kept the final scene intact.

During this time, Kelly sent me presents. Little treats. Manila envelopes filled with pictures. Each night, I lay in bed and stared at the ceiling, twirling her necklace in my hands. Staring at our memories together. I listened to her music.

I fell asleep with a smile on my face.

THE REAL KELLY TROZZO
TheInsideJuice.com Interview 2019

INSIDEJUICE: How did you feel after the VMA performance?

TROZZO: After that, I took some time to consider my options. The backlash was incredible. I was the biggest trending topic in the world. Everyone was so shocked to see their goody-two-shoes princess kiss three girls and go down on a guy in a Styrofoam bathroom stall. The online hysteria, the headlines, the attention—my army was growing, and my troops were preparing for battle. I just needed the right solider to make it complete.

During that time, I reread my favorite book, *Pay Me, Alice.* I couldn't stop staring at the author's photo on the jacket. And I couldn't help but wonder if he loved the real Alice enough to make that ultimate sacrifice. Maybe I would never know what it's like to be loved like that. Was I not good enough? Was I not beautiful enough? I'll admit, I wondered what it would be like to have someone like that. Someone with soft green eyes and a broken past. Someone who knew what it was like to make a real sacrifice.

THE REAL ALICE
NEW MEXICO, 2015

SIXTY-EIGHT DAYS SOBER. The gun shop was another cliché. The walls were lined with dusty deer heads. An American flag. A series of torn NRA posters. The employee wore a camo hat and a week's worth of scruff. He had a wad of chewing tobacco in his cheek and a bad attitude.

"You looking for something specific?" He eyed me suspiciously.

I browsed the filthy glass counters.

"That one." Bob pointed to a handgun.

"Can I see that one?"

The man unlocked the case. He handed me the gun.

"You ever shot a gun before?" he asked as he spat brown juice into a Styrofoam cup.

I ignored him, turning the metal over in my hands. I focused on the growing pit in my stomach. My hands began to tremble. I dropped the gun back onto the counter. The man chuckled. Rolled his eyes and sneered.

Bob's hand gripped my shoulder. "Try again."

I reached for the gun. As soon as I touched it, an image appeared. Sara's husband was looking down the barrel with fear in his eyes. He backed away. Power surged through my heart, my arms, my hands. No more trembling. I was strong. Confident. Poised. Sara was next to me, smiling.

"Do it, Kaleb. Do it. Save me."

Bob's hand fell off my back.

"Hey, man." The employee backed away from the counter. The smug look on his face was gone. He avoided my gaze. He'd underestimated me. I had his attention. I liked that. I held the power.

I set the gun back on the counter, handed the man an envelope of cash.

"$500 for the gun and bullets, $500 for you."

He flipped through the cash. "You're not going to kill anyone, are you?" he asked, nervously.

I felt Bob behind me, awaiting my answer.

"Of course not." I grinned. "It's just for protection."

THE REAL KELLY TROZZO
TheInsideJuice.com Interview 2019

INSIDEJUICE: Is that why you hired author Kaleb Reed to document your comeback?

TROZZO: In a sense.

INSIDEJUICE: What was it about his book that engrossed you so much?

TROZZO: Have you ever read a story that lingers far after the final page? I'm not entirely sure why I'm so obsessed with *Pay Me, Alice*. Maybe because the protagonist is so damaged, so relatable, but what he does at the end, it just makes sense. That's what real love is. And then it dawned on me...I've been thinking about fairy tales all wrong. Happily ever after isn't about convincing a knight to rescue you from a tower. That's too easy. No. It's about real sacrifice. It's what my mom and no man could ever do for me. Without sacrifice, their love and affection were just empty words.

Lizzy: I'm sorry, but look at it from my perspective. Did you read her posts? Or the stuff from the KTroop fan club? Kelly turned her fans against me. She was the reason my show got canceled. She was the reason Barry turned his back on me. She said she was looking out for me, but she wasn't. She was punishing her best friend.

Jez: Kelly taught her followers that short-term pain equates to long-term glory. Not everyone has that type of vision. Some people are just concerned with ratings, record sales, and double taps—scared little sheep. The KTroops needed to teach Lizzy a lesson. Sadly, she was a very slow learner.

Twenty-four days sober. I wrote five pages in the morning. I left the coffee shop by 10:00, drove through Los Angeles, then back on the freeway. Home by 1:00. I watched television until the sun went down. Ordered takeout. The food had just arrived when I heard the notification and a new text message appeared on the screen. Music to my ears.

The thrill of my mission.

I stared at the phone resting on the table.

A nervous ache trailed by eagerness.

It was time. My leader had called.

Her message: *Go read the obituaries.*

Our second morning in New York. We were lying in the hotel bed, sheets wrapped around us. She stared at me suspiciously.

"Okay. There's just *one* more problem I had with your book."

"Kelly," I moaned.

"I didn't like the reasoning behind Alice's infatuation with the obituaries. There has to be more to it."

"There's not," I said, yawning. "It's early. Go back to bed."

She rolled her eyes and sat up.

"Okay, okay." I wanted to please her. "It's about attachment to the physical world, and the obituaries put everything into perspective. How fleeting the human experience is. Death is coming for us all. Now will you stay in bed?"

"You're really going to give me that shitty book club answer?" She got out of bed. "Is that all you think of me?"

"Fine, fine." I conceded. "There was one scene that got scrapped." I sat up, rubbing the sleep from my eyes.

I had her attention. She wasn't leaving. "Anyway, in the scene, Alice was reading the paper and she closed her eyes and envisioned how she would die. From his hand, repeated blows to her face. She saw her name in black ink, what the few lines would say. That's when she knew. Like really knew. There was only one ending with her husband. Always. One day her husband was going to kill her."

Kelly looked dissatisfied. I grabbed her hand.

"More than that, she read the obituaries to prepare. So when AJ put his message in the paper, he was giving her a lifeline. You can choose me. You can escape this fate. You have a choice, Alice. Choose me. Choose life. Choose love."

I drove to the nearby gas station, dropped in the quarters, opened up the newspaper case. Grabbed a paper, flipped through the pages. Advertisements fluttered out onto the cement. I scanned the obituaries, looking for the full-page ad. There was nothing.

What was I looking for?

And then I saw it.

A black and white picture, front and center. Her favorite painting. Perseus holding a shield, the head of Medusa carved into the metal. Angels were placing a crown upon his head.

Andromeda was naked, tied to the rock. At the bottom of the painting was the mouth and claws of a monster, rising, ready to devour the chained beauty. There was an address inside the monster's mouth. I ripped the clipping from the newspaper and got into the car. A rush of adrenaline coursing through my body. I was prepared for the ending she created. I was ready to see her. I opened the glove box to make sure.

The gun was still there.

The Real Kelly Trozzo

TheInsideJuice.com Interview 2019

INSIDEJUICE: What did you want Kaleb to capture through this process?

TROZZO: I wanted to produce something they will never forget. Something that will be passed down through generations. Not just some performance that steals headlines for a week. Not some boring biography or tell-all bullshit. I want to go down in infamy, preserved like the great myths of old.

Lizzy: I was so angry when I got to New York. Kelly should have apologized. My show was canceled, my career was in shambles. But no…Why should she care about her best friend? She was so wrapped up in her little book project. You know what she told me? That it was for the best. That by the end of all this, I would be immortalized. That we would finally be free. Are you kidding me? Pardon my language, but she had lost her fucking mind! Then she confessed the whole crazy idea. Recreate her favorite story? Conspiring to kill? I laughed at her. How could she think that would cheer me up? That was the reason we got into a fight. I was mad at her. But she was obsessed. That book poisoned my best friend's mind!

THE REAL ALICE
NEW MEXICO, 2015

SEVENTY-THREE DAYS SOBER. It was hard for me to look at Sara, sitting across from me at the diner. She was stunning, with her faded crewneck sweatshirt and messy bun. She ordered a coffee, one creamer, and sourdough toast with a side of avocado. She was reading the paper, the obituaries. I read current events. It was our routine, and I clung to it like it was the last drug I would ever take.

"What do we have today?" I asked.

"Alice Beth Daniels, a beloved mother of six, grandmother of twelve. Apparently, she handled all the family responsibilities when her husband, Allen Jeffrey Daniels, nicknamed AJ, was in the military. She died in surgery."

"Not bad."

"Wait——" Sara's face was animated. "Listen to this. The kids used to recall their father making silly bets with their mom, and if he won, he would grab her by the shoulders, kiss her cheek and yell, 'Pay me, Alice!' And guess what?"

"What?"

"Those were the last words their mother spoke before she died."

261

Sara took a deep breath and folded the paper before her emotions got the best of her. She grabbed the avocado to spread across her toast.

"Can I ask you something?" she said playfully. "What would you write if you were doing my obituary?"

If she had only known how often I thought about that. Every time she left me. I imagined it would be the last time I would see her. No one would call. She would miss our daily breakfast. And I would wonder. But I wouldn't know for certain, until I read her name in the paper or saw it on the news. And I would write her obituary because her husband wouldn't, and I knew how much it meant to her. I would say that Sara had beauty that could make a man drive seven hundred miles without thinking. She could get a drug addict to stop using. She could make you seem worthwhile, stronger than you actually were. That when she loved you back, it was like feeling the sun on your face after spending years in a cold and lonely prison.

"I'll never have to write yours," I said, sipping my coffee casually.

"Well, if you did."

"But I would gladly write your husband's," I offered.

"What?"

"He deserved it. That's what I would write."

She looked at me strangely. "Kaleb."

"I'm leaving, Sara."

She scoffed. "Where?"

"Home. Somewhere else."

She grabbed the butter knife and avoided my gaze. This was the part where she should fight. She should say no, and of course, I'd listen. Because I was looking for any reason to stay. I would remain with her in this town until the end of days. Even if she was married. I would take what I could get. It was better than the life waiting for me back home. I would continue to be whatever she wanted me to be. I looked down at the newspaper.

No.

Not this time.

Those are the thoughts of a weak man. I wouldn't listen to them. Not anymore. I needed to be someone else. I needed to be what she needed. Not what she wanted. She was trapped. She had to find what Alice Daniels had, or her obituary would never have a happy ending. I could save her.

"Promise me something," she said, her gaze moving back up to mine. "If something were to happen to me, will you write it? Will you write my obituary?"

She was trying to make me hurt. Like I needed this to be any harder. Yet I was glad she did. It was a test. I would be stronger. Better. For once in my life, I would stand tall. I reached for her hand. "Of course I'll write it."

Then I pulled my hand away. "I'll miss you, Sara," I said warmly. Then my tone turned cold. "But I have to leave." We locked eyes, and I saw the color drain from her face. She had never seen this person. But it was who I needed to be. Who I needed to become. To protect the woman I loved.

I got up from the booth.

I had rehearsed this. It had to be fast. It had to be clean. I couldn't turn back. She looked at the bill. I always took care of the bill. It was expected. All the lunches, all the coffees, all the breakfasts at this lonely diner. It wasn't just a gesture—it was a statement. She figured I would always be there. I would always be waiting in the wings to comfort her. To say it was going to be okay. To coddle her, hold her, uplift her. But not this time.

"I think you can pay this one."

The bell on the front door chimed for the last time. Bob was perched outside, a pencil to his crossword.

"How did she take it?"

"She took it well."

"Good. You're doing the right thing."

"You sure?"

"Trust me. She'll thank you someday."

I reached into my jacket pocket. The gun was still there.

The Real Kelly Trozzo

TheInsideJuice.com Interview 2019

INSIDEJUICE: It seems like you have more to say about your decision to hire Kaleb Reed.

TROZZO: I do. I want to tell people how I found his book. It's significant.

INSIDEJUICE: Please.

TROZZO: It was three days after my suicide attempt. I was sitting on a park bench, in this beautiful state of bliss. And I was staring off into the horizon with bandages around my arm. On the bench next to me, a lovely girl was reading a book. I was drawn to the cover; the artsy way "Pay Me, Alice" was written inside a skull and crossbones. I don't know why, but something inside me told me to talk to her. So I did.

I asked her if the book was any good and she nodded, giving me a confident "Yes." I asked her what the story was about. She was extremely passionate about the plot, talking with her arms and smiling as she described it. There was something about her, something alluring. She had these warm brown eyes and beautiful dark blonde hair.

She finished explaining the storyline, and then she asked about me. She told me she was a big fan, and she wanted to know what I was working on. I was polite, but I was much more fascinated by the book. I asked her what about the novel she liked so much. She explained that it was a heartbreaking love story, but it was still happy in a way, and that there was hope even though there was death. I could tell she was holding back, so I said, "There must be something else."

She admitted that she recognized herself in the love interest and that she was quite fond of the narrator. And as I stared at her beautiful smile, for a brief second, I was envious. There was this peculiar happiness and love radiating from this woman. She looked content and joyful, and that made me jealous. I wanted her life.

That's when she handed the book to me. "You should have this," she said. "I've read it twice already."

I tried to refuse but she was adamant. As she got up to walk away, something told me to ask for her name. She turned around and said, "Sara." Then she gave me a smile. "Or, as this book refers to me, Alice."

The address Kelly gave me was forty minutes east. It was a rest stop along the highway, a diner with a fluorescent sign and an empty dirt parking lot. The sound of the nearby highway drowned out the chirping crickets. Dim stars flickered underneath the dome of the city smog. I knew why she chose this place. In her imagination, it was the perfect reproduction of a scene from her favorite book—Alice and AJ's little heaven. The best Hollywood could do. But it was nothing like the real one. The sign on this diner was refurbished. The real one was faded, chipped, weathered from years of sun and neglect. This was for passing truckers, people outside the city. Mine was for locals within. Drifters who spent months at the motel next door.

But this wasn't my story anymore.

I grabbed the gun from the glove box, stuffed it into my coat. The metal pounded against my pumping heart. This was the role I was meant for. My tense steps pounded on the gravel.

The bell chimed.

She was alone.

The same way I found Sara.

As I once described it.

Kelly looked fatigued, yet calm. She was dressed in a black peacoat and red jeans. Her hair was wet, and she wasn't wearing any makeup. I felt nostalgic. I knew it was temporary. When she bestowed her gifts, and she expected something in return. I crawled into the booth. The aftermath of a breakdown showed in her eyes.

"Are you okay?" I asked.

She gave me a faint smile. "I have to be fast."

I grabbed her hand. "What do I do now?"

She took a deep breath as our fingers interlaced. She squeezed my palm, restoring our connection. Latching onto my soul. What we had was real. Bonded by our darkness. Our unworthiness, our brokenness, this dark ball of energy cut off from its creator. It was the force that guided our actions. This thing that made us do shit that hurt us. And no matter how hard we searched, how much shit we consumed, we would never cover up the shame. We would never fill these giant holes. It was a fool's errand. We would always be seeking. Always be addicts. Until we lifted the veil. Until we discovered a veil to lift.

"I'm ready, Kelly."

She smiled. "You know why I liked your book so much? Because AJ really loved Alice."

I nodded.

"People have always taken from me. They've always loved themselves more than me." Her voice trembled. "I think parents are supposed to teach their kids about love, and I don't think I ever learned."

I nodded again.

"Kelly, what's going on? I thought—"

She held up her scarred arm. "I was free, Kaleb. I was free." Her eyes met mine.

I reached over and pushed strands of blonde hair from her eyes.

"My heart just kept cracking that night, and it finally opened," she said, as I glided my thumb across her soft hands. "And I was free. I didn't need the world to love me anymore. I was enough." She paused and tried to compose herself. "But it came back."

"What?"

"The monster, Kaleb."

"Kelly, what happened?"

"Promise me that you'll finish the book."

She gave me a half-hearted but genuine smile. "I wasn't always truthful with you, but I want you to know that I do care."

She looked at me with those crystal-blue eyes. I never had a countermove. Never had a chance. From the very first moment I saw her on the screen. She was supposed to find my book. She was supposed to find me. Transform me. I was supposed to protect her.

She took a deep breath. Her hands slipped from mine. Our connection was lost. I looked up, confused. She had practiced this. Her eyes hardened. She got up from the booth. Her gaze moved to the door.

"Please finish the story."

She pulled out a gift-wrapped package from her coat and dropped it on the table. "This is for you."

Hands in her pockets, she walked away.

"Kelly!" I yelled. "Where are you going?"

Her hand lingered on the door. "I'll be back. I promise."

I returned to my apartment. I sunk into my couch, staring at the gift. I held it in my hands, flipped it around. Undid the twine and recycled paper. It was a copy of *Pay Me, Alice.* There was a note on it. *I've missed you.*

I browsed through the book. A photo fell out. It was the picture of Kelly and I in Philadelphia. I liked that she printed it. It meant something to her. I turned the book over. Why would she give me a copy of my novel? It was dirty and worn, creases on the matte cover. There were rips. Scuffs on the spine. This wasn't the copy sitting on her nightstand. This one had been crammed into bags and backpacks. Read hundreds of times. I started flipping through. There was a highlighted passage at the end of the book.

What would he do for the girl he loved? Anything. Everything. Who could he become? How far could he go? There was only one way to find out.

I searched through the pages for something else, but that was it. Then flipped to the end of the book. Then I saw it. Handwritten words: *Go find your sunrise.*

This was Kelly's penmanship.

I leaned back on the couch.

But how?

The truth struck me.

Why did I ignore the signs?

It was my first night in New York. The first time I met Lizzy Michaels. Her TV show had been canceled and Kelly threw a party in her hotel suite to cheer her up. Her eyes lit up the second Lizzy arrived. That affection never left her face. Kelly clung to Lizzy, her arm tucked into hers, never leaving her side. I was jealous at first. I wanted time with her. I had been waiting all night, but her attention was solely on Lizzy. My curiosity grew as I watched the two interact.

She introduced us.

"This is the writer I was talking about."

Lizzy forced a smile. She was cute, sandy blonde hair, perfect TV face. She looked innocent and candid, the new teen star. No tattoos or scars. A boy was standing next to her. Kelly leaned over to me and whispered, "I think she likes him."

I nodded and pointed to Lizzy.

"And you like her."

She beamed. "Yes, I do. She's like my sister."

I saw Kelly whisper in Lizzy's ear. I caught the words leaving her lips.

"Play it cool."

Kelly put her arm around Lizzy, and they skipped away, laughing.

Later, I saw Lizzy by herself. She looked agitated. She didn't want to be here. She was texting in the small kitchenette. When I approached her, she looked uncomfortable, offended. "So you two have a special relationship, huh?"

Lizzy stared into my eyes. It almost scared me.

"Don't let anything happen to her, Kaleb."

It was nearing 4:00 a.m. and Kelly and I were drunk on the couch. Everyone else was asleep or gone. We were passing a bottle back and forth and staring as Lizzy danced with the boy she liked. I was drunk and wanted to go to the bedroom with Kelly. My head was numb. The vodka was going down like water.

"Who is she to you?" I asked through slurred speech.

"I love her, Kaleb." Kelly paused, and the bottle lowered. "I would do anything for her."

I looked back and forth between the two girls. The truth struck. "You said you had a third gift from God on the night you made that scar…an angel."

A grand smile flooded her face. "Yes, Kaleb. An angel found me that night. An angel dragged me to the car and took me to the hospital," Kelly said, her voice dreamy. "An angel was with me that night. An angel saved my life. And I will never let anything bad happen to her."

Then her eyes turned cold.

"Lizzy has always been my something bigger."

Jez: Imagine if your best friend betrayed you? How would you feel?

The Real Kelly Trozzo
TheInsideJuice.com Interview 2019

INSIDEJUICE: Why are you smiling?

TROZZO: I'm thinking about the day I posted about Kaleb's book. How easy it was getting his attention. I recorded numerous videos and posts, one for every social network I had. I knew he would receive a flood of notifications and messages from my fans. He had no idea what I had in store for him. I took him out of his comfort zone. I pushed him as an artist. He evolved and was better for it, and in the end, he fell in love with me. But he will never know his place in my something bigger until the very end. Until it's too late for him to refuse.

THE REAL ALICE
NEW MEXICO, 2015

EIGHTY-NINE DAYS SOBER. The sun was setting on the construction site. The structural beams of the house were intact, blocking my view of the cliff. But I knew he was there, just around the corner, smoking his cigarette. He would never see it coming. The gun was in my hand. I held the power. I reached for the car door.

No. Stop. I can't. This couldn't be the only way. I needed to breathe. I needed to think. My hands were shaking uncontrollably. I could go back to Sara. I would find another way. There must be another way. I put my hand on the steering wheel.

"Where do you think you're going?"

I could feel Bob's cold breath.

"Go away. I'm not strong enough."

"I'm not going to let you off that easy, Kaleb."

"I'm not a killer," I protested.

"You coward. Think about her bruises," he seethed. "Think about her face. You're going to let him get away with that? You remember your mom at that beach house, don't you? Her swollen face, pretending to smile? Do you remember your dad, sitting on the porch doing his stupid crossword puzzles?

You didn't do shit, did you? Just like now. Imagine his fist, his knuckles, striking Sara's face. Again and again. "

"Stop it."

"Again and again."

"Stop," I whispered.

"And the bullies will always win."

I was rocking back and forth. Bob's hand fell on top of mine, and I felt my heart go cold.

"If it weren't for the bullies getting you expelled, you would have driven your brother to school that day. Instead, he had to carpool, and that drunk driver killed him. Your father was right to blame you. But you had a chance to make it right, and you let him off. The killer is still out there. And your father. Don't get me started. If you had stood up to him, maybe your mom wouldn't have endured so much pain. But they all got away with it. Now is your chance to redeem them all. To do what we set out to do. To finally be a man. To be the protector you've been afraid to become. This is your destiny. Become the person you were meant to be."

"I can't."

"Do you love her?"

"Yes."

"Then fucking prove it!"

"I can't."

"Do it, or else."

"Or else what?"

"Or else face me, you fucking coward. I dare you."

"Stop."

"Turn and face me like a man," Bob screamed.

"I can't!" I cried. "I can't."

"Then you have no choice.

"Will you leave me alone?" I mumbled.

"There's only one way to find out."

I rip open the motel blinds. The sirens howl in the distance. They are music to my ears. They are coming. I must be quick about this. I crack open the last bottle of vodka. Pour it over my book in the trash can. I watch the flames cascade over the skull and cross bones, melting the matte finish. The pages shrivel under the roaring flames.

I drop the silver sparrow in the toilet and watch it spin around and around until it disappears. The last keepsake is gone. There is nothing left to cling to. Nothing to tether me to this world. Nothing left to fight for. It's time to say goodbye. I sit down with the gun clutched in my hand. I have a new purpose now. The sirens are getting louder, closer. I stare at the empty chair across from me, waiting for his arrival.

THE REAL KELLY TROZZO
TheInsideJuice.com Interview 2019

INSIDEJUICE: When you say something bigger, are you talking about your purpose, your legacy?

TROZZO: I guess you can say that.

INSIDEJUICE: What will be your legacy?

TROZZO: I don't know yet. We'll have to wait and see. But I'll tell you this. My greatest fear is my star dying before it has a chance to shine. My entire life, people have tried to dim my light. Before I go, I want my star to gleam so bright that it has no other option than to burn out in one last flash of brilliance. And if that happens, death will truly be my happily ever after.

———

Jez: If anyone knows what happened to Kelly it's Lizzy. She was in the tower with her.

Lizzy: I've had enough. I want to leave. Please. I want to leave.

"AJ was *your* character. Your sacrifice. That was our work." Bob seethed in the passenger seat. Rain poured from the sky. I was swerving in and out of lanes, windshield wipers on high. Twenty minutes. Ten minutes. Five miles until Kelly's exit.

"I know."

"Drive faster."

Pedal to the metal.

"This is your job."

"Faster."

I pulled into Kelly's driveway. Two cars were parked there: a Bentley, freshly waxed with chrome wheels, and the two-door pickup truck. I approached the entrance. Dropped the large brass handle on the thick oak door...one knock, two knocks. I was holding Kelly's copy of my book in one hand, my gun in the other.

"Are you prepared?"

I am.

"Then what the fuck are you waiting for?" yelled Bob.

The door was unlocked. I pushed it open.

"Kelly!"

The sound of the creaky hinge echoed. It took a second to adjust to the light.

"Kelly," I yelled.

I looked down at the white marble floor, and the book and gun slipped from my fingers.

THE REAL KELLY TROZZO
TheInsideJuice.com Interview 2019

INSIDEJUICE: There's still something you're not telling me. I think there's more to your relationship with Kaleb Reed.

TROZZO: He's my solider.

INSIDEJUICE: Can you elaborate?

TROZZO: It means he'll do anything I ask of him.

INSIDEJUICE: And what have you asked of him?

TROZZO: Kaleb exceeded all my expectations. He saved young Zoe at her concert in Los Angeles. Then he chased Princess Jade into the tower, battling toe-to-toe with her monster. And as the sun rose and the curse retreated, I wondered if I had pushed too far, if he would abandon his post, if his loyalty would waver. He had every right. I was deep into my morning meditation when I heard him enter the room. He looked drained, emotionally and physically. My broken and damaged soldier, staring at the cursed princess with such love and compassion, wanting more than anything in the world to save her.

His green eyes were fierce, stronger than I gave him credit for. He knelt down next to me, put his hand on my face, and wiped a tear from my cheek. He finally understood why I gave him my favorite sparrow necklace. Others might see him as a monster. But in this story, he is my hero.

Jez: Read the ending, detective. Do you think she made it better? I think so. But maybe I'm biased.

The Final Scene of *Pay Me, Alice*

The basement pulses with loud music. AJ sees Dan's shadow in the small room that serves as the club's makeshift tattoo parlor. Dan's left shoulder is exposed—the tattoo he knew so well, the serpent and Celtic knot twisted together. It is the same image etched on Alice's left shoulder, in the exact same spot. They were eighteen years old when they got them, in love, and impulsive. At one point, Dan must have seen the beauty that was Alice. But somewhere along the line, he stopped trying. He stopped loving her. Dan stopped seeing what AJ saw. That Alice was perfect. That she deserved to be cherished and exalted. She deserved someone who would make her shine brighter and not cower with fear.

The gun is clutched in AJ's sweaty hand as he leans against the wall. He hears the sound of a tattoo needle against flesh. Two people walk by in the hallway. The club is too dark. The music is too loud. No one notices the weapon.

AJ no longer requires anything in return. He knows he won't live long enough for the reward. He wants Alice to live, and do things, and be somebody…and stop running from him, from herself, from everything she was too scared to face. He squeezes the handle of the gun one more time, staring at the man who can take that away from her. He knows his fate. He hopes Alice will find peace. He hopes she will find happiness in the future, even if it isn't with him. This is his sacrifice. She doesn't owe him anything. Nothing. They are even now, all squared up. He loves her—that is all that matters. He puts the hood of his sweatshirt over his head and walks into the room. Alice's husband looks up. Their eyes meet. Both of them pause.

And the tattoo needle stops.

The light of the chandelier reflected off the growing pool of red. Flashes of light lingered in my vision. The sound of the gunshot rang in my ear. Blood poured out of Barry's mouth. Crimson stains flowed across the floor, running to the soles of my shoes. Barry keeled over, his eyes staring back at his killer. He opened his mouth to speak, gurgling. Behind the smoke of the gun barrel was a steady hand and blue determined eyes.

Kelly stood proud as the final sliver of smoke faded into nothingness. A man stood next to her, dark hair, shaved head. Scar under his left eye. Noah Tash.

"What the fuck, Kelly!" Noah screamed.

Kelly stared at me; the gun still pointed at Barry. "I knew you would come."

More blood gushed out of Barry's mouth.

"You fucking bitch," he slurred, clutching his bleeding stomach.

"You will never hurt her like you hurt me," Kelly shouted.

She pulled the trigger again.

POP.

The recoil jerked her body back.

Barry's eyes went wide, and more blood poured from his mouth.

Again.

POP.

Blood spattered. The bloated body landed on the marble with a thud.

Barry was dead.

Silence.

Stillness.

Noah paced with his hands atop his head. "What the fuck! You crazy bitch!" he shouted.

Kelly gazed down at the body of her manager.

Satisfaction.

Remorse.

Confusion.

Her eyes were darkening.

Finally, she looked up at me, grinned. "Kaleb, I'd like you to meet Noah." She pointed the gun at him. "My treacherous ex-lover. I've invited him here tonight so he could watch our enemy fall. And what happens next is up to you, Kaleb."

"How long?" she asked Noah, her gun pointed at his chest. "How long were you sleeping with her?"

"Get that fucking gun away from me," he yelled.

"It's time for your atonement, Noah."

"Barry was right. You're a crazy bitch!" Noah screamed. "Put it down."

Kelly cocked the hammer.

Noah's hands went up. "Fine. Fine. Okay. Fuck." He took a deep breath. "After she came back from New York."

"Why?" Kelly asked through gritted teeth. "You could have chosen anyone. But you chose her."

Noah chuckled. "Wait, you don't know?"

"Know what?" The gun began to tremble in her grip. Blood was running across her shoes.

"You still think I came to the investment dinner to find you, don't you? Oh, Kelly, you were so obsessed with all this bullshit." He pointed to me. "So obsessed with that twisted fucking book. You never saw your best friend double-crossing you."

Bob was moving around the room, his hat tilted low. He walked behind Noah, holding up his finger. "Listen. You need to know the truth."

Noah laughed. "Don't you see? She sent me. Your precious Lizzy was the one who found me. She came to *my* club and asked me for *my* help. She paid me to go to the dinner and find you. To pretend like I had come to apologize. To start our relationship back up. She used me to get to you. Just like Barry. She wanted me to control you. Manipulate you. Force you to back off. All she cared about was protecting her precious little show. She didn't care about you. She was protecting herself. She even knew about your mom. She and Barry were working together."

"You're lying."

"But you know what?" Noah smiled, his certainty building. "I started to enjoy using you again. I liked watching you spiral downward. And I think you liked it too. Kill Barry for you? You think you're worth it? I'm not like this crazy asshole."

The gun shook in Kelly's hand.

Noah paced around her. "You know, I only came up with the idea to sleep with Lizzy after you invited this asshole into your house. I wish I could say it was difficult." He shook his head. "She was almost as easy as you were at sixteen. So naive. So innocent. Hopefully, she won't turn out as batshit crazy and stubborn as you. She's in the car right now, waiting for me."

Kelly's eyes closed. A tear rolled down her cheek.

Noah moved closer. "But it's not too late," he whispered.

The gun lowered in her hands.

"There you go, Kelly. Give me the gun. It's not too late for us."

Bob moved closer to me. I glanced down at my gun on the floor. I could feel my hands start to pulse with power. "Steady, steady."

Noah moved closer to Kelly. "I know you still love me. I was your first. That's why you won't hurt me." He was almost touching her.

"Steady," Bob said.

Here it comes.

Rage.

Spots of red.

Noah stopped, holding his hand out to her. "So what are you going to do?"

A grin stretched across Kelly's face. "What I planned, silly."

Noah took a step back, eyes wide.

Kelly tossed me her gun.

"This is my story, Noah. And in this version, there are two heroes. I've done my part. Now my solider will do his." She nodded at me, then gazed back to Noah. "Lizzy won't be safe until you're gone as well." She moved up the stair, then stopped, turned. "And you're wrong," she said, "you were hardly my first."

Noah and I locked eyes. Two predators in the wild. We both watched Kelly ascend the steps.

"Don't fall for her shit, man," Noah said. "You're a pawn. She's using you. That's what she does. You don't think I got the same proposition? But I wouldn't do it. That's why she went out and found you."

"He couldn't do it because he is weak." Bob's voice came from behind me. My finger curled around the trigger. "You're stronger than him, Kaleb."

But I've been here before.

"Finish this," Bob ordered. "Do it now."

A scream rang out from upstairs.

Noah met my gaze. "Kill me or save her."

"Do your fucking job," Bob shouted. "She gave you a chance at redemption."

Music began playing upstairs.

I aimed the gun at Noah's heart.

I wanted this.

I wanted him to pay.

"Pull the trigger."

I closed my eyes.

Kelly screamed again.

My eyes jolted open. My gaze moved up to the tower. A sudden force struck me. Noah pinned me down. The gun flew out of my hands. We wrestled, rolling through puddles of blood. I put my hands on his neck, squeezed. His forehead smashed into my nose. I released. He grabbed me, flipped me over. He was choking me, his eyes full of rage. My own reflection staring back. Kelly screamed again. I looked up. Noah's hands still wrapped around my throat.

Then I saw her.

A thin blonde girl, slowly climbing he steps. Lizzy was going to the tower.

Jez: Lizzy and Noah were careless. I caught them kissing outside her house. Do you want to see the pictures?

Lizzy: I had to do something. One day Kelly was going to regret destroying her legacy. Yes, that included her best friend's career. That's why I messaged Noah. I sent him to that investment dinner.

Jez: There was no satisfaction in showing Kelly the photos. But she handled it with such grace. As she cried, she told me that AJ must have felt the same way. It was poetic how she said it. How strong AJ must have been to watch the girl he loved return to the enemy every night—to watch Alice choose evil over love. And yet, AJ never gave up on her. His love was too strong. That's when she turned to me and said, "I want to be that person."

Lizzy: Okay. Fine. I was jealous of her. Noah told me I was special. That I was just as beautiful as Kelly. I wanted to believe it. I wanted to believe that I was just as good as her. But it wasn't true. He's always loved Kelly. Everyone loves her. I will never be loved like that.

Jez: Kelly wrote, directed, and produced her final act. You see what she wanted you to see. The world is reading what she wanted you to read. She conquered death. Look what is happening! Look at the mania she ignited—a headline befitting of a real princess. Her final masterpiece.

Lizzy: I was angry when Kelly texted Noah to come over. That's why I went along. Then I saw Kaleb's car pull up. I heard the gunshots.

Jez: I was four hundred yards away from Kelly's mansion that night, hiding in the bushes. Lizzy was so pathetic, cowering in Noah's car, shaking. She winced when she heard the gunshot.

Lizzy: You don't think I've done this before? You don't think I know what it's like to walk in and see your best friend lying in a puddle of her own blood? To hold her pale, lifeless body? I know what that's like, and I couldn't go through that again. I couldn't save her again. I just couldn't.

Jez: It wasn't until the second gunshot that she opened the car door.

Lizzy: I don't remember leaving the car. I was under some spell, some enchantment. I don't remember walking up those stairs. Or stepping over Barry's body. I don't remember walking past Noah and Kaleb. I just remember her screams. That music.

Jez: I guess it comes down to—who do you believe?

Lizzy: When I walked in the tower room, Kelly was cutting herself, screaming. She was gone. It was madness, and I was terrified. She just kept shrieking, asking God to give her gifts, slicing away at her flesh as her music played in the background. But then she saw me, and she stopped. She ran over and reached her hand out, blood dripping down. I flinched at her touch. I couldn't help it. She scared me. But then something unexpected happened. She grabbed my hand with real strength, and for a second, there was clarity, and I saw my best friend. I saw her. The sweetest girl in the whole world. The one who took me under her wing on my very first day on set. My best friend. And with her hand in mine, she smiled and whispered. "It's your time to shine, Lizzy." Then she told me to go.

Jez: Did Lizzy do it? Oh, that's an interesting theory. It's plausible. In her jealous rage, Lizzy finally snaps, shoving Kelly off the balcony. But I'm afraid I don't know what actually happened in that tower, detective. Kelly wanted it this way.

Lizzy: How can you even ask that? I didn't push her. You have to believe me. But what I did was worse. Far worse.

My head pounded from Noah's fists. My shirt, my arms, my hands were all soaked in blood. Somewhere in the distance, sirens screamed. Noah released his hands from my throat. He glanced to the tower, then scampered away. I picked myself up off the bloody floor. Reached for the bannister. Stumbled up the steps. When I made it to the tower, familiar voices stopped me in my tracks.

"What have you done?" Lizzy cried.

"I did this for you," Kelly's voice was mumbled, muted.

"You're scaring me, Kelly."

"I did all this for you," Kelly pleaded. "All for you. I love you, Lizzy."

"No. Stop."

"Stay by my side. Stay with me. I love you."

"No. I have to go," Lizzy's voice got louder. "I have to go."

"Lizzy, please," Kelly cried. "I love you."

Lizzy ran from the tower, looking at me with frightened eyes. Blood covered her shirt and jacket. She didn't speak. She was in shock. Her face was pale. Her body trembled. She ran past me without saying a word.

I walked into the room. The song was on full blast. Kelly wasn't on the bed. I went straight to the bathroom. There was a bloody knife on the floor. I picked it up, wheeled my head around. The curtain gently blew in the breeze. Soft sobs rang from the balcony. Her naked body was perched on the ledge. Kelly was staring at me, the night sky and stars behind her. There were gashes across her chest and her blue eyes were blank.

But she was still alive.

She put her hands around her exposed breasts, leaving red, bloody imprints on her skin. Whimpers. Soft tears. Her lips quivered. Blood dripped down her arm. Her hair was wild, thrown to the side. Her eyelids drooped. Her small body swayed back and forth. She was fading. But not gone. It wasn't too late.

"Come down, Kelly."

She didn't respond.

I reached out my hand. This was my chance to make amends. I couldn't fail, not again.

Her eyes opened, stopping me in my tracks.

"Please, come down."

"I knew you'd come," she managed to say through the hysteria. I could barely make out the words. "Write our story," she whispered. "Free yourself."

"I'm not leaving without you."

"Please protect her," she cried.

"I will." I inched my hand back toward her. "Come down."

"Make sure she's okay," she struggled to say. "Make sure she's safe. Make sure evil doesn't hurt her. Promise me, Kaleb. Promise me!" she screamed, sending knives into my gut. But I wouldn't give up hope. I still believed we could fight this. Our story wasn't over. The ending wasn't set. We could be free.

"I promise, Kelly. I can't lose you, not you, not now."

Just for a second, her eyes flashed. Cobalt blue. I saw the

real her. The one I loved. She whispered, "I told you I would break your heart."

She reached out for my hand. Our fingers touched, one last time. I tried to hang on. A small grin formed in the corner of her mouth. Her eyes closed. Hands folded into her chest.

Darkness.

THE REAL KELLY TROZZO
TheInsideJuice.com Interview 2019

TROZZO: May I ask you a question?

INSIDEJUICE: Fire away.

TROZZO: Notice the painting above us, a depiction of the tale of Andromeda. Usually, I like to ask people which one they identify with, the hero, the damsel, or the monster. But considering everything I've just shared with you, I'd like to ask, which one do you think I identify with?

INSIDEJUICE: It's hard to tell. I feel like you've contradicted yourself so many times.

TROZZO: Exactly. That's the beauty of all this…We are all complicated, broken creatures. I'm the damsel who submits to the monster. The princess who seduces the knight in shining armor. I'm the monster that lives within. The enemy that gives our champion a purpose. And I'm the hero that will rise above it all. The woman who will control her own destiny. The princess who slays her own beast. I will break the chains of the people I love. And because of that, I won't be just another girl who died famous. My story will be written in the skies.

THE REAL ALICE
NEW MEXICO, 2015

I PICKED UP THE gun off the warm dirt. The last ray of sun dripped away from the horizon. I stared at the edge of the cliff. Alice's husband was gone forever. There was an emptiness. A hollowness in my soul. A void. My heart was still beating wildly. What do I do? Where do I go? A raspy voice rattled in my thoughts.

Leave.

My heartbeat slowed.

Go.

Where?

Anywhere.

I threw the gun into the ravine.

The car door slammed.

The open road.

Find solace.

Find the blank page.

Write.

Do something meaningful.

Find me in the wilderness.

I looked to the passenger seat. It was empty. I put my foot

to the pedal and drove. I rolled down the windows. Mile after mile of desert.

Go north.

Further and further. I was going to a place I had always dreamed of. Eventually, my hands stopped shaking. My mind felt clear and lucid. Like something had fallen away. A strange sense of freedom. Temporary lightness. I had done it. Bob had honored his promise. He had left. He was gone.

Or so I hoped.

Three days after Kelly's death. Detective Donaldson took a seat at the interrogation table. Defeat was written on his tired, droopy face, his low sagging eyebrows. In a few minutes, my lawyer would arrive and our visit would end. They had no choice but to release me.

He reached for his pack of cigarettes. It was empty.

"Just my luck." Donaldson shook his head. "You know after this, we can't help you, Kaleb. I hate to say it, but you're safer in here. You have no idea what's happening out in the world. It's madness."

I didn't say a word.

There was only one place I wanted to go.

Into the abyss to finish Kelly's masterpiece.

"Oh well, you'll find out soon enough." Donaldson gave a half-grin. "You know, when I met you, I was certain we had our man. Covered in blood, shaking in your car, mumbling her name. I thought we caught a lucky break. Thought I'd crack you on the first night."

He looked off in the distance, thinking. "Oh well. Guess I'll have to keep investigating, right?" He chuckled.

I didn't respond.

He leaned back in his chair. "You know, I did some digging. Read an interesting missing person's report about a man in New Mexico. Case remains unsolved. Local police didn't seem to care too much. You wouldn't know anything about that, would you?"

I didn't respond.

"It's funny. Your ex-girlfriend lived in that town with him for a bit. I got a hold of the transcripts when local police interviewed her. She was convincing. I'll give her that. Her husband was a gambler, heavy drinker, couple of domestic abuse charges on his record. Who was going to miss him, right?"

Donaldson smiled, picking up a copy of my book. "Man, you sure painted a picture in this thing. If Kelly Trozzo had never found it, I wonder if your dirty little secret would have surfaced."

A well-dressed man with a black suit and briefcase stepped into the room. "Don't say anything, Kaleb. You're being released."

Donaldson smiled at me. "Enjoy your freedom while it lasts, Kaleb. But let me ask you one more thing before you go." He turned to my new lawyer. "Don't worry, he won't need you for this."

He shifted his gaze back to me, unblinking. "Was it worth it? Was she worth it?"

"You don't have to answer that," said the lawyer.

I waved him off. "It's okay. I won't be able to answer anyway."

"And why is that?" Detective Donaldson humored me.

"Because my final task is not yet complete," I said.

"Oh," Donaldson snickered. "You mean you haven't written her little autobiography? Or is this the new task of taking care of the ex-boyfriend?"

I smiled. "No. No. There is something much more important at stake here."

Detective Donaldson rolled his eyes. "And what's that?"

I stood up. He followed suit. We were face to face, our
noses nearly touching.

I leaned forward, whispering. "I am going to kill the man
responsible for everything."

The helicopters hover above the motel. I pace around room, the gun in my hand. I turn on the television. There are pictures of the rundown motel. Breaking news scrolls on the lower portion of the screen. *Police have surrounded Kaleb Reed.* It ends here. Detective Donaldson will have his man. Dead or alive. Dead. I stare at the chair in the corner. He is coming. I can feel his power, his dark vibrations lingering in the air. I am ready for him.

I place my finger on the trigger.

He appears on the chair across from me. Crossword tucked in his armpit. Hat pulled over his eyes and mangled face.

"I can't believe you came here," he scoffs. "Aren't you tired of this dump?"

I don't have to look. I know he is smiling.

"I am going to kill you tonight," I say, sternly.

"We'll see about that."

"But first I need to ask you a question."

I can hear him chuckling.

"Why did you come back?" I ask him. "Why did you return to Sara's house that night?"

He chuckles again. "Do we really need to do this again? Fine. Because you asked me to come," Bob says. "You always ask me to come, and we always do this game. You pretend to not want me. And I convince you otherwise. "

"And where did you come from?"

"You created me."

"Why?"

"To protect you."

"I don't need you anymore."

"Then why do I keep coming back, Kaleb? You need me. You've always needed me to clean up your mess," he said. "To take care of your pain."

I don't say a word.

"Do you remember the first night you met me? Do you remember the party? Couple months after your brother died. You were so pathetic. This weak, frightened kid. Couldn't stop hearing the screams of your mom outside the hospital room. Seeing your father standing next to your lifeless brother." Bob stands. "I couldn't even look at you that night we met. Cowering from life. Do you remember what I promised you?"

I don't say a word.

"Nothing, huh? How about I remind you?" He moves closer.

His voice rises. "I told you I would make you strong. That I would help you become a protector. I would help you be a fucking man."

"But you didn't! Look at me!" I scream, putting the gun to my head. "Look what you've done to me."

"Please." He circles around me in the chair.

The gun shakes uncontrollably in my hand. "Don't come any closer."

"Are you blaming this on me?" he sneers. "You didn't ask for my help. This is what happens when you do things without me."

"Lies," I scream. "All lies!"

"You forced Kelly to take matters into her own hands," he seethes. "You had all the time in the world to take care of it. And you failed her. Just like you failed your brother. Like you failed your mother. You couldn't protect them, could you? Not without me. You just sat there and watched."

"Stop it!" I yell.

"You need me."

"No. You hurt me."

"You deserve it. You need to be reminded of your weakness." Bob's hand falls on my shoulder. My eyes roll back. My heart throbs, then freezes over. The air is pulled from my lungs. Images appear. I see Sara crying, her beautiful face overrun with sadness and fear. I see my brother in the hospital with black eyes and bandages on his head. I see Kelly's dead body. Crimson blood on cold cement, streaking across her driveway. *Stop it. Stop it. I don't want to see.* I feel pain. I feel hurt. I can feel it all. Then he takes his hand away. I don't feel it anymore.

"You see? I protect you from that. You need me. In fact, the one thing you ever did right in your life, I was there. I was leading you. Guiding you. But you tried to run away. You tried to find yourself a home. You tried to stay sober without me. But you need me. You've always needed me."

"Face him, face this shit." I look in the corner of the room. It's Nathan. He looks up from his newspaper. "You face this. Don't be a fucking coward."

"Don't listen to him," Bob snaps.

"He *is* the pain!" screams Nathan. "Face him."

"He doesn't have the guts. Isn't that right, Kaleb? You'll never look at me. You can't. You're afraid."

He's right. I won't face him. But I *can* do this. I cock the hammer back on the gun, press it firmly against my temple. "You and I are finished," I scream.

Donaldson's voice sounds from outside. "Come out with your hands behind your head. We have you surrounded."

I will not come out. Not this time. It ends here. "I'm killing you." I close my eyes. Clench my teeth. It will finally be over. The pain. I won't have to feel again. I won't have to fight him again. This is it.

"Wait!" Bob yells with urgency. "Give me another chance. We can still make a difference. There are still people out there that we can protect. We can redeem your failures. You and I."

"No," I cry. "I'm not falling for this again. Look where I am!"

The bullhorn blares. "This is your final warning."

Bob laughs. "Fine, pull the trigger. Do it," he froths. "Let the bullies win. Give up, you coward. But at least look me in the face before you do it."

I can hear movement outside. They are getting closer. I close my eyes. I can't look at him. I can't. I won't.

"He'll never do it," Bob snickers. "He's a coward. And I will live on."

My stomach lurches at the truth.

Bob laughs and laughs. He knows he has won. If I don't face him, he will endure. He will reside in someone else. In the collective soul of this world. Bringing pain to everyone and everything he touches.

I know what I have to do.

I won't hide any longer.

It ends with me.

"No." I shout over his laughter. "You die tonight."

And for the first time, I turn and look at Bob in the eyes.

A piercing scream rings in my ears. The air is ripped from my lungs. Fear floods my body. Bob's eyes are dark. They penetrate deep within my soul. His face is battered, damaged. He is laughing and I am so fucking scared because I don't want to be bad and evil like Bob. My darkest fears are moving through me like a living, breathing thing. It's chaos. It's madness. It's the worst thing I've ever felt. The fear of never being worthy, never being good, never being whole. That no one will ever love me. I'll always be tainted and damaged and alone. That I will always destroy the good things in my life. That there will be nothing good inside me anymore. I will become darkness.

"Keep going," I hear Nathan yell above the screams.

Bob's face is melting away like black candle wax. I can feel the pain of my father's hand. Bottling up those tears. Scared of not being a man. Scared of not being strong enough for him. For everyone. I let my brother down. I didn't protect my family. I let them all down. I will always let you down, Nathan. I'm horrible. I'm evil. I'm not worth anything.

I see my brother reaching for me, telling me to hold on.

I see my fingers running along Kelly's scar.

I see myself sitting across from Sara at our favorite diner.

I feel Nathan's proud hand on my shoulder. I hear Sara's voice. Just a little longer. It feels like I'm dying. I'm so scared. And I must keep looking. I must let all the pain and suffering devour me.

I surrender.

A flash of light.

Darkness shrieks.

Strength begins to build.

Real power.

I turn to Bob. The voice comes through me. *I created you. You lived inside of me. But you are not me.* The dark mass inside me pulses one last time, pure evil shrieking as it meets its death. It screams and throbs and my heart cracks and tears open as the last of Bob's face melts away. My father is staring back. I see his tired, broken face. I see all his pain, and sorrow, and regret. I see his guilt and shame. Then he disappears. The dark mass detaches from my heart.

Stillness.

Just my breath.

Something has been lifted.

An open space where darkness doesn't exist.

Freedom.

I can feel my heartbeat. The motel room is empty.

The door bursts open. Detective Donaldson leads a team of men in Kevlar Vests, their guns drawn. Donaldson stares at me, his dark brown pupils widening. Both of us pause.

And the gun falls from my hand.

THE REAL ALICE
LOS ANGELES, 2017

SIX HUNDRED AND EIGHTY-NINE DAYS SOBER. I was standing at the podium, my book in hand. It was my first signing. It wasn't a very big crowd. Only a handful of people. I didn't care. It wasn't about that. Nathan was in the back, drinking out of a Styrofoam coffee cup. I took a deep breath, opened to the page. I was about to begin the reading when I saw her walk into the bookstore.

Everything in the room stopped.

She came.

After everything we had been through. She had returned. She was wearing jeans, a plain white shirt, her hair pulled up. She had never looked more beautiful. She had never looked stronger.

"I had a passage picked out," I mumbled. "But I think…" I watched her move through the bookstore, into the aisle. "I think I'll read something special to me. Something I've wanted to share for a very long time." I flipped open the book, pulled out a piece of paper hidden in the flap.

"This epilogue was never published. But I have been waiting for the right moment to reveal it."

306

Sara sat down. Her gaze was fixed on me.

I read: *"Alice's routine was consistent for the past month. She never left the house for more than ten minutes. She was crippled by uncertainty, paralyzed with self-doubt. She didn't know who she was anymore without her husband. Without his permission. She had seen the police on television. A homicide in his tattoo parlor, two bodies found.*

There was no freedom in her husband's death. Somehow, he was still there. She still wore her wedding ring. He had built an invisible wall around her life. Years of abuse could do that to anyone, she told herself. But he was dead. He would never hurt her again. And yet, five weeks later, she couldn't leave the house. She still needed permission.

It was her birthday that day, September 9th. The first birthday she had spent alone since she was seventeen. She poured coffee into her thermos and opened up the door to grab the newspaper. As soon as her hands touched the plastic film, she felt better. It was the one thing she had left of her old life. The last of her precious routines. She unrolled the paper on the kitchen table and opened up to her favorite section. She scanned the names and sipped coffee. She closed her eyes and put herself back into the café, reading her favorites to AJ. He always amused her. He always wanted to make her happy. He would do anything for her. He did. The ultimate sacrifice. His life. She opened her eyes. Looked down on the page.

The thermos fell from her hand, sending a wave of hot black coffee across the paper. Her hands flew to her mouth in shock. It's not possible.

He knew. He knew everything. He knew her better than she knew herself. He knew exactly what that asshole had done to her soul. And now he was giving her another lifeline. He was giving her permission. The sign that she needed. Even after his death, he was thinking of her. One final birthday present. She looked toward the bedroom. She wouldn't need a thing. Just one bag. Just a car.

Without warning, a lightness consumed her. Anxiety and fear evaporated off her body like dew off the morning grass. A grin stretched across her face. She stared down at the words in the paper one last time.

Go find your sunset, Alice.

This was the last time she would ever read the obituaries."

The bookstore crowd came back into focus. A few claps sounded. My eyes went straight to Sara. A tear fell down her cheek. She lifted her hand up, smiled. Her wedding ring was gone.

Lizzy: Kelly attended that book signing. She asked me to go, but as usual, I made up some excuse. She told me all about it after. . . She stood in the back with a wig and sunglasses on. There, she watched her favorite author narrate a deleted scene that left her in tears. But according to her, that wasn't even the best part. The best part was getting to see the real Alice and AJ reconnect after the signing. Apparently, she even followed them to a nearby lunch spot so she could watch them interact. She said it was the most beautiful thing ever, watching them light up around each other, even after everything they'd gone through. To her, it was the greatest love story of our time. It was finally a fairy tale she could believe in.

Jez: Kelly emptied the hidden safe behind her painting on the night of the murder. There wasn't much in it... A box full of childhood pictures, a postcard, her copy of *Pay Me, Alice* and a gun. She and I were the only ones who knew the password. . . Well, maybe Kaleb as well. The password was Alice's birthday, after all. Now that I think about it. . . Perhaps the safe isn't empty any longer.

Lizzy: A week after Kelly's death, I received a package from her. It was a wrinkled postcard from the castle we always wanted to visit in France. On the back it said, *This was my sunset. Now find yours, Lizzy.* I just wish I knew how much that trip meant to her. How much I meant to her. We should have gone. I should have made the time. I should have been a better friend. I know she wanted me to shine. I know she wanted me to move on. But I just…I just can't. Not with thousands of paparazzi lining up outside my house. I feel so trapped. Maybe it's the guilt or shame. Maybe I'm not ready to face the world without her. There is nothing left inside me. What if my star died with her?

Jez: That's everything I know, detective. Our work here is done. As for the KTroops, our work is just beginning. As their new leader, it is my duty to lead her fans and continue fighting the evil in this world. Starting with our old friend, Noah Tash. I'm confident his atonement will be our next headline.

THREE MONTHS AFTER KELLY'S DEATH

I am a free man. Unpunished for my role in this story. For now, at least.

I should thank my lawyer. You should have seen him in the courtroom. He had a forensic psychologist testify that I was extremely intoxicated and suffering from extreme delusions while writing my blog. The content will not be admissible in court. I have proven myself to be a very good storyteller. Until that is a crime, I deserve to keep doing what I do best. My lawyer's words. Not mine.

Donaldson was there when I stepped out of the courtroom. He had a cigarette to his mouth, a smug grin on his face. His eyebrows raised. He was wearing the same cheap button down he was wearing on the night we first met. He might be the only one who understands me. The only one who can see through the lies. He's never been a gray area kind of guy.

In the end, I wrote the book Kelly paid for. She got the headlines she wanted. A publisher is more than willing to pay now. You should see the offers that are coming in. Fiction, non-fiction…I'll let you decide.

The death threats have subsided, replaced with fan mail

and other strange letters. Thank you all for your support. The KTroops have made me a hero. I'm not sure I feel like one. They shower me with praise, love and affirmations. Just like their leader once did for them. I'm famous now. But none of that matters. I don't care about the talk shows and television specials. I don't care about the big fancy house I live in now. I miss my tiny apartment.

The grass is always greener.

Sara reached out to me. She said she had been following the news. Hoping for the best. She apologized for our latest run-in outside her house. There was nothing to apologize for. I was being guided by a dark hand. We messaged for a while. She can tell that I am doing better. That I'm sober. That I'm writing. She wants to meet up. I'm not sure I'm ready. I'm not sure we have a future anymore.

No more fantasies.

But today is a celebration for Kelly. She left a will. The castle would be given to Jez and her friends. They plan on carrying her legacy for as long as the house stands. The party is small. There is only thirty of us, the regulars, sharing memories and laughter. Her music is playing in the background, not the teeny bopper stuff. The new Kelly. That was her art.

She would have liked the scene—her illusionists, all dancing and smiling, drinking and celebrating. It is difficult walking through the house, past the memories, past the marble that was once covered in blood. I look up the staircase toward her tower room. I was never her protector.

Jez gathers everyone around the pool. They hold red Solo cups filled with Kelly's favorite concoction. They stare at me as I un-crumple a piece of paper I had written a few hours before.

I begin: "The average person would say I didn't know much about Kelly because our relationship was built on a lot of…illusions. But I did know Kelly. We all did. This fantasy, these illusions, that *was* a part of Kelly. She was nothing and everything at the same time. She had moments where she loved in ways I couldn't imagine. Unconditional and selfless. And the world loved her for it. They loved the fantasy and the real moments in between. They loved what they saw on the screen. They loved her words of strength. She empowered us to be better, to stand up to our bullies, to be heard. We loved how she danced with lightness, even when her world was much darker. We loved how her eyes made us feel seen. They made us all feel special. They made us feel vulnerable and ambitious. We loved her loyalty, her passion, her smile."

"Our relationship was a testament to her transformative power. Kelly showed me her demons and shadows, helping me unearth and understand my own. She took me on a journey. The first time I came here, she told me that I was going to fall in love with her. She was right. It was a selfish love, at first. I loved what she could offer me. Just like a story I once wrote. A story that connected us. But as I got closer to her, I loved her for different reasons. Kelly and I were fighting something together. I loved her because she believed in me when no one else did. She made me stronger. I wanted her to beat the odds. I wanted her light to overpower her demons. I wanted her to find the freedom that she longed for.

"Kelly was talented. She was an artist. She had a gift, and she believed it was selfish to not give that back. I liked that.

"None of us are childhood friends or longtime partners, but that's how she wanted it. She thrived on people coming and going, brief moments of connection. She loved her fans. She loved giving community to the lonely. Strength to the weak. Affection to the wounded.

"She loved being a leader.

"More than anything, she wanted the people who were supposed to love her to do just that. But as we all know, life is messy and unfair. Despite that, Kelly had brief moments where her inner light shone brighter than anything. I consider myself lucky to have witnessed a few of those moments. We are all lucky to have known her."

"To Kelly." We all held up our glasses.

I lock eyes with Lizzy. She takes a deep breath, smiles.

"To her something bigger."

I walk into the kitchen, where Kelly had put the blade to her flesh. I stare down at the spotless tiles that bore no evidence of that moment. That story still makes me smile. On the surface, it seems morose, but I love how she talked about freedom. About being connected to something bigger. To anyone fighting demons and darkness and shadows, it gives them hope. Kelly wants that story told for a reason.

The windows are open, and a light breeze wafts in and strokes my face, carrying the smell of flowers. The trees outside sway, casting shadows across the room. I can see small motes of dust floating in the deep beams of sunlight. It is beautiful. I feel my breath move the particles away from the sunlight, and a stillness sweeps through me. My thoughts stop. There is a second of lightness and happiness. Just for a second, a brief moment of openness. That is heaven. That is her happily ever after.

Then my thoughts return, and I don't feel it anymore. The stillness is gone.

The sound of stomping boots thuds through the house. Screams follow. The police order everyone to get down, stand aside. They are coming for me. I close my eyes and fall to my knees, my hands behind my head. There will be no fight. I will go quietly.

Thank you all for your love and support.

Please forgive me for my sins.

ACKNOWLEDGMENTS

"Shadowy material resides inside of all of us, but the man who is willing to face his own capacity for darkness will discover his deepest inner goodness and the presence of the divine within him."

—Richard Rohr

This novel has been on a long journey to get here. It has gone through multiple title changes and editors. It has been rejected and rewritten. It has been abandoned and picked back up again. But through all the setbacks, I've always believed in the story. I knew that there was something I needed to say through this book.

Steven Pressfield taught me that the more resistance you have to a piece of art, the more important it is to your soul's calling. I felt a great deal of resistance with this book, both in writing it and having people read it. Channeling Kaleb was frightening at times. It seems that every time I captured his voice, I was strapping on a harness and diving into a black hole. Thankfully, I was able to emerge with a piece of art that I'm proud of.

For me, the story has always been about our collective shadows. We are all wounded, men and women, victim and bully. We all have scars and pain that dictate our actions and keep us away from God's calling for our lives. Scars that make us operate out of fear and insecurity rather than love. But if you are willing to face those shadows, you will come out on the other side transformed. You will come face to face with our creator.

Thank you to my friends and family who were able to tether me back to earth while I worked on this.

Thank you to my writer's group for the feedback (Collette, Carlos, Annoushka), as well as my early readers (Kalee, Erica, and Alisha).

Thank you to all the professionals who lent their editorial skills and insight, including: Allison Itterly, Monica James, Julie Mosow, Annoushka Lyvers, Lindsay Means, and last but not least, Julie Tibbott. Each of you gave me honest feedback that helped shape the book.

Thank you to my design team, Anamaria Stefon for making an amazing cover and Vanessa Maynard for her interior design inspiration.

Thank you Adam Richardson for being so cool and answering my questions about police procedure.

Thank you to Joe for always letting me bounce ideas off of you.

Thank you to my parents for all your support.

Most of all, I want to thank my wife, my partner, my everything. Thank you for your unconditional faith in me. For always pushing me. For allowing me to turn on dark, suspenseful movies when I'm writing thrillers and Harry Potter when I'm writing children's books. For allowing me to run scenes by you when I'm lost in my own thoughts. There are countless chapters in this book that were influenced by our brainstorming sessions. Thank you for truly understanding why I do this. You have always had faith.

Finally, thank you God for tasking me with this. I believe our job as artists is to grab an idea and get it down before it returns to the mysterious vortex. But if you grab that idea, be prepared for anything. Be prepared to strap on your armor and go into battle. Be prepared to encounter every part of yourself. Be prepared to transform.

ABOUT THE AUTHOR_

Kyle Rutkin is a digital storyteller and author in Orange County. To stay up-to-date on giveaways and news about his next release in this series, please visit shediedfamous.com or follow him on Instagram at instagram.com/kmrutkin.